Running Through the Wormhole

Kate Abbott

BLACK ROSE writing™

ISBN: 978-1-61296-488-1

PUBLISHED BY BLACK ROSE WRITING

www.blackrosewriting.com

Printed in the United States of America

Suggested retail price: $18.95

Running Through the Wormhole is printed in Times New Roman

Running Through the Wormhole

Chapter One

Phoebe

Run with me wherever you go, just play dumb, whatever you know.
~Tom Petty

The mist was becoming a light drizzle. Her breath was even and her footstrike against the damp asphalt regular. Ten miles into a planned twenty-to-thirty-mile overnight run. Midnight Friday and the traffic on the neighborhood roads was very light. Finishing this run would give her the mental confidence to approach the overnight hours of the one-hundred-mile trail run she had registered for several months ago. It would represent a victory over sleepiness and fear of darkness and, most of all, the wheedling voice in her head that insisted that this was foolishness and cajoled her into doubt, saying things like: "Phoebe, you don't need to do this; you know you can't finish this."

A vibration from her wrist Garmin signaled mile eleven. She took a swig from her water bottle and adjusted her headlamp. A pick-up truck appeared ahead and passed with a quiet hum, the first vehicle she had seen in some time, probably someone heading home from a late dinner or a movie. A half mile later, she passed her sprawling white house and smiled at the warmth of the lighted windows in the TV room. Her teenagers were engrossed in Grand Theft Auto, their heads bobbing animatedly. Phoebe continued without stopping; she was checking in with them hourly and had exchanged texts with them forty-four minutes ago. Laughing, she had told them before she started this venture, "if you don't hear from me each hour, call 911 and tell the cops to find your crazy mother."

Phoebe was by nature cautious, headlamp, reflective vest, cell phone. Although she ran every day without exception, she varied her route, time and distance. She much preferred to run in the morning but this run was intended to test her mental fortitude and to challenge her circadian rhythm in a manner similar to the upcoming race. Phoebe loved the outdoors, taking note of the birds and other wildlife, even roadkill, and marveling in the changes of the seasons. This early spring evening, the peeper frogs were out in full force, their chorus echoing in the neighborhood.

As she neared the intersection of the local street with a slightly busier one, she saw a red pick-up truck pass slowly through the intersection, too slowly she mused, for that hour. A faint alarm pinged some part of her brain as the truck passed out of sight. It looked, she thought, a lot like the truck she had seen a few minutes before.

"Maybe you should bail on this run," said the voice of doubt. She made a left turn, planning to run for a half mile or so to the intersection with Branch Street, which ran in front of her house.

"I can always just stop at home," she told herself.

She was close to the turnoff for Branch. Branch had no streetlights and was normally dark. There was a utility right of way some hundred yards or so into Branch where occasionally someone would park, maybe to look at a map or a text or to drink beer, leaving cans behind that she would pick up on her morning runs and take home to place in her recycling bin. Glancing to the left, about to turn, she saw the twin beams of headlights abruptly shut off. The truck was in the right of way spot, parked facing out. The dome light flashed off, but not before she saw two profiles.

She stopped short and reversed direction. Panic rose in her throat. She mustn't lead anyone to the house. She thought of her children and wished she were sitting on the couch or maybe reading her youngest a story, snuggled up for the night in her queen-size bed.

"Think, Phoebe. Don't panic. Make yourself inconspicuous."

She tore off her reflective vest and put it in her windbreaker pocket. She switched off her headlamp and wrapped it around the water bottle, unconsciously creating a weapon. She took out her phone to text the kids; it had been almost an hour since their last exchange. She observed the "No Service" message with growing fear. Running from here to the gas station a mile and a half away was an option but time was short. Did she really want the kids to realize their mother was missing and grow frightened? They could be counted on to play Grand Theft Auto for a while after the hour mark but her eldest was cautious and easily alarmed.

The best thing, she reasoned, was to take the long way home. It was about a mile and, most importantly, at least in her near panic state of mind, there were woods along the way in which she could hide, woods that contained a faint path to her back yard. She had explored those woods with the children, looking for turtles and toads. She retraced her steps back to the intersection where she had seen the truck roll pass, too slowly, a few minutes earlier, and made a right. Home was a mile away.

There were streetlights here, the few that there were in this neighborhood. A driveway was blocked off with yellow tape. She could smell fresh asphalt. She passed several more driveways and as the road sloped gently downhill, a dome light in a vehicle parked ahead on the left winked off. A pick-up truck. The Thai lemongrass soup that she had eaten for supper rose in her throat. She willed herself to keep moving. Surely the man walking towards her lived in the house with the newly paved driveway and had parked on the street instead.

He passed her wordlessly, cigarette smoke fluttering around him. Dark clothes, mustache, maybe five foot, ten inches, average build, her rational mind recorded. Alright, even if he had belonged to the pick-up that was stalking her, where was the other guy? Down the hill she ran, her breath ragged. She willed a car to pass, any car that was not a pick-up truck with the profile of men. Another quarter of a mile and she was crossing a stream, a stream that was loud with water from the recent rain and, she supposed, in a detached fashion, perhaps snow melt. The peepers were nearly deafening.

She found it impossible to run now, her heart was racing beyond what any physical exertion would cause. She sensed more than heard, someone approaching from behind. She turned and with dread, regarded the man walking next to her.

"Nice night for a walk," he said in a conversational tone.

She looked at him and almost returned the pleasantry.

"What are you doing out here alone?" he asked in a low voice, less friendly now.

He was wearing an improbable outfit for a walk. Dark, heavy sweatpants and sweatshirt, hood pulled down low. Taller than the man she had seen a few minutes earlier, clean shaven and no smell of cigarette. He had stopped in front of her, still slightly to the left.

"If you don't get the fuck away from me, I am going to scream," Phoebe said through gritted teeth.

"Don't scream, lady, don't scream." He began to step towards her, raising his hands, on which he was wearing heavy, white, cotton gloves.

"Those don't look like running gloves," Phoebe's inner voice recorded inanely. "Of course they aren't running gloves, stupid, he means to hurt you, maybe kill you."

Phoebe began to scream while stepping toward the white glove man. He started and took a step back. She turned and sprinted back the way she had come. She raced towards the bridge over the stream, glanced over her shoulder and saw him running, picking up speed as he went. Placing her hands on the metal guardrail, she threw her legs over the side and dropped into the water, thinking that she could fade into the woods and lose him.

The water was icy cold and she slipped on the rocks, stumbling for what felt like hours until she found her balance and dragged herself through the waist deep water and deeper into the woods. She heard a car door slam and muted, angry voices. Had the white gloved man been joined by cigarette man? Did they mean to follow her or would they just leave? Surely they had only been the neighborhood to rob houses, what would they want with her; she did not have a penny on her.

Her inner voice mocked: "Money is not what they are after."

The underbrush was deep along the edge of the stream and brambles snatched at her hair and hands. She could hear splashing behind her and imagined them both, intent on hurting her, raping her, probably killing her, plunging angrily after her. Her mind went to the kids. Had an hour passed and had they noticed? Would they call 911? What would they tell the cops? If she did not return and the cops could not find her, would they think that she had abandoned the children and take them to a foster home for the night? Her husband was thousands of miles away on a business trip in Asia, unreachable except by email. A day or more would pass before he could get home, even if they could contact him.

A sob escaped her. Why had she embarked on this ridiculous training run? It seemed so unimportant now, an exercise in vanity, a cute story to post on Facebook to share with her running friends. She clawed her way through the brambles and onto a faint path. She slid in the mud and fell to her knees. As she scrabbled to get to her feet again, a hand clamped onto her right foot. It felt huge and iron-like. She kicked with all her might but it felt like flutter against that hand, a hand, she saw as she turned her head reluctantly, that was wearing a white glove.

"You got that stupid puta?" panted cigarette man as he joined his companion.

"Please don't hurt me," she said weakly. "What do you want with me, what did I do to you?"

Phoebe's inner voice, the doubting little sick shit that woke her at night to fan her anxiety, said: "I told you not to do this run. Now look at the mess you are in. Do you really think that a one hundred and twenty pound, forty-four year old woman is any match for these animals?"

"This is not personal," said white glove man and he grabbed her by the ponytail with a savage yank.

He hauled Phoebe to her feet and began to drag her deeper into the woods. Cigarette man took the opportunity to give her a kick in the ribs that made her cry out. Boots, steel toed boots, her rational mind catalogued. White glove man pushed her to the ground, her head struck a log and her vision wavered. Part of her prayed silently that she would black out, that she would be spared the memory or experience of whatever torture was in her future. Another part of her mind focused on the kids, on each of their faces, the sound of their laughter, as if to replace the upcoming horror with those sweet memories.

White glove man began to drag her running tights off. The ground beneath her was damp and spongy and she imagined her blood soaking into it, darkening the moss. She thrashed about and he became entangled in the stretchy material. The one foot that still wore a running shoe made contact with his mouth and she felt his teeth give. White glove man cursed violently, spat blood and tore the remainder of her running tights off. He dropped his sweatpants, revealing black boxer shorts, which he yanked down. He threw himself on top of her.

Phoebe screamed. She fought and wriggled but white glove man punched her several times in the face. She felt something warm run down her cheek. The pain in her face was quickly replaced by the pain of the man thrusting himself savagely into her. Her vision swam. She heard, improbably, music and the clink of glassware. Perhaps that was her mind distracting her, or maybe this was all some sort of awful nightmare.

She moved her head towards the imagined noise and saw a dim light through the leaves in the clearing.

"Fight, Phoebe, don't leave your children."

Resolve washed over her and she struggled to clear her mind of what is being done to her body, to focus on the light. Cigarette man had been holding her shoulders but he eased up, perhaps in anticipation of his turn to violate her.

"Your hand, Phoebe. What is in your hand?" Phoebe was not sure if the voice was in her head or someone was speaking aloud.

The hand held water bottle, strapped with velcro to her arm and around which she had wrapped the elastic band of the headlamp. It was metal and glass and a tiny little object in comparison to the men abusing her.

"Now, Phoebe, now!"

White glove man was climaxing. Phoebe swung her hand with the water bottle and headlamp as hard as she could at the side of his head. The impact was so hard that she felt her shoulder pop. White glove man raised his head to look at her, confused, and slumped onto her. She struggled to slide out from under the dead weight but cigarette man pinned her with his booted foot on her chest, unbuckling his belt.

Phoebe closed her eyes in resignation, she was no match for these two. Her life was about to be snuffed out here, to what end, her beloved children left without her. Maybe not knowing what became of her and thinking she left them would be better than them knowing what really happened that night.

Phoebe heard a thud and white glove man moaned. Phoebe opened her eyes and then blinked in shock. White glove man's head absorbed another blow and he clutched at his head and he stumbled backwards. Phoebe scrambled to stand up, staring in astonishment at the third man who was punching and kicking white glove man in the head with calm fury. White glove man had stopped moving.

"Take the knife off my belt and finish off the other," said the third man.

Phoebe gaped for a second or two and then grabbed the large knife in the scabbard on the man's belt. Without further thought, she plunged the knife, over and over, into cigarette man's back.

"That oughta do him," her rescuer said.

Cigarette man fell heavily on top of white glove man. Neither one of Phoebe's attackers were moving. Phoebe considered the pair for a moment and tried to control her breathing. Her heart was pounding in her chest. She thought she might be hyperventilating. She got her breath under control and then sank to her knees, suddenly aware of her naked lower body. She looked about for her running tights, but they were not visible in the clearing, which seemed much larger now.

"Here," her rescuer said, taking off his overcoat and draping it over her shoulders. She flinched at his touch and shivered violently. He stepped back from her.

"We've got some clothes out back but first, have a sip of this." His voice was gentle.

He pulled a flask from his hip pocket and offered it to her. The first sip was tentative and the taste burned. The second was a long draught and a tiny bit of her mind relaxed.

They were standing at the edge of a clearing, larger than the one Phoebe had been dragged into by white glove man and cigarette man. Music and laughter drifted through the night air, competing with the sound of the peepers. The drizzle had become lighter.

"Come along now, let's get you some clothing."

Phoebe shook her head in confusion and fought to keep from screaming. She was not going anywhere with this guy.

"Wait here, then." His voice was still calm.

Phoebe watched the man take a path at the edge of the clearing. A light blinked in the forest ahead of him. A minute later, he appeared with a young woman who was carrying a lantern.

"Fern will see you get some proper clothing."

He started away but Phoebe clutched at his arm. "Who, who ARE you?" she stammered. "And what is this place?"

He turned back to her. "My name is Petrel and this is my place. You are safe and welcome here." He went back the way he had come.

Fern was a slim woman, with a bob haircut. She wore trousers and a light jacket. She regarded Phoebe carefully, studying her bruised face in the flickering lamplight.

"Let's get you cleaned up and dry."

Phoebe was trembling now. Her teeth chattered with fear and cold. Perhaps this was what it was like to be dead, or maybe she was hallucinating. Fern took Phoebe by the hand and led her down the path where the man had gone. A small cabin came into view. There were lights and the sound of voices. Glasses clinked. Fern led her past the cabin to a smaller building, more of a shack.

Fern opened the door to what appeared to be someone's sleeping quarters. She drew a long match out of her jacket pocket and lit a kerosene lamp. Pointing towards a trunk she said: "See if something in there suits you. I will fetch some warm water for you to wash."

The door slammed shut and Phoebe was alone in the lamplight. There was a mirror on a nail above the trunk. Bracing herself, she looked at her reflection. Her frightened eyes stared back, a large welt on her cheek, her nose slightly askew with a river of dried blood running beneath it. Her hair was knotted, her jacket was gone and, aside from her Balans running socks, she wore only a torn t-shirt from a 5K race in 2006 over her running bra.

Phoebe opened the trunk. Inside neatly folded were dresses and slacks, sweaters and shirts. She selected a pair of slacks and a sweater, pausing an instant before choosing a cloche hat.

Fern returned with a large pot of steaming water, soap and a sponge. A towel hung over her arm.

"Do you want me to help you? It looks like they hurt you bad."

Phoebe could only nod, her eyes filling. Fern helped her wash her bruised face and gently untangled her hair. She rinsed the blood off Phoebe's hands as the image of the knife plunging into cigarette man forced itself into Phoebe's exhausted conscience. When Phoebe removed her t-shirt, Fern's eyes widened at the bruised ribs on her right side. Phoebe could only dab at her most wounded place, wincing in pain and shame as she did so.

As Fern helped her into the borrowed slacks and sweater, Phoebe asked: "How did Petrel find me?"

"He was out watching for the law," Fern responded. "He had heard a couple of sheriff's deputies were roaming around earlier. Looks like we won't have to worry about them any more."

This made absolutely no sense to Phoebe. Something was clearly very wrong.

"Thank you for your kindness," said Phoebe. "I must get home to my children. I live just through these woods."

Fern looked perplexed. "There is nobody living in these parts."

"Aren't we in Fairfax?"

"Yes, but the nearest farm is a thirty minute ride from here."

Phoebe felt a ringing in her ears and swayed, trying to keep her balance. What was this woman talking about? This could not be real. She hoped that she would wake up soon, in her own bed.

"Come now, let's get you some food and drink. That'll help you mend."

Phoebe followed Fern to the cabin. Inside it was warm, the candlelight kind and the conversation animated. Petrel was behind a wooden bar. He set a plate in front of her, chicken and potatoes and vegetables. A mug of what looked like beer appeared alongside her plate. At first, the notion of food appalled her but then, she attacked the food and gulped the beer.

"There, that helps, no?" said Petrel.

He smiled at her. She took her first real look at the man who had fallen upon her rapist. He was probably in his fifties and not a large man, dark eyes and hair, with a day or two beard. His skin was tanned. His eyes seemed kindly, if a bit sad.

"Thank you," she said.

"No thanks needed. Those varmints needed to be put down, for both our sakes." He spoke as he refilled her mug and her eyes grew heavy. She allowed Fern to lead her upstairs to a small bedroom with a single bed. Phoebe was asleep before her eyes closed.

She slept fitfully and nightmares left her exhausted. Her children, pursued by cigarette man and white glove man. Petrel and Fern butchered by her tormentors. Phoebe running desperately through the woods, trying to find her house in the thick underbrush. The police, summoned by her children's frantic 911 calls combing the roads and streams in the neighborhood and finding her lifeless, violated body. Her hands, slick with cigarette man's blood as she plunged the knife into him, over and over.

Chapter Two

Phoebe climbed out of her sleep like a swimmer surfacing after a long dive, sheer will driving her to wakefulness and forcing her eyes open. She was on her back in the woods, damp earth pressing into her naked lower body, a terrible ache between her legs. The peepers' song was very loud. She looked around her before she moved and saw she was alone in the dark.

She eased her aching body to a seated position. Her handheld water bottle and jacket were next to her. She grabbed for the jacket and fumbled in the pocket where she kept her cell phone. She snatched the phone to her chest. Gasping, she opened it and saw a text from her eldest.

"U ok mommy?"

Fingers shaking she wrote back. "Fine, home soon. How is game going?"

The phone chirped almost immediately, "kk, was worried. I am winning xoxox."

A sob of relief caught in her throat. She listened closely to the night. No sound of crashing angry men. Only the falling rain and the peepers. She unwound the headlamp from the water bottle, noticing that the water bottle cover was streaked with what looked like dried blood. She found her tights but one running shoe was gone. She pulled the tights on and stumbled in what she hoped was the direction of her house. She tripped over a downed tree and cried out in frustration. Finally she was rewarded by first a glimpse of the white siding, then her back porch.

She walked around the house and peered into the family room window. There were the two dark heads of her older children, engrossed in their game. She fished the key out of its hiding place and suddenly stopped, thinking of her bruised face and nose. She could not let the kids see her in this disheveled state; she had to clean up and have a story.

She went around the back of the house to the garden hose, washing her hands and face as she combed her mind for a plausible story for her missing running shoe, rat's nest hair and bruises. She sifted through the jumbled events of the evening, carefully avoiding any thought of Petrel and Fern and the plunging knife and the two bodies.

A mewing kitten by the bridge. The pitiful sounds sent her searching and she went into the water. It was much deeper than she anticipated because of the recent rains. She lost her shoe and fell face first into the water, bruising her nose and banging her ribs. And what of the kitten? That was the tough one. She did not want the kids out searching for the damn kitten in those woods. In fact, she did not want the kids in those woods ever again. Okay, she found the kitten and as she was walking home, came upon a dad whose kitten was missing who was ever so happy to have found the darn cat. Not a story that would hold much water with the law, or with any adult, but it would fascinate, and satisfy, her animal-adoring offspring.

She kicked the sole running shoe off outside and unlocked the door. The older kids glanced up at her and went back to Grand Theft Auto. Her eldest, Eileen, turned back.

"Mom, why are your face and hair so messy?"

"It was raining pretty good for a while and I got caught in it."

From her middle child, Kendall, "Can we have popcorn?"

As she put the popcorn bags into the microwave, Eileen came into the kitchen.

"Mommy, are you alright? You look kinda funny. Are you going to run all night?"

"Oh, honey, it's really raining and it is getting colder. I took a little fall and got a bit banged up, in fact I hit my face on the ground so I'm going to call it a night."

Eileen seemed satisfied so Phoebe omitted the story of the lost kitten.

Phoebe went upstairs and peered in on her youngest. Damien was sleeping peacefully with his pillow pets. She took a long, hot shower. She was trembling again, despite the near scalding water. She felt a scream rising up in her throat and she stuffed her hand into her mouth to stop it, biting her fingers.

The smell of burning popcorn pulled her back from the horror in her mind. She forced herself to be calm and went downstairs. She opened the kitchen window to let out the smell. Her ribs screamed in protest and her shoulder twinged. She quickly yanked the window shut when she remembered what had happened out there in the night. She double checked all the doors and windows, took two Percocet left over from her last c-section, and ordered Kendall and Eileen to bed.

The second sleep of this endless night was, thankfully, dreamless.

Phoebe awoke to the sigh of the ancient lab member of the family, Roxie, curled around her and twitching in her sleep. She touched the old dog's silken ears and sniffed her paws, which always smelled, inexplicably, of Cheetos. She breathed the familiar scent and its odd comfort. For an instant, all seemed well in her household. Then the memory of rape and murder slammed into her consciousness, almost knocking her breath away.

"Come on, Roxie, let's take you out."

Roxie groaned and complied, clambering down from the bed. Avoiding the bathroom mirror, Phoebe peed, wincing at the knifelike pain this caused. She dry swallowed several Bactrim from her medicine cabinet and emerged from her bedroom to the faint sounds of cartoons.

She tousled Damien's bedhead. He was engrossed in Sponge Bob and barely gave her a glance. The older two slept on, hibernating teenagers that they were. She smiled at both sleeping forms, quietly closing each door. She snapped Roxie's leash on and led her out to do her business. It was a classic spring morning. The birds were out in full force.

The old dog ambled along Branch Road, sniffing contentedly. Phoebe shuddered as she passed the right of way, but it was empty, save for a faint tire track in the grace and two Budweiser cans, which she absently picked up.

Coffee dripped from her Keurig. She took her bold roast onto the porch and looked out at the woods behind the house, green and silent. She peeked once more at the kids, took the meat-cleaver from her kitchen drawer and slipped it into the waistband of her yoga pants. Roxie looked up at her with mild surprise as she put the leash back on her but got off the couch and headed into the backyard.

The path into the woods was very faint. Several downed trees blocked their way. She climbed carefully over them. The ground sloped down towards the stream, which she heard before she saw the water sluicing over the rocks. Phoebe stood in the small clearing and studied the ground closely. The ground was muddy with many footprints and one spot where there was an indentation. If she closed her eyes, she could see the men falling atop one another as they died.

A few branches were broken off the underbrush beside the stream. A grey and blue object was submerged in the water. Her missing running shoe. She fished it out and shook it off. A glint in the sunshine at the edge of the clearing beckoned and, upon closer inspection, revealed itself to be a large knife. She picked it and tested the blade. A prick of blood on her thumb.

Back in her laundry room, Phoebe studied her ruined running tights and blood stained water bottle holder. She drew the knife from the pocket of her windbreaker and threw all these items into a large, black garbage bag. She tossed the bag into the back of her wagon. Her sensible car for sensible moms. She fought hysterical laughter. Should she take the stuff to the dump, or to a more distant place to be discarded? Burn them?

Maybe she should call the police, report her attack? That was what good citizens did. But how could she explain what she had done, or maybe what she and Petrel had done, to white glove man and cigarette man? Whatever was she going to tell David, who only barely tolerated her running and would have frowned upon her leaving the children unattended to run at night? David was due home on Tuesday; she had some time to figure that one out.

Absently turning bacon in the frying pan and stirring pancake mix her mind drifted to the memory of the little bar in the woods. Was that merely product of a traumatized mind? Perhaps another walk with Roxie was warranted to inspect further, to see if there was any sign of the place. Were Petrel and Fern the stuff of a dream? As the kids tucked into their Saturday morning breakfast, Phoebe turned on the radio and listened to the weather report.

After loading the syrupy plates into the dishwasher and reminding the kids that it was time to practice their instruments, Phoebe once more leashed Roxie, who groaned as she climbed off the sofa. This time, rather the faint path from her back yard, she went out to Branch Road and entered the woods a quarter of a mile up Branch Road via the larger path that was occasionally used by the county Park Authority to tend to downed trees.

She followed this path, which ran some hundred and fifty yards into the woods and opened into a small clearing. Phoebe carefully inspected the area. A few pieces of charred wood and some bricks were in the southwest corner of the clearing. She pushed one of the bricks aside and saw the glint of old brown glass half buried in the damp earth.

She flickered back to the memory of a roofing contractor who had some years before come to give David an estimate on shingles or a new roof or some such thing. David was forever making plans or getting estimates, most of which never went beyond the planning stages. The roofer was an older gentleman, maybe in his late sixties or early seventies and he was commenting on the neighborhood.

"Oh yes, there used to be a speakeasy here. When they started construction in this neighborhood in the sixties, they came across hundreds of glass bottles. Back from Prohibition days, I suppose."

She had thought the memory quaint, and even recounted the story to her middle schoolers, to give them some truck in history class. "My house used to be a speakeasy…"

Back in the house, Phoebe googled "speakeasy" and "Fairfax, Virginia". The only hits she got were advertisements for a local bar called "Speakeasy Live" that catered to George Mason and NOVA students. She supposed that she might have better luck in the public library newspaper archives. The thought exhausted her and she stretched out on the couch and fell asleep to the tinkling of the piano.

Her eyes blinked open to the face of her youngest.

"Can we have pizza for dinner?" he asked.

She glanced outside and saw that it was twilight. She had slept for five hours. She ordered two pies and sat down to her computer. When she logged into her email, she saw a message from David, sent the previous evening.

"Hi, babe. We finished up earlier than expected and I will be home Sunday. See itinerary. xoxoxo."

She studied the flight information, noting with some dismay that David would be home by the next evening.

Phoebe could only pick at the crust of the pizza. The kids did not notice. David would have scolded her for not eating.

Her most immediate problem was getting rid of the items in the garbage bag in the back of the wagon. The second issue was her bruised cheek. David was very sensitive to marks on faces, a trait that she had at first found charming and then annoying, as each playground bump on the kids was the topic of intense cross-examination. The battered ribs might be hidden for a few days; David preferred the lights out for moments of intimacy.

She cringed at that thought. Should she go and have a rape kit taken? Could she stand to subject herself to bright lights and prying questions? What of her privacy, was there really any privacy at all even in the medical records maintained by her physician? She supposed she should have an AIDs test, and a test for other STDs but, thankfully, she had not had a period in nearly a year and assumed that she was in early menopause.

What would she tell David? He would criticize her for running alone, at night, leaving the children at home. Her heart began to race as she anticipated his accusatory glare. But if she did not tell him, how would she handle the sex he would invariably expect when he returned from one of his business trips. She took another Percocet and had two glasses of wine, which quieted her mind enough to allow for a fitful sleep but left her feeling vaguely nauseous in the morning.

She awoke before it was light and let Roxie out to do her business in the front yard. No walks in the woods today. Checking to be sure all three kids were fast asleep, she eased the wagon out of the driveway and onto the entrance ramp to Route 66. She exited at Business 234 in Manassas and drove at speed limit down the nearly empty street. The Super K had several dumpsters behind the store, next to a blue clothing donation box. She parked next to the dumpsters, leaving the wagon running, and removed the black plastic bag from the back. She walked towards the donation box, quickly checked for any other activity in the area, and tossed the bag containing the tights, knife and blood stained water bottle into the dumpster.

Belatedly, she thought she should have separated the items and placed them in different dumpsters, maybe in different locations. She cringed as the notion of security cameras flashed through her mind. Dunkin Donuts black coffee in hand, she stopped at a CVS to buy foundation and concealer, hoping that jet lag would keep David from studying her face too closely. She hated wearing make-up.

Back at the house, the kids were stirring, inhaling shredded mini-wheats and quibbling over who had the next turn at the controller for Grand Theft Auto.

"Who wants to go to the library?"

"I do, mama," chirped her youngest, "I want to research how to be a dolphin trainer."

Phoebe showed Damien the mammal section of the Centreville Library and approached the greying Asian man staffing the information desk.

"I am looking for information on Prohibition in this area, in particular, I am interested in speakeasies in Fairfax in the 1920s."

He regarded her solemnly. "What is speakeasy?"

"A bar where moonshine was served, during the time when alcohol was illegal."

He turned to his computer, jotted down a number. "Follow me. I show microfiche."

Phoebe groaned inwardly. She had hoped for a hard copy newspaper. The Asian man led her to a table in the back of the reference section, opened a file drawer, and pulled out a sleeve containing rolls of microfiche.

"Newspaper from Fairfax, 1920s. All we have."

He pointed to a microfiche reader and drew away, back to his desk and questions about *The Hunger Games.*

She eyed her youngest, sitting cross legged on the floor and pouring over photos of whales and dolphins as she began to feed the fiche into the reader.

Forty-five minutes later, she was bleary eyed with her efforts, perusing countless engagement announcements and advertisements for auctions when a line jumped off the microfiche feeder.

"Petrel Johnson, 63, Questioned in the Murder of Deputy Sheriff."

On April 13, 1929, Fairfax County law enforcement officers arrested Mr. Johnson on suspicion of the murder of a deputy sheriff who had been sent to investigate claims that a speakeasy was in operation in the backwoods of Lee Pines, in the county of Fairfax. The body, which had been stabbed multiple times, was found on April 10 off a logging road near Lee Highway. Further investigation revealed an illegal speakeasy being operated under the direction of Mr. Johnson, some half mile from where the body was found. A second deputy involved in the investigation has disappeared and has not been heard from since the evening of April 10.

Phoebe scrolled through several more weeks of trivia. From May 3, 1929 the headline read: "Sheriff's Deputy Still Missing."

Despite an exhaustive search of the woods and roads of Lee Pines and along Lee Highway, no trace of missing deputy Earl Sandford has been found. Volunteers and deputies are frustrated at the lack of progress in the investigation while the Fairfax County Prosecutor has yet to issue an indictment against Petrel Johnson, although the search for the missing deputy and for evidence in the murder of Deputy James Arrington did include the premises of Johnson's speakeasy, which has been shut down. A source in the sheriff's department indicated that several patrons of the speakeasy as well as Johnson's common-law wife, Fern Irving, vouched for his whereabouts on the evening in question.

She looked through the rest of 1929 and 1930 but found no further mention of the deputies, Petrel or Fern.

"I am hungry, Mama," her youngest pleaded and she was shocked to see that it was well past noon, close to the hour that an airport taxi would deposit David back into her life.

As the wagon idled in the drive-through line at Popeyes, she checked David's flight status on her cell phone. Mercifully, a delay in departing Nairobi had caused him to miss his connecting flight in Amsterdam.

"Sorry babe," he soothed from AOL. "Will now arrive Monday morning around nine."

"No worries," she responded. "All is well here. xoxoxo."

Another eighteen hours for the bruising to fade.

She wondered if she would be able to stay in control, act normal. She was grateful for the kids, their predictable needs and wants. Even her eldest, with whom she had felt a pronounced sense of oneness from the moment she fluttered in her womb, had not sensed anything amiss. Hopefully, she could fool David as well.

Folding laundry, she glanced out the window towards the woods. Her conscience prickled at the thought of Petrel and Fern, their kindness and, even though her rational mind told her that her life could not possibly have intersected with theirs, she was glad there had been no reference to a prosecution. She went back to her computer and this time, searched "Petrel Johnson." She stared at the results, which included an obituary dated January 14, 1943, and briefly detailed the life and death of a resident of Fairfax, Virginia, who claimed as his wife a woman named Fern but who had been married to Veronica Johnson, who died of influenza in 1917.

Chapter Three

Monday morning came early. Almost reflexively, Phoebe followed her normal routine of walking and feeding Roxie. She woke Eileen, whose pre-high school routine took nearly an hour. Flashlight in hand, phone strapped to her waist belt and reflective vest glowing she went for a run. She supposed she looked like a yellow highlighter. She battled her inner voice, which was telling her not to run, that it was not safe. But Phoebe knew she would fall apart if she let fear rob her of what she loved. She was barely holding on as it was. Her ribs ached but it felt good to run.

The sky was lightening as she ran east along Branch Road. She passed a dog walker and another runner. They exchanged their regular greetings. She fretted a bit over how the reunion with David would go and then realized with relief that she would be at work when he got home.

Two miles along Branch Road, she doubled back to ensure that she would be able to kiss Eileen goodbye. Three-quarters of a mile from the house, her watch gave her a few extra minutes. As the sun peeked from behind a grove of trees, she turned left to run down a side road. She had been down this road many times, usually rewarded by a glimpse of the shyer animals, foxes or raccoons and once, a coyote. Mostly though, she liked to run this particular road in search of the ghosts who haunted the Civil War field hospital that her gossipy neighbor Layla claimed had been here. She would picture the tents, the wood smoke and the nurses and doctors moving among the wounded.

Although she liked to imagine that she "felt" something, just like her running friend Moises claimed to feel ghosts at Manassas Battlefield, the truth was that it was just a quiet little gravel road.

A robin and a cardinal flickered in the underbrush. It was quiet, save for the birdsong, which struck her as strange: the rush hour traffic on the highway was normally audible here. There was a small field to the right and she smiled at the butterflies dancing above the new grass. Her ankle rolled in the soft gravel and she began to fall. A veteran of many running falls, she waited for the inevitable impact as her mind considered first: "How much is this going to hurt and will I be able to hobble home?"

And then, the vain query: "Did anyone see me go down?"

Her right knee and hand took the brunt of this one and she rolled to her side, thinking to catch her breath and figure out if there was any damage. She smelled spring dirt and looked through the grass. A movement caught her attention and she watched, hoping that a rabbit or fox sighting would be the reward for the skinned knee and hand.

A pair of mud stained bare feet came into view. Her eyes slid upwards and she saw the hem of what looked like a muslin skirt. She blinked in confusion.

"Are you alright, ma'am?"

A tentative voice. Phoebe looked above the hem and straight into a set of wide eyes. Thirties, slight build, dark complexion, recorded her rational mind. Hair wrapped and tied in a scarf. The woman held a metal bucket in one hand, and blood stained rags in the other. Phoebe smelled wood smoke.

"Ma'am? Yer gonna catch the grippe laying on this cold ground."

Phoebe lurched to her feet. She heard male voices. Some hundred yards out into the field, she saw a tent and five or six men lounging on the ground outside the tent. Some had crutches, others bandages. There were tables here and there, most occupied by a prone form.

The woman gestured towards a wood fire with a kettle suspended over it.

"I'm fixin to wash these bandages. Scouts say more wounded is coming presently. If you are alright, that is."

Phoebe shook her head slightly and looked to the left. The ranch home that had been there, complete with barking collie, was not to be seen. The gravel road where she had tripped was a faint track. She must have hit her head in the fall and started to hallucinate.

"Nurse, nurse," an urgent voice pleaded from somewhere inside the cabin.

The woman dropped her bucket and hurried towards the door, Phoebe wandered behind. A dozen or so pairs of eyes tracked her progress. The stench of sick was almost breath taking. She fought back a gag as a hand reached out to clutch her hand.

"Nurse, Tommie here is real bad off. Can't you help him?"

She turned and saw on one of the tables a dark haired man/boy whose pasty complexion stood out against his fever bright eyes. What remained of his right arm was a stump, oozing green pus with angry red streaks reaching his chest.

"Hold on, let me get the nurse."

"Won't do no good," said Tommie's companion, "she won't waste her medicine on him. Says the laudanum has to be for them that gots a chance."

The voice dropped to a whisper. "Tommie has the look of death now. Can't you just spare him some kindness? He misses his maw something awful."

Tommie's eyes were half-closed, his breath shallow. Phoebe ignored his awful smell and took his good hand in hers. His eyes opened and met hers, widening slightly.

"Can you help me? I know I'm fixin to die, but please listen. That Sorel, you hafta help her." Tommie gestured towards the cabin, his voice now a hoarse whisper.

"Sorel is my half-sister and she followed my unit. I know she's spying for the yanks and maybe that's the best thing, being that she's a half breed. She won't tell me nothin' but I cain't die without makin' sure someone looks out for her. Crazy slave catcher is gonna come for her…."

Tommie's voice trailed off, as if the effort of his words were too much for him. Phoebe thought of all the boys who had died in Iraq and Afghanistan, far away from home and without the comfort of their mothers. She kneeled down next to the makeshift hospital bed and took Tommie into her arms, stroking his lank hair and kissing his pale forehead. He sighed and his frail body leaned into her.

She rocked him back and forth and whispered to him softly the line from *I Love You Forever* she had recited to her babies each evening before kissing them goodnight.

"I love you forever, I like you for always, as long as I am living my baby you will be."

A tear dripped from the end of Phoebe's nose onto Tommie's shoulder. Tommie shuddered and his breath rattled in his chest. Phoebe sensed Sorel's gaze and met the woman's eyes. A long moment passed, and then Sorel reached down and closed Tommie's eyes.

Tommie's companion drew out a piece of paper and laboriously wrote, "Thomas Evanston, died of his wounds on 13 April, 1864." He tucked the paper into the pocket of Tommie's ruined uniform pants.

Sorel turned back towards the cabin. Phoebe touched her arm.

"Talk to me. I promised Tommie I would help you."

Sorel picked up a large bucket and handed it to Phoebe.

"Let's fetch us some water from the stream o'er there."

Phoebe fell in step with Sorel and they walked down a faint path that led down downhill towards a stream.

"Sorel, you need to get away from this place," said Phoebe. "Do you have Union contacts?"

Sorel looked at her from under her dark lashes and nodded shyly.

"Can they help you?"

"I dunno."

"Listen, you give them information, right?"

Sorel nodded.

"Tell them you have information but first they need to move you to a Union hospital."

The insistent neighing of a horse interrupted their conversation. Sorel started, eyes widening in alarm.

"That ain't no ambulance. Mules pull the wounded here, and take them away, to home or to be buried."

She clutched Phoebe's arm.

"Oh please Lord, don't let that be Mastah White, looking for bounty for runaways."

"Stay here and out of sight. Let me go see what this is about."

Phoebe snatched the nurse's cap from Sorel's head and the blood stained apron from her waist, filled the water bucket, and began trudging back to the cabin. Three men on horseback stood in the clearing.

"Where is the surgeon in charge?" one man demanded of several patients.

A man with a bloody rag on his head answered. "He went out with the mule wagon yesterday to fetch some wounded."

The man spotted Phoebe.

"Nurse, where is the doctor in charge of this hospital?"

He swung down from his mount, his white gloved hands handing the reins to one of the more mobile patients.

Phoebe swallowed hard and answered.

"I expect him back soon with more patients. That's why I went to fetch clean water." She tried hard not to look at his white gloves.

"Are you the only nurse here?" the man demanded.

"Why, yes I am. Some of the local housewives come from time to time to help and bring food but I am the only one assigned here."

The man eyed her critically, eyes lingering on her forearms, pale in the early spring sunlight.

"I am looking for an escaped slave, a half breed name of Sorel. I hear tell she might be passing herself as a nurse."

"I have seen no such individual." Phoebe answered as firmly as she could. "There is a larger hospital, some miles out past Manassas though, you might want to check there."

"Search the hospital!" he commanded the other two men.

Phoebe moved from patient to patient, checking bandages and whispering words of encouragement. A few minutes later, the men emerged.

"No sign of her here. Be warned though that if you should see such a person, you are obliged to inform the authorities."

Phoebe nodded but said nothing, watching as the men mounted up and rode off to the west.

An hour or two passed and the sun drew higher in the sky. Finally, Phoebe took the water bucket and headed back to the stream. She crossed in ankle deep water to the eastern bank, looking for any sign of Sorel. The woman poked her head from behind a large tree.

"Was that them? Did they have dogs?"

"Yes and no. Sorel, you must find your way to a Union hospital. Do you have any idea where that might be?"

"I think it is near the mouth of the Occoquan River."

Phoebe considered this, searching through trail maps in her mind.

"Sorel, can you tell east from west?"

"Yes, ma'am, from the track of the sun I can."

"If you head southeast from here, you will run into it, probably about fifteen or eighteen miles from here. Then just follow it south. I don't know how far to the mouth, maybe another ten or twelve miles."

"That will take me a week or so, traveling at night." Sorel shuddered. "I hate the woods at night."

"When do you next expect to see your Union contacts?"

"I don't see them. Tommie's friend, he would write information for me to give them and I would hide it a basket one of the housewives would bring with food."

"Why is this man so desperate to find you?" Phoebe asked.

Sorel smiled sadly.

"I bore him a boy child after he forced himself upon me. I sent the child north on the underground railroad before he could sell him and then I followed Tommie until I found him here, hurt real bad. The doctor in charge told Mastah White that the south badly needed my services and that it would not be patriotic to prevent me from serving these lads. I buried that doctor yesterday; he fell to camp fever."

"I don't think we can wait for the housewife for you to be on your way. You're in danger here, Sorel. Wait here til dusk. I'll get you what I can from the hospital in the way of provisions."

Phoebe made her way back to the hospital, willing herself to walk calmly, speaking to the patients, ministering as best she could. She found some hard tack and a spare blanket, a tin cup and a pair of socks.

"Nurse?"

It was Tommie's friend. He pressed some coins into her hand.

"Please, give these to Sorel. Tommie would want it this way. She was very kind to all of us, she don't deserve to be dragged back to Danville."

Phoebe took his calloused hand in both of hers and smiled.

As dusk fell, Phoebe took the meager items to Sorel. She untied her running shoes and gave them to Sorel. They were a little big but at least they would provide some protection. Sorel seemed bemused. Phoebe supposed Sorel would walk in the water as much as she could to hide her scent. Sorel took the little bundle and slipped wordlessly into the darkening woods. Belatedly, Phoebe wished she had found a candle to accompany Sorel into the darkness.

• • •

Phoebe felt the grass pressing against her cheek and watched a blue swallowtail butterfly dart along the horizon. She became aware of gravel pressing into her side and shakily drew herself to her feet. The collie in the ranch house to the left began to bark. A garbage truck ground its gears in the distance. She glanced at her watch. Ten minutes to get home before the school bus arrived.

She mustn't think about the runaway slave or the dying man. It was not real. Phoebe fought hysteria as she trotted home in her bare feet. She ignored the toe she stubbed on the pavement. She needed to focus on getting through the day.

Lunches tucked into backpacks, kids kissed, wave to the bus driver. Shower and dress. Absently sipping Earl Grey from her silver travel mug, Phoebe started the wagon and headed to work. As she waited at the light, a wave of nausea washed over her, her hand shook and hot tea dribbled onto her skirt. Was this the aftershock of the rape and the trauma? Were the necessaries of daily life and her family distracting her from the reality of the bloody knife, the torn running tights and the bruised ribs?

A horn blared behind her and she pulled onto the shoulder. She turned off the engine. And what of these episodes, these visions? Were they symptoms of PTSD, a way of her mind escaping from what had happened? After all, any sane woman, any responsible woman, would have reported the rape, would have been to see a doctor, would have changed the locks on the house, and, most of all, would have a plan for what, and how, to tell David what had happened. But what of the man she had killed, she was sure she had killed him. She had washed his blood off her hands. Where were the bodies? What if no one believed her or worse, thought her unstable and took the kids away? Her heart raced and her hands were slick with sweat as she gripped the steering wheel.

She must do nothing, behave as normal. It had worked so far with the kids; David might not notice anything was wrong. Maybe see her doctor, ask for an AIDS test citing a one-night stand, or find a therapist to talk to about these episodes, describe them as flashbacks. Was Phoebe hurting future victims, or past victims by not coming forward? But how was this even possible, when Phoebe and Petrel had killed the men who had attacked her?

Phoebe started the wagon and continued to her office. She pulled into the parking lot of the building that housed the law firm where she worked part-time, mostly researching and writing briefs and memoranda. The firm specialized in school board and home owners association cases. The details and nuances of the cases intrigued her and the partners valued her work. On Monday morning, only Nancy, the office manager who also functioned as a paralegal, was in. The other attorneys were all in court or off at depositions.

She returned Nancy's greeting and asked after Nancy's mother, who had recently been placed in assisted living and was struggling with worsening dementia. Then, citing her need to finish an Amicus Brief in *Nicolson v. Loudon County Board of Education*, she closed her office door and logged into her computer. Rather than firing up Westlaw, though, she pulled up a trail map of Virginia. She studied the Occoquan River and smiled when she realized that her calculation of eighteen miles to the river mouth had been off by a mere mile. Then she caught herself and gave herself a rough mental shake. That was some sort of dream, or PTSD moment. You did not give directions to a ghost fleeing a slave-catcher.

Phoebe's cell phone buzzed and David's voice jarred her.

"I'm home. Dontcha think you could've waited to see me? I've been gone for two weeks!"

"Sorry," she murmured. "It's just that I've got to turn this Amicus Brief in by noon and I am stuck on this one issue. How about we have a late lunch?"

"Ok, I'll be waiting for you and I'll be hungry."

Phoebe hung up and sighed. She supposed her marriage was a decent one. Nineteen years, three kids, a comfortable life style. David had his faults, those really annoying habits. She knew she had hers too. Littering the living room with shoes, a tendency to buy way too many jackets he never wore and stuffed all the closets with, that vile way he cleared his throat in the bathroom. He had a bit of a temper too, and sometimes drank too much, but for the most part, he was attentive and he helped with the kids if she asked.

She liked it when he traveled for work. It gave her a sense of calm and control, and, most of all, freed her of the need to answer to him, to explain herself, to constantly have to agree with him. No, there was absolutely no way she was going to tell him what had happened. It would cause him to ask too many questions, and she would have to justify herself. Most of all, she hated having to justify herself.

Chapter Four

David greeted her at the door with a hug and a kiss, both of which she returned. She handed him a bag.

"I got some sushi from Wegman's, and a salad."

"Sounds perfect." He beamed. "Do you want a beer? I see there's one more Sam Adams Cherry Wheat in there."

His voice was hoarse. Maybe he got a cold on the airplane. He had several days beard growth.

"Say," he grabbed her face in his hands, "do you have a bruise on your cheek, Phoeb?"

"Oh, I got up to take Roxie out, she was whining to go and it was still dark. I thought the bathroom door was open and I ran right into it."

No sooner had she said that then she realized how completely lame it sounded, the oldest line in the book. She braced herself for the inevitable cross examination. But there was none. David turned away and pulled a beer stein from the cabinet.

"Want to eat outside?" Phoebe asked. "It's so nice out."

She updated him on the kids' antics and activities while they ate. He laughed at the funny bits and frowned in concern when she told him about an incident with a teacher. It felt normal, almost, if she weren't hiding from her husband that she had been raped and had probably killed a man or two. She fought hysterical tears that threatened to bubble up from somewhere deep inside.

Phoebe usually enjoyed sex with David. Of course, nothing was new anymore and sometimes she just wanted it to be over, but for the most part, she thought, it was a healthy physical relationship. Now though, the very thought of anyone touching her, penetrating her, made her heart beat in fear. How to avoid it, at least for a few more days, became the only thing she could think of as she rinsed the dishes from their lunch and placed them in the sink.

"Do you want some coffee?" she asked.

"I would rather have something else."

David cupped her buttock in his hand and she willed herself not to flinch and steeled herself for what was next.

Her cellphone chimed in her purse and she made herself step casually away from him and glanced at the phone.

"I'd better take this. It's the school."

Never had Phoebe thought she would be glad to hear the school nurse tell her that Damien had a fever of one hundred and two and was vomiting. He needed to be picked up as soon as possible. Smiling ruefully at David, she slipped out the door.

The little guy was wan, complaining of a sore throat. She sniffed his breath, thought she caught the tell-tale odor of strep. She phoned her pediatrician on the way out of the school. She carried Damien in her arms. He clutched her neck and rested his feverish cheek on her. An hour and a half later, her suspicions confirmed, she picked up an antibiotic from the drive through at CVS and drove home, a dozing child slumped in the back seat.

David met her in the driveway, concern creasing his face. He carried Damien into the house and laid him on the couch.

"Does he need anything?"

"Maybe some popsicles and Gatorade, and that alphabet chicken noodle soup he loves."

"I am taking the wagon," he said. "Don't know the truck will start since it has been sitting a couple of weeks. Don't want to get stuck and need a jump."

Phoebe thought that slightly odd; he hated driving her car and besides, he knew that she regularly started his F-150 when he was away. She said nothing though, just nodded as he grabbed her keys from the counter.

The rest of the evening was normal enough for a house with a sick child, and a mother who might be quietly losing her mind. Soup, medicine, homework for the older two, hamburgers on the grill. By the time she got the little guy to sleep with a second dose of penicillin on board, David was snoring in their bed. Jetlag had caught up to him she told herself.

Phoebe, on the other hand, was wide awake. She paced around downstairs and chased the older two to bed. She tidied up the kitchen and made school lunches. Finally, she sighed and sat down to her computer. She was still not sleepy so she googled "Danville." About four hours southwest, it had been the last headquarters of the Confederacy and had remained segregated until after the passage of the Civil Rights Act in 1964. No wonder Sorel did not want to go back to that city. Searches on "Sorel and Danville" produced no meaningful results. Finally, she researched "Thomas Evanson" and did get a hit, which was a link to blog containing a listing of Confederate soldiers lost in 1864.

"Thomas Evanson, born 1840 in Bedford, Virginia, died of his wounds, April 1864 in Fairfax County."

Google maps informed her that Bedford was some forty miles northwest of Danville.

Phoebe was lost in thought at the kitchen table when she heard a faint cry from upstairs. She looked in on Damien, who was feverish again. She gave him some children's Advil and lay down next to him. She fell into a dreamless sleep, one in which she slept so hard that she woke with drool on her stuffed animal pillow.

The next morning the older two went to school, David went to work, and Phoebe stayed home with Damien, whose energy level improved by the hour. She did some work on a memorandum in support of a homeowners association that had moved for foreclosure on a condo, the owner of which was eight years behind in homeowners' fees. Later in the afternoon, she took Damien out in the jogging stroller for a couple of miles. The field where she had met Sorel and Tommie was quiet and the collie outside the ranch house barked at her. The stream she had plunged through in her efforts to get away from the white glove man was a mere trickle, and no pick-up trucks stalked her.

David called her at six, telling her that he needed to meet a client for dinner and would be home before ten. She was in bed by nine forty-five, and when he came into the room at eleven, she feigned sleep. She listened for David to fall asleep, praying that he would not reach out for her. He was soon snoring. She could not sleep so she slipped out of bed and went downstairs. She took out a legal pad and made notes, every detail she could recall about these people from the past, all that she had learned on line and at the library.

The next morning, the little guy was well enough to go to school and she left the house at seven-thirty. She did not go to her office, however, but instead headed south on Route 29. Her yellow legal pad was tucked into her briefcase.

Bedford was about a hundred and seventy-five miles south and she was at the town museum before eleven. It opened at twelve so she walked around a bit to stretch her legs from the drive.

She texted David. "Meeting with a new client in Madison. See you for dinner. XOXO."

"Ok," came his immediate response. "Drive carefully."

An older woman with tight grey curls unlocked the door to the museum promptly at twelve. Phoebe wandered through the building, which was a converted house with three floors. Display cases housed uniforms, artifacts and photos of the Revolutionary and Civil Wars and a sign indicated that further information was available in the archives. She trudged down the stairs and asked the curator if it was possible to research an individual who had served and died in the Civil War.

"We'll see what we've got. We're in the middle of scanning older information but the complete set of our holdings are still hard copy family papers and newspapers."

The woman let her into a back room, where file cabinets were labeled by dates.

"You're welcome to look up the name on our database." The woman gestured at a MAC on a small desk.

The name Thomas Evanson came up under "Civil War Losses, 1864, location of grave unknown. See *Bedford Bee*, June, 1864." The link to the newspaper was empty. Phoebe consulted the file drawer for

1864. The newspaper was yellow with age and protected by a plastic sleeve. The article was small and on the bottom of the back page.

"Bedford Family Mourns Beloved Son."

Thomas Evanson was reported died in a field hospital on April 13. Mr. Evanson was the son of Jessie and Mildred Evanson. He leaves behind two sisters and three brothers. A stone marks his intended resting place on the family farm but his body has not yet come home as the hospital was taken over by Union troops and no burial records have been located. Mr. Evanson had been engaged to Miss Martha Williams of Bedford.

A later issue of the *Bedford Bee* had a listing of escaped slaves. There were rewards offered for the return of some of them, including: "Sorel, half injun, property of Jessie Evanson and her boy child, property of James White." She took a photo of the list of names.

Phoebe mused over this information as she drove north. If she had dreamed of Sorel and Tommie, or for that matter, of Petrel and Fern, why had she found records? How had these souls wormed their way into her subconscious? She pulled the wagon into the driveway at five-thirty and greeted the kids, who, although they feigned homework, she knew had been playing video games until they heard Roxie bark when she opened the door.

David came home moody and late for dinner. He snapped at the kids and answered Phoebe's questions about his day in monosyllables. She gave up trying to talk to him and went upstairs to fold laundry and supervise Damien's bath. She heard his truck pull away from the curb and felt her anxiety level rising. She hated when he got like this. He could be quite unpleasant sometimes. She wondered if something had happened at work.

David shook her awake. The alarm clock read thirteen minutes after two. She smelled whiskey on his breath and braced herself for an argument.

"How was your client? The one in Madison?" He sneered at her.

"Fine, I suppose. Still hasn't committed to a retainer. Has a kid with autism and the school won't…"

He cut her off with a laugh that sounded more like a bark. "You are lying. I can always tell."

"You can look though my notes if you don't believe me," she offered, edging away from him.

He pounded the bed with his fist. She shrank back further.

"You are just so stupid."

Phoebe got up and went into the bathroom, locking the door behind her. She hoped he would not get loud. Sometimes he did and if he woke the kids that would be a whole different problem. She waited for a few minutes, but there was no further noise from the bedroom. She slipped out and went downstairs to the couch.

Further sleep eluded her. She thought about what David had said. Why was he so sure she was lying? She did have notes from the client in Madison, from the week before. She hoped that she had not written down the date, and even more, she hoped that he would not ask to see them. She hadn't thought it necessary to create a more detailed story. Ordinarily, he wasn't interested in her clients. She tore her notes from the museum and the library off the legal pad and hid them in the china cabinet, inside her grandmother's soup tureen.

Roxie started to bark. The sharp yelps made her jump. Shushing the old dog, she got up and made tea, taking it with her as she snapped Roxie to her leash. Roxie must need to go outside. Sometimes, she did not make it through the night without an accident.

The night air was damp and loud with the peepers. Phoebe shuddered at the sound. She suddenly felt that white gloved hand clamp her leg. She heard the laugher at the speakeasy and smelled the wood smoke at the field hospital. She shook herself and came back to the moment. Roxie shuffled along and did her business. Everything was fine, she soothed herself. And that rustle in the underbrush was just a rabbit.

Back inside, she took a Xanax and considered once again whether she should talk to a therapist. But still, she came up against the same issue. How could she tell anyone about the murders? A therapist might decide that a report to the police was warranted. She had no way of guaranteeing her safety from prosecution. Her privacy might not be respected. No, that was not the thing to do. She was on her own with this one. She finally slept on the couch for a little while.

David did not stir when she tiptoed into the room to shower and dress, nor did he emerge to say goodbye to the kids. Although it was her day off, Phoebe went to the office and worked, rather distractedly, at research on whether a homeowner's association was permitted to request the city to enforce a noise ordinance against a family with a child who screamed and ran around for most of the night, causing the shared wall of the townhouse to shake, at least according to the neighbors. The child's parents claimed that the boy had autism and that they were doing the best they could to control him.

She gave up and went home at two. David called her and they exchanged pleasantries. No mention was made of the night before. Maybe he did not remember? But she knew he did, and that at some point, he would bring it up again. She knew him too well to imagine that he would simply let it go. She also knew that at some point, she would be expected to make love with him. The idea still repelled her. She wasn't sure that she'd ever want anyone to touch her again. She felt hopeless.

The kids came home and she smiled at their antics and queried them on their homework. The afternoon gave way to evening and she made dinner. Steak and potatoes, and a green salad. David came home, demeanor benign. He complimented the meal and helped with the dishes.

Phoebe fell asleep reading Damien a story. The smell of his just shampooed hair comforted her and he wrapped himself around her. A hand shook her shoulder.

"Phoeb? You gonna avoid me?"

She went into her bathroom and brushed her teeth. In the other room, she could see David waiting for her in their bed.

"Hey, babe. I'm sorry about last night. I had a bit too much to drink and I was talking shit."

"It's ok," she murmured, settling into her pillow. He began to caress her shoulders and breasts. She willed herself not to flinch, not to pull away. He was clearly aroused and she made herself touch him. She blocked the white glove man from her mind but she could not get her body to respond to her husband.

When he entered her, she was dry and unready. She forced herself to move in some grotesque version of what used to be pleasurable.

David didn't notice. He was in his own place. He climaxed loudly and she rolled away from him, padding silently to the bathroom. Tears coursed down her face as the shower steamed. When she shut off the water, she heard David snoring in the other room.

The next morning, she was gritty from lack of sleep. Her eyes ached and her mouth was dry. As dawn broke, she ran a few miles. The light sweat and clear air lifted her spirits slightly. She made coffee and roused the kids.

David came downstairs, smiling.

"Morning, babe," he enthused.

She handed him a cup of coffee.

"You're up early," she said.

"Yes, I've got an early conference call with Singapore."

No mention of the night before. Good. He had been fooled into thinking that all was well. He had to think that, would always have to think that. Her inner voice was vehement. She could not have explained why. Nor did she let herself think that perhaps her good marriage and normal life were actually not so great. She was going to block out all these things that had happened, shut down the memories. She would burn the notes in the soup tureen.

Phoebe looked at the calendar in her office. She was startled to see that the following week was spring break for the kids. She penciled in a couple of days off, maybe make two long weekends of it and do some day trips or a mini vacation. She called David.

"I was just about to call you," he said. "I am going to have to go to Singapore. There is a problem with the plant there."

David was a senior vice president for a large, European-based drug company called Parlington. He traveled frequently for meetings and to troubleshoot major equipment and personnel issues. Although the company was not bound by U.S. labor laws in its overseas locations, the shareholders demanded regular reports on labor conditions and monitored the press, even sending independent observers into sites. She imagined that this was one of those types of problems.

"Ok," she said. "When?"

"They are booking me on a flight tomorrow. Right now, I figure a week, maybe ten days. Long flight."

"That is too bad," she replied. "Next week is spring break and I thought we might.."

He cut her off. "Sorry. Can't be helped. You do something with them. Maybe I'll be back before it is over."

That evening the air was thick with tension, as it frequently was before David went on one of his trips. Phoebe focused on dinner and laundry and getting the kids to do homework. She avoided his path and finally he settled down. Two suitcases sat by the front door.

"Did you book your cab for tomorrow?" she asked.

"No," he said. "I have a meeting in the office in the morning. I'll take a cab from there."

"Do you want me to drop you at work? That way you can leave your car here."

"No thanks, babe. It will be fine in the parking lot at the office."

This was odd. Normally, he wanted his car driven while he was away, to keep the battery alive and to keep the milage on the wagon down. She said nothing, though.

"Let me say goodbye to the kids tonight." He went upstairs.

When she came back from her run in the morning, his car was gone. Her phone chirped.

"Sorry I missed you. Will email you when I get there. xoxox."

She texted back. "Have a good trip. Luv u."

Phoebe spent some time looking up places to take the kids. Maybe go to Williamsburg, or to the beach, if the weather looked good. She looked at the map, eyes drawn to Bedford. There was a WW II Memorial there and a good sized lake, Smith Mountain Lake. She had a neighbor who talked of vacationing there. The website for the state park on the lake advertised cabins for rent.

She took the kids to Friday's for dinner.

"What do you say if we take a couple of short trips next week," she said. "We could go to the beach or maybe stay in a cabin near a lake."

"Do they have boats?" asked Damien. "Can we swim?"

Chapter Five

On Saturday morning, Phoebe and the kids were southbound on Route 29. They stopped for lunch in Charlottesville and were checked into a cabin at the park by early afternoon. The kids poked around the cabin, which was simple but adequate. The day was warm, nearly seventy degrees. Phoebe put the groceries she had purchased on the way down into the refrigerator.

They explored the park. The trail map showed a network of one to three miles trails most of which ran along the lake. Birds sang and the occasional boat passed. There were a few other hikers and teenagers played Frisbee on the beach.

The younger kids took their shoes off and waded into the water, assuring her that they would only go in up to their knees and then claiming to accidentally fall all the way into the water. She spread out a blanket and felt a bit of the tension that had gripped her for days let go. As the sun set, they gathered themselves up and went back to the cabin.

Roxie snored on the porch. Hamburgers sizzled on the grill and Phoebe poured herself a glass of Malbec. She listened to the kids playing hide and seek in the trees at the edge of the clearing. Even her teenagers' voices had a child-like quality.

She nestled Damien into his sleeping bag in one of the two bedrooms. His hands were grimy, a sock was missing and his shirt was grass stained but he had fallen asleep on her lap and she did not have the heart to wake him up. With an admonishment to the older two not to stay up too late playing Nintendo, she drowsed on the sofa bed in the living room.

Roxie's whine woke her. Faint light came in through the curtains in the kitchen window. She took the old dog out in her bare feet; the damp chill of the dew made her shiver. Coffee started, she peeked into the room where the older two slept soundly on the queen bed, arms and legs flung about. Closing the door quietly, she opened the door to the smaller bed room.

The sleeping bag was empty. Phoebe checked the bathroom and the porch. She pulled on her sweatshirt and stuffed her bare feet into her running shoes. Had she locked the cabin door last night? She could not remember. She began to search the area behind the cabin, where the kids had played the evening before.

She did not want to shout for him, not so close to the cabins. After all, people were sleeping. One of the hiking trails ran about fifty yards behind the cabin. She walked up and down it for a few minutes. What looked like a scrap of cloth caught her eye, hanging from a low branch a few feet off the trail. A grass stained child's sock. Terror raced through her as she brought the sock to her nose and inhaled her child's scent.

"Don't panic. He has to be close. He was talking about exploring before he went to sleep."

Damien was fascinated with animals, surely he was right around here someplace. She called his name. Bird song was the only response. The water. What if he went down to the water? Maybe someone came into the cabin. Should she have locked the door when she went out looking? And her cell phone was back in her purse.

She tried to visualize the trail map. The thing to do was to search each trail, working her way out from the cabin. She started on the trail that ran east around the perimeter of the cabins towards the campsites. The sun was coming up and the water shimmered. Ahead on the trail, there was a circular opening in the trees and blue sky above. She felt her vision slide to the right and her foot catch on a root. She was off balance and stumbling through the opening in the trees.

She righted herself, avoiding what she was sure would have been a nasty fall. To the left of the trail was a small graveyard with several headstones. The park brochures had noted that the Bedford area was dotted with tiny family gravesites, some of which dated back to the seventeenth century. They had been left undisturbed even when the land was sold. She blinked; her eyes must be adjusting to the brightening sun. She blinked once more, and became aware of a figure kneeling next to a tiny stone with a lamb on the top.

Phoebe stopped short, not wanting to disrupt someone in mourning but fighting the urge to shout, to ask if anyone had seen a small barefoot boy. The woman turned towards Phoebe. Her face was lined and the color of milk chocolate. Her hair, flecked with grey, was coiled neatly.

"Excuse me but I can't find my son," she blurted.

The woman regarded her calmly.

"You don't say. He done wandered off now?"

"I don't know. I woke up and he was missing." Phoebe's eyes were filling. "He is only seven and I am afraid he is lost. Have you seen anyone this morning?"

"No, I don't imagine I have. Been setting' here a while visiting with my lambs."

She gestured towards the headstone with the chipped lamb on the top which Phoebe now saw read, "Elsie and Noah, gone so soon."

"I am sorry for your loss," said Phoebe.

"It is alright, child. It was a long time ago. They took sick in the winter of 1852. The grippe was bad that year."

Oh, God, Phoebe thought. Not again. Not with Damien missing. She felt her mind slip. Fighting panic and trying to keep a slight grip on her sanity, she found herself making inane conversation with the woman.

"Do you have other children?"

The old woman smiled. "Why yes I do. I have Sorel, she a fine young woman. She works with me now, at the Evanson's place. She fixin to make me a grandmother."

This is it, thought Phoebe. I have officially lost my mind. Her face felt wooden but she kept talking to the woman.

"My name is Phoebe and I am pleased to meet you. My son who is missing is named Damien."

"They call me Raven. I keep one eye out for him. He can't have gone far, now."

"Thank you," said Phoebe. "If you see him, can you please ask him to wait here for me?"

Raven nodded and turned back to the headstone. Phoebe continued down the trail, which seemed wider here than it had been before. The campsites, which should have been ahead a few hundred yards, were not there. Instead, the trail ended and she saw a log cabin with smoke coming out of the chimney. Two mules were tied up in a lean-to behind the house.

She shook her head and backed away. She turned back toward the trail. Raven was walking towards her.

"Yer young un is just up ahead."

Phoebe gaped at her and then clasped for her hand. "Thank you!"

The woman stepped back and then looked into Phoebe's eyes. A gentle smile touched her lips. "Keep him close now."

Phoebe darted up the trail. Damien was sitting next to the headstone with his hand on the lamb.

"Mama! I was looking for you."

Phoebe sank to her knees and drew him close to her. She kissed the top of his head and studied the children's headstone, which looked more worn to her now.

"Did you get out of bed and go outside?"

"I had a dream, mama, that you and I were walking in the forest. We found some beautiful snakes, all different colors. Then, we picked up a rock and there were these little mice that turned into puppies. I went to find the puppies. I heard them barking and I followed them on the path."

"Oh, honey, I don't want you to go outside without me, or your sisters."

"I wasn't alone, Mama. I was with a little boy and a little girl. They played with the puppies with me and showed me the forest. It was so pretty. Where did they go?"

Phoebe could only stare at her son. Half dreading the answer she asked: "Did you see anyone else, sweetie?"

"A nice old lady. She was smiling at the boy and girl, but when she touched them they disappeared. She seemed so sad when they left. Then she told me that you were looking for me, and not to leave you alone, that I needed to look out for you. She sat with me a while next to this stone. I told her that I played with her children and that made her so happy. What is this stone? Are these graves?"

"Yes, they are. The stones are in honor of people who died a long time ago. A place where people can remember them. Maybe her children died and she buried them here."

Damien studied the headstone for a long moment and touched the lamb. He buried his face in Phoebe's chest.

"I won't leave you, Mama."

Phoebe took his hand in hers and led him back to the cabin. She ran him a bath and started breakfast. She found both his grass stained socks in the bottom of his sleeping bag. Her hands shook as she buttered the toast.

David called that evening.

"How is my family?" he boomed. "We have a busy day today. How do the kids like the lake? Have you been hiking yet?"

"We are having fun and the weather here is great. Here, the kids want to talk to you."

She handed the phone off and each child spoke to David.

She washed the dinner dishes and sipped a glass of wine. She mulled over the day. She had read somewhere that some people were more sensitive to spirits. The characters from the past had done her no harm. She felt no fear of them. She was mostly concerned that they were the product of her unstable mind. She was not sure how she felt about Damien having experienced her visions. She supposed that a child was probably even more open to other souls, or the spirit world, though she had never identified with a religious group, nor had she exposed the kids to such notions. Maybe Damien had read her mind.

Phoebe gave herself a little shake and faced what really bothered her. She had never told David where she was taking the children, or when. She thought about this for a long time and then used her cell phone to do some research.

Phoebe slept curled around Damien, nose buried in his hair, inhaling his slightly stinky boy breath with adoration. She woke before dawn and eased herself out of the twin bed. Roxie yawned and walked outside stiffly. Coffee brewing, she found a large flashlight in the cabin pantry and began a careful search of her car. Once again, Google proved accurate, and she found, as described, a pager sized GPS tracking device under the back bumper of the wagon.

She considered ripping it off and depositing it at the dump just outside the park entrance. No, that would not do. David knew she was here. Best that she kept to her plans for a long weekend with the kids.

She gulped her coffee. Why would David feel the need to track her movements? She had never lied to him about what she was doing or where she was going, well at least not until this past week. They had a decent marriage, not perfect, certainly, but they were stable, committed to the kids. Maybe she did not always enjoy his company but what couple who had been married as long as they had been, could stand each other all the time?

Her mind raced a bit. Was she in some sort of danger? Did she need protection, a gun maybe? Or was all of this a by-product of the rape, and the vision of that knife in her hand, plunging over and over into cigarette man's back?

Phoebe wished suddenly that there was someone she could talk to. Her parents were elderly, her siblings distant. Although she had friends from college and from law school and several running partners, she was truly close to no one. Her life revolved around the kids, her job and her running.

Ah, well, she sighed to herself, even if I had a really close friend, all this stuff is just over the top. Anyone I told this to would think I had lost it. After all, she herself was pretty sure she was out of her mind.

A day of wandering the trails and picnicking on the beach was a distraction. Phoebe knew that she was so lucky with her children. They were all she needed. Maybe she needed a break from David, some sort of separation to sort through her feelings. A period of time without him. She could get some counseling. She took them out for pizza and then gave in to their pleas for ice cream.

Phoebe woke to the tapping of rain on the cabin roof. It was still dark. Damien twitched next to her and rolled onto his side, muttering something about a banana. She stroked his hair.

Her terror at not being able to find him still wrapped icy fingers around her heart. The rape had been awful but the thought of her kids lost or hurt was a thousand times worse. She slid out from under the quilt and padded into the kitchen to let Roxie out.

She frowned. Roxie was not snoring on the couch, nor was she sleeping with the girls. The cabin door was locked. She opened a can of dog food; as deaf as she was, Roxie would always rouse to the smell of Alpo. No response. She looked for her sweatshirt and the flashlight and then hesitated. She would not leave the kids alone in the cabin to search for the dog.

The door to the porch was locked. It was still dark and she could not see anything out on the porch. She checked each window, feeling silly. Roxie had certainly not gone out a window. One of the windows in the girls' room was open a half inch at the top.

Phoebe had still not turned on any lights in the cabin and she made a cup of tea by the ambient light of the microwave clock. Uneasy, she settled onto the couch, tucked her feet beneath her and wrapped herself in an afghan.

The rain was steady. She thought she would wait until it was full light and then take the kids with her to look for Roxie. She should call the park rangers; maybe they could help. For the first time in her life, Phoebe wished she had a gun.

"Mama."

Damien appeared in front of her. "I saw them again, Elsie and Noah."

"What were they doing, honey?"

"They played with me in the woods. I wanted to go swimming but they said there was no place nearby to go swimming, which was kinda weird cuz we went wading yesterday."

"Well, the lake hasn't always been there. It was built in the 1960's. And sweetie, you were dreaming."

"They told me they were always here. Their mama comes to see them sometimes. She is sad, but when they sing to her she stops being so sad."

"That would make a mama very sad. Mamas don't usually bury their children."

"I am hungry. Can I watch Sponge Bob?"

Phoebe made scrambled eggs with cheese and toasted some English muffins. The rain had stopped and the sky was light. She looked out onto the porch. No Roxie.

Come to think of it, where was Roxie's leash? Once again, she searched the small cabin. Nothing. She took her cell phone into the bathroom and called the park rangers.

The ranger who answered was cordial and took a description of Roxie. When Phoebe mentioned that Roxie's leash was missing, concern came into his voice. He was headed right over.

She met him outside, on the stoop, explaining that she did not want to alarm the kids. She locked the door and together they examined the perimeter of the cabin. Phoebe pointed out the window she had found open earlier and the ranger knelt down to examine the ground beneath the window. Wordlessly, he gestured to a footprint in the soft ground. The roof overhang had protected it from being washed away by the rain.

"Any of your kids have feet this size?"

She shook her head.

"I'm going to call the troopers. You folks stay inside and I'll have Angie come up and sit with you until they get here. I'd rather you not go looking for the dog yourselves. If she's in this park, we'll find her."

He waited until a short blond woman arrived. She, too, wore a pistol on her belt and a look of concern. Phoebe imagined this might be the most excitement the rangers had seen in a quite some time. They sat at the kitchen table. The girls woke up and came into the kitchen.

"Mom, what is going on?" demanded Eileen.

"Roxie is missing and the rangers are going to look for her." Eileen raised her eyebrows.

"What do you mean, missing? How did she get out?"

"We are trying to figure that out. When did you two see her last?"

"She was on the couch when I brushed my teeth," said Kendall.

"Did you guys hear anything last night?" the female ranger asked. "Any barking or doors opening? And did either of you happen to open the window in that bedroom?"

Eileen looked at Phoebe.

"Mom, what is really happening here?"

There was a knock at the cabin door. Two Virginia state troopers came inside. That got Damien's attention.

The troopers established that Eileen was the last to go to bed, around midnight, and the Roxie had been on the rug between the twin beds in the smaller bedroom. When Phoebe got up at six, Roxie and her leash were missing. No one could say for certain that the window had been closed when the girls went to bed. Roxie, though hard of hearing, would generally bark at a stranger, but she might not have considered the cabin a place she needed to protect. Roxie was not fond of the rain; it bothered her arthritic leg, and she had never wandered away from her family or her food bowl.

"Anything else, amiss, ma'am?" asked one of the troopers as his partner headed out to radio for another car to help search the park.

Just about everything, thought Phoebe, but she shook her head.

"Say," Phoebe asked the female park ranger, "is there a story behind the gravestones down that trail?"

She pointed towards the trail where she had found Damien the day before.

"Why yes, there is," smiled the ranger. "I did my Masters' thesis on this area in the 1800s and the interactions of the slaves, the whites and the Monacan Indians. I believe, based upon the records I found and the folks I interviewed about what their grandparents and great grandparents had passed along, that those children's mother was a former slave who was purchased by a Monacan Indian who then married her and took her to live with his tribe. Before 1824, this would have made her free. In those days, the law allowed a person to free a slave by marriage and then the children of the marriage were born free. Of course, that changed in 1824 with the Racial Integrity Laws, which prohibited intermarriage and would have called into question whether the children of such a union were free."

"How did they die?" asked Damien.

"I don't know. A lot of children died back then, many of diseases like mumps and chickenpox. The stone has no date, so we can't be certain of when they died, or how old they were. And that is the only stone in the little graveyard that has names on it, so we don't know who else might be buried there."

Not wanting to tie the ranger up all morning, Phoebe told the kids to get dressed for a trip to the library in Moneta. Maybe they could research this a little more, or at least find something to read or a movie to rent. She gave the ranger her cell phone number and loaded the kids into the wagon.

Someone, most likely David, was tracking this movement. Again, she considered removing the device but did not want the ranger to see her do this.

The girls were delighted that there was internet access at the library. Damien was absorbed by a book on elephants. Phoebe browsed through some best sellers. Her cell phone buzzed.

"We found your dog, ma'am," said the trooper.

"Oh good," Phoebe replied. "Shall I come and get her?"

"Ma'am, I'm sorry to have to tell you this. We found your dog down at the beach with her throat slit. She had her collar on and the leash was nearby."

Phoebe tried to wrap her mind around this image.

"What? Who would do such a terrible thing? She was a faithful old girl; I got her before the kids were born."

Phoebe's voice cracked. Whatever would she tell the kids? She stepped outside the library and sank onto a bench.

"Ma'am? We'd like to examine her further, if we can have your permission. The vet who takes care of our police dogs will see that she is returned to you along with her leash and collar. I know you don't want those kids to see her like this."

"Thank you for that. I think I'll take the kids home today. I don't want to stay in that cabin another day."

"Probably best. Please give me your contact information. I'm going to call over to Fairfax County. I have some friends up there. They'll touch base with you this evening, make sure everything is alright."

Phoebe though of Roxie as a puppy, a brown ball of fur who chewed everything in sight. Shoes, toilet paper, underwear, socks, even a couch; nothing was sacred. She never lost her patience when the kids mauled her, drooled on her, stuck their hands into her food bowl.

She pictured trusting Roxie, obediently trudging along on her leash down to the beach. A hot white flash of rage seized her. Her hands shook and she wiped her eyes. She wished she had a cigarette.

An older gentleman passed by and looked at her face. "Are you alright?"

"I've had a bit of a shock, that's all." She smiled, a feeble attempt. "You wouldn't have a cigarette would you?"

He tapped one out of a battered pack of Marlboro Reds and lit it for her. Her hands still shook. She inhaled and looked up at him gratefully.

The man studied her. "Been a few years since you had a smoke, looks like."

"Yes, probably twenty, maybe twenty-five years."

"Well, I sure hope that whatever's troubling you, it don't stay long."

Phoebe went back into the library and collected the kids. She led them to the wagon and then stopped. A few yards away was a bench. They sat down.

"Guys, I have bad news about Roxie." Damien's eyes welled up.

"The troopers found her near the beach. It looks like she went for a walk and had a heart attack. She was an old lady."

Eileen looked at Phoebe in disbelief. Phoebe shook her head slightly and willed her eldest not to ask a long list of questions. Kendall was weeping and clutching Damien.

Damien looked up. "Do you think she was scared?"

The question floored Phoebe. He answered his own question.

"Elsie and Noah were with her. They're probably playing with her now. She'll always be there. It's a nice place."

Phoebe hugged each of them. "She loved us. She was part of our family. The park rangers will return her to us and we can bury her."

She studied her trio. "Let's go back to the cabin and pack up our stuff. We can come back and visit another time."

The ride home was quiet. Roxie's spot in the back of the wagon seemed huge and empty. The kids dozed, listless. No texting and no music. Ordinarily, Phoebe would have relished this and engaged them in conversation but now, she just wanted to be home.

She stopped for gas in Amherst and used the restroom, stuffing the GPS into the sanitary napkin disposal in the ladies' room. Belatedly, she regretted her impulsivity. She probably should have left the GPS somewhere in the cabin. Her stomach began to ache. She was more afraid now than she had been during the rape.

Home. But was it even a safe place? What did she really know about safety? If someone had raped her in her own neighborhood, and then stolen her poor dog right out of a cabin while she and the kids slept, how could they be safe? If only she had not gone running that evening at all, or even if she had reported the rape, things would be so different. She wondered, not for the first time, who she had offended so much as to hurt her or kill Roxie or maybe even lure Damien out of the cabin.

Chapter Six

Phoebe did what she did best. She fretted and she made lists. Goals, really, to distract her terror and growing sense of loss of control. First, to change the locks on the house and have an alarm installed. She made those calls from the car and arranged for immediate installation.

The next thing was trickier. She needed to arm herself. She knew nothing about guns and would need training. In the meantime, mace or pepper spray. And you better believe, she was carrying a knife. And the kids, what to tell them, to give them enough information without scaring them. She considered sending them to visit her mother in Pennsylvania for the remainder of spring break week. She hated to let them out of her sight though.

Eileen, like her mother, was anxious by nature but she was smart and intuitive. When they got home, Phoebe pulled Eileen into the garage and told her that the troopers had told her that someone had taken Roxie out of the cabin. She left out the bit about the slit throat.

"Did the person who took Roxie hurt her?"

"We don't really know. They are doing an autopsy. Please don't scare Damien and Kendall with this. We just don't have enough information right now."

She explained about the changing of the locks and the alarm system. She hoped that would assuage Eileen's fears.

"Mom, we need to get another dog. One that can protect us, warn us if someone tries to get into the house."

"Yes, we should get another dog. Let's take it one thing at a time though."

The alarm company showed up an hour later. They installed a system that detected motion as well as any attempts to open doors or windows. They also changed the locks, adding an extra deadbolt with a separate key.

Phoebe sat at the kitchen table. She reached for her computer but then hesitated. If someone had placed a GPS on the jeep, who was to say they were not monitoring her computer, her phone? She had purchased the MAC about five years ago at the mall. She did not password protect it or her phone. She hated having to remember passwords and besides, she did no on-line banking. Who would care about her personal email and her Facebook account? She did her work on a separate laptop that had been issued by her law firm and was networked to their system and required her to use a password.

Her smart phone was new. David gave it to her for Christmas. It had a lot of fancy features. Eileen would tease her about not using the phone for all the things it could do. She went upstairs and logged into her work lap-top. Fifteen minutes of research and she was armed with the knowledge that installation of a key stroke logger onto her home computer involved downloading a simple piece of software. There was a more subtle product, visually unapparent, that would feed her emails, her phone call log, her texts and any photos she took with the phone to another account.

The doorbell rang. Phoebe opened it to a middle aged man who showed her his Fairfax County detective's shield and introduced himself as Todd Nichols. They went out to the porch, out of earshot of the kids. He told her that his buddy down at the lake, Trooper Weyson, had called him and asked him to check up on her. She told him that she had changed the locks and installed an alarm system. He nodded approvingly. She hesitated, and then told him about the GPS and that she had removed it and had then thrown it away.

Nichols thought for a moment. He met her eyes.

"Who is the first person who comes to your mind as wanting to track you?"

She swallowed, feeling very guilty.

"My husband David."

She explained that David was away on a business trip, and that he had known that she had taken the kids to the lake without her having told him.

"How did you make arrangements for that trip?"

"I did some research on line and made a few phone calls," she replied.

"If I were you I'd get that phone and computer looked at, maybe not use them until you are sure they are not being monitored."

Phoebe sighed, staring out into the woods. Nichols shook her hand and gave her his card, urging her to call him any time she was worried or had any questions.

"Can you give me a photo of David?" he asked. "And the make and model of his car."

Phoebe pulled out her phone reflexively but then Nichols held up his hand. Phoebe went into the house and pulled out a photo album from their trip to Disney World the previous year. She also pulled from her file drawer a manila folder marked "cars".

"He drives a 2007, Ford F150," she said, showing him a copy of the registration.

Nichols left and Phoebe went back out to the porch. She needed to really think about that gun. She consulted her work laptop once again, and learned that in Virginia, it was surprisingly easy to obtain a gun and that getting a carry conceal permit would not be a problem for someone with a clean record. Obviously, she would need some training and some time to get comfortable with the idea of carrying, and maybe even having to shoot someone. Pepper spray she could find at Walmart. She had one in her purse, one in her car and one in her nightstand before nightfall.

She settled in with the kids to watch *The Walking Dead*. Normally she would have been engrossed in the characters but her mind drifted to who and why. The most obvious answer was David but the why just would not come. First, he had been the one who brought Roxie home and spent hours teaching her to retrieve that damn tennis ball. Second, even if it had been David, she could not imagine that David would have wanted the kids to have been traumatized, particularly given the gruesome way the poor dog had died.

How well did she really know David? That was a good question. They had been together a long time. While their relationship was not without strife, for the most part, they got along well. They never argued about money or the kids. David was not terribly interested in her day to day activities, but neither was she interested in his. Their conversations would revolve around the kids' lives. They would occasionally go out to eat, or see a movie. In the nice weather, they attended barbecues in the neighborhood and hosted similar events from time to time. David had always traveled a lot for work and there had been a slight increase in the lengths of his trips over the last year.

David's company was based in Sterling. There was the annual office picnic and Christmas party, which they usually attended, although, come to think of it, she did not think they been this past Christmas. Of course, David had mentioned some layoffs; maybe the principals decided that it was not a year to have a big party at the Air and Space Museum. She knew his co-workers in passing. David liked to go fishing. She never went because she got horribly seasick, but the girls went once or twice. They were bored though, and were not interested in slimy fish.

Phoebe had never poked around in David's drawers, or looked at his phone or computer. Until today, she had never considered that he would do such a thing to her. Why would he want to frighten her? What could he possibly be looking for? She could not think of a single thing. Her life, frankly, was on the boring side. She liked it that way. Maybe it wasn't David at all.

"Mom," said Damien, "are you listening to anything I am saying?"

"Sorry, sweetheart. I was thinking about something. What did you say?"

"I said, can we make some more popcorn? And, I miss Roxie." His brown eyes brimmed with tears.

"I know, so do I. More than you know. Tell you what, let's make some popcorn and I will pull up the animal shelter's website. Let's see who might be in need of a home."

He brightened. They regularly scrolled through the animals at the shelter. Rabbits, cats, guinea pigs, dogs and once or twice, a goat or a pot-bellied pig. She brought down her work computer and he frowned at her.

"I thought we weren't allowed to touch your computer for work."

"My MAC is acting funky, very slow. Let's try this one tonight."

The girls joined them as they poured over the website. Not surprisingly there were quite a few dogs, mostly pit bulls and pit bull mixes. Phoebe had always been leery of those with children. Probably too many horror stories and not enough facts in her mind about the breed. Before the bowl of popcorn was half finished, she had promised a visit to the shelter the next day.

Phoebe did not think she would be able to sleep but she did. She woke once when Damien's footfalls echoed across the hardwood of her room and he bounded into her bed. She wrapped her arms around him and stretched her feet out feeling for Roxie's soft fur at the bottom of the bed. She blinked awake, awash in sadness. She regretted ever begrudging the old dog her early morning walks or hogging the bed.

Fully awake, she made her way down to the kitchen and brewed some herbal tea. Her cell phone showed seven missed calls. David's cell phone. He had not left a voice mail. He almost never called when he was overseas, except from a company phone, not his cell. Almost without thinking, she dropped her cell phone into the toilet. Kendall had a phone that she never used. Phoebe would use that one, or the land line, until she could buy a new phone, one that was on a different account.

She started with his dresser drawers. David's drawers were always chaotic. Unmatched socks and underwear were stuffed randomly into different drawers. Pocket litter and change were piled deep into several drawers, old receipts going back probably ten years. Matchbooks, random yellow sticky notes with indecipherable scrawl. She did not know what she was looking for.

She found shotgun shells in a bottom drawer. David did not have a gun, at least as far as she knew. He had never even mentioned guns. Wedged between two drawers, like it had gotten caught and shoved back, was a set of papers stapled together. She eased it out. It was a contract and price list for an updated bathroom and kitchen. The address listed was 134 Eastern Shores Road, Virginia Beach. VA. David had signed it in 2011.

Google earth pulled up a single family house two blocks from the beach. The image was a bit blurry but there was a blue pick-up truck parked in the driveway. Phoebe felt dizzy and vaguely sick. Next she looked up tax records for the property and found that it had been purchased for $735,000 in 2010 by David Rivers and Annette Peterson. She wrote down the address, no need really, she had memorized it, probably forever. She then jammed it back into its spot between the drawers.

"Really, David?" she thought. "I would have respected you more if you had hidden it more carefully."

Next into the browser went "Annette Peterson." Lots of hits so she added Virginia Beach to her query. A Facebook page showed a thirty-something blond, very tan. Lots of beach shots for profile photos. She looked closely at one of the photos. Annette was beaming into the camera, a glass of white wine raised, a male arm around her shoulder, an arm which, Phoebe was quite certain, belonged to David.

"How cliche, David," she thought.

A little blond piece on the side, a beach house. The picture had been posted on August 7, 2012. She was sure that if she checked her appointment book, she liked a written appointment book, always had, she would see that it showed David on a trip that day. She wondered why she was not angrier. It dawned on her that she did not really like David that much at all. That realization was almost a relief. But the kids, the kids would have loved a beach house.

The animal shelter opened at noon. Phoebe and the kids were there by a quarter after. They spent an hour and a half getting to know the half dozen pit bull mixes. One tan and white puppy would not leave the girls alone. He trotted after them, licked their hands and faces and barked for more belly rubs. A home inspection was required to adopt a pit bull. Phoebe filled out the paperwork. The volunteer assured them that it would not be more than a few days for the home visit.

The next day was Wednesday. Only a few more days of spring break. Phoebe studied the weather forecast for Virginia Beach. She told herself that she would not go anywhere near Eastern Shores Road. Using her work computer, she booked a suite in one of the high rise hotels in the heart of the town. They could eat in some of the restaurants, she could run on the boardwalk.

They were on route 64 on Wednesday morning, almost to Norfolk, when Kendall's cell phone rang.

"Phoebe," said Nichols, "are you driving?"

She explained where they were. "Can you pull over and stop and get out of the kids' earshot?"

She pulled off at the next exit and sent the kids into Starbucks with their computers. She told them she had to return a phone call and would join them for a treat in a few minutes.

"David does not work at that drug company," said Nichols.

"What? How can that be?" replied Phoebe, dismay in her voice.

"They wouldn't give me any details other than that he stopped working there two years ago last August. Human resources said it was confidential. I have a colleague who retired from the PD who works in their security department; he may be able to give me more information. What sort of information do you have about this trip to Singapore that he told you he was taking?"

Phoebe explained that the trip had come up fairly suddenly, but that was not abnormal, given that his other trips were not always planned in advance.

"I didn't take him to the airport though. He told me he had a morning meeting at the office and that he was planning to leave his car in the parking lot at work and take a cab to the airport."

"How about flight or hotel information?" asked Nichols.

"Normally he will email me that information, sometimes when he gets to wherever he is going. He usually calls me or emails me a few times on each trip."

She considered this for a moment. "He did call me, not from his cell but I can't recall what number came up. It was when we were at the lake. Of course, that was when I realized he knew we were there even though I hadn't told him we were going there. I can't tell you what the number was because I drowned the phone."

"If you get me that phone, maybe we can get some information off it. Any other contact with him?"

"Just a bunch of missed calls from his cell the day we came home. Actually, more like late in the night when we came home. That was also weird. His cell phone won't normally work overseas because he does not like to buy the additional international service."

Her voice trailed off. "I don't actually know where he is."

"I don't like the idea that you are going to out of the area," Nichols said.

"But I promised the kids," she pleaded.

"Alright," said Nichols. "Don't ignore anything that seems strange."

• • •

Phoebe and the kids walked along the beach. The day was warm and the breeze was gentle. Phoebe bought a kite from one of the boardwalk stands and Damien and Kendall took turns running along the shoreline, trying to get the kite into the air. There were a few other people walking along the beach, as well as a couple of dogs jumping in the surf. Phoebe thought of how much Roxie had loved to chase a stick into the water.

"When does dad get back from his trip?" asked Kendall.

They were walking up from the beach. The kids pleaded with her for money to play arcade games.

"I am not sure. He said probably a week or maybe ten days," Phoebe replied.

Phoebe ordered a sea breeze from a restaurant adjacent to the arcade. She sat in the sun and watched the kids.

Kendall's phone rang in her purse. It was the state trooper from the lake. He told her that the results of Roxie's autopsy were in and that the local vet would cremate her. He went on to say that they were not sure where she has been killed but it was not at the beach where she was found.

"Why?" asked Phoebe.

"Well she had pretty much bled out before she was left at the beach. There was very little blood at the scene."

"Thank you for letting me know. When will her remains be ready so I can come down and get them?"

"There is one more thing, Ma'am," said the trooper. "A couple of folks spotted what may have been your husband's truck in the park the day before and early in the morning that you noticed her missing. Funny thing is, one of the witnesses said a woman was driving the truck and she was alone."

Phoebe absorbed this as he told her the vet's office would contact her when Roxie was ready.

The next two days were blessedly uneventful. Phoebe had picked up some brochures from the hotel lobby. One was for the Great Dismal Swamp Wildlife Refuge. About an hour southwest of Virginia Beach, it featured guided bird walks, hiking trails and hinted at black bears. The latter immediately caught Damien's fancy and the girls were persuaded when she suggested that they see who could take a photo of an owl, alluding to a prize for the best picture.

A cheerful college aged guide with a pixie haircut led them on the tour.

"Please stay on the trail," she cautioned. "There are water moccasins and other snakes."

Much of the tour was along wooden planks raised above the swamp. There were indeed many birds, and Phoebe imagined that if it had been any warmer, the mosquitos and black flies would have been feasting on their winter white skin.

Damien ran ahead and the girls lollygagged behind with their cameras. Phoebe admired the sun glinting off the water and turned to point it out to the girls, hoping they might get a nice shot. The wooden walkway had disappeared, as had the girls. Phoebe heard a faint buzz in her ears and thought vaguely of mosquitos. She glanced forward to where Damien had been and saw only a mucky path. She shook her head, trying to clear her vision.

She saw movement up ahead and breathed a sigh of relief. Damien, she thought. But it wasn't. It was a tall black man with a pronounced limp. He was leaning heavily on a walking stick. He started when he heard her and turned, fear creeping across his face. He wore a muslin shirt and torn cotton pants. He was barefoot and one foot was terribly swollen.

"Are you alright?" she called. "What happened to your foot? Do you need help?"

He gave her a look of astonishment. "Ah cut it in dah wahdah."

She approached. "Have you seen a doctor?"

He gave her a look of incredulity. "Do yah no know where we is? Ain't no doctah for more 'n a hundred miles and he jes see white folks."

He winced and she saw pus ooze from the top of his foot.

Phoebe groaned inwardly. She had hoped never to have this happen again. Why was she a magnet for these characters? Were they lost in her world or was she in theirs? What did they want with her? She thought of her notes in the soup tureen, she supposed that she would be updating them later. As she had with the others, she interacted in the hopes that this man would soon disappear.

"Let me see that foot," said Phoebe. "Sit down on that log. And did you happen to see a little boy?"

"A little white boy?" He snorted with laugher. "Here? Not a chance."

Phoebe reached into her purse and pulled out a tube of Bacitracin. "Here, clean that cut off and put this on it."

He regarded the tube with suspicion. She dug further into her purse and found her bottle of Bactrim pills. She always carried them to ward off those pesky urinary tract infections. She shook two out and handed him her bottle of water.

"Here, take these now and then two each day for a week."

He squinted at the medicine bottle and she realized that he either needed reading glasses, or perhaps could not read. He pointed at the date at the bottom.

"What do dis mean?"

"The medication expires in July 2014," she said. "Next year."

"Dat ain't nex yerah." "Dat don't make no kinda sense. Must be some powerful magic. I thanks you."

He hauled himself to his feet. "You go on ahead a ways, you find yer young uns."

He limped forward into the swamp. He spoke over his shoulder. His eyes were piercing.

"And you watch fer dat woman. She evil pure. She need to be marked."

The clouds moved away from the sun and the water glistened once more. Phoebe turned to look for the man but he was gone. Thank goodness. She looked ahead and saw the wooden planks. She heard the girls laughing and walked ahead to join them.

The jeep was parked at the Visitors Center. She went into the building and approached the elderly volunteer behind the desk.

"Sir," she asked, "what is the history of this area? Did anyone live here?"

He smiled. "Now that is quite a story. For as long as I can remember, and I grew up in Suffolk listening to my great grandparents talk about the old days, folks went on about the Dismal Swamp Maroons, escaped slaves who used to live in the swamps here. It was practically inhabitable. Bears and alligators kept the slave catchers away. No one dared go into the swamps. A type of trade system developed. The maroons would harvest wood and make shingles and trade for other goods. It went on for several hundred years. It was all local lore until a few years ago, when some archeologist found actual evidence of the community. They're still excavating and it is kind of under wraps but I imagine we'll hear more about it in the years to come."

"Fascinating," mused Phoebe. "Thank you so much."

"Mama," said Damien. "Did you see the man with the gross foot? It was really yucky. He told me to wait for you and the girls and to watch out for snakes. Do you think he was bit by a snake?"

Chapter Seven

David and Annette

For most of his marriage, David had considered life rather dull. He had a decent career at Parlington. He traveled a lot. The kids were not really his thing. Sure, when he was around, he went through the motions, went to a school play, checked homework. He mostly liked to stay in the garage, tinkering around with old car engines that never seemed to work regularly. The kids did not gravitate to him. He figured he was as boring to them as they were to him. Of course they really got to him sometimes and he would lash out, particularly if he had a drink or two on board. Phoebe always looked the other way, blamed his outbursts on work stress.

When he and Phoebe first got together, it was exciting. She was hot and things were steamy between them for a few years. Before the kids came along, they traveled and went to concerts. Not that things were always that smooth; she could really get on his nerves. Who could blame him if he snapped once in a while, said cruel things. She suggested once that maybe he was depressed, he should see a shrink. He thought that was ridiculous and yelled at her about it. She never brought it up again.

When the kids were babies, Phoebe was always exhausted. She never wanted him to touch her. At first, he pursued her more but then, he lost interest, at least for the most part. Besides, she had gotten way too skinny for his taste. Their coupling became sporadic, scripted but neither one of them cared enough to talk about it. He thought about leaving her but that seemed like too much work and he figured it would be too disruptive for the kids and very expensive.

He had brief but torrid affair with a red-headed summer intern. She eventually bored him but his libido spiked for a few months. Once or twice when he fucked Phoebe he pictured the intern's red pubic hair and round ass. It angered him that Phoebe would not respond to him like the intern had and he was rough, jamming himself over and over into her until she cried out. He tried flipping her over and going at her from behind but she wriggled her way out from under him and locked herself in the closet. He jerked off and then had a couple more drinks to dampen his anger.

After that, he traveled as often as they asked. He was vaguely ashamed of himself and increasingly discontented. He was drinking more and occasionally dabbling in recreational drugs.

In early 2010, he was doing a pre FDA inspection at a factory outside of Bangkok. His job was to anticipate violations that the FDA guys would flag. He was willing to look the other way for little stuff. Record-keeping that was less than perfect or a few missing lab tests. This factory had not been inspected for at least a decade. He found rampant lack of documentation and use of substitute ingredients in US bound drugs. Many of the technicians had no training records and in some cases, lacked adequate identity documents.

This situation, he told local factory management, was a potential shutdown scenario. Not only would the factory fail FDA inspection, Parlington's shareholders were sticklers about underage workers and safety. The managers smiled and nodded. They protested that they had not had any problems with the previous inspection and cited the high cost of making all the recommended changes.

David was firm and told them he was going to issue them notice requiring that the violations be addressed within thirty days or a corporate stand-down on work at the factory would be issued.

He went back to his hotel room and drafted his report. He planned to send his preliminary report back to Virginia before he got on the plane. It needed a few more details but he was hungry and wanted a drink. He had some pad thai and a beer at a restaurant across the street from his hotel. After dinner, he walked into the red light district. He enjoyed people watching but the sex shows advertised were lame. On his first trip, he had quickly learned that once you set foot into those places, they would have you watch a show and then shake you down while promising more exciting entertainment.

He sat at an outdoor bar and had a drink or two. That was as much as he could remember the next day. He woke at two in the afternoon. His head ached and his mouth was like cotton. He was completely naked. He staggered into the bathroom to piss. He stood under the tepid water in the shower until his head cleared a bit. He ordered some food. He had missed his flight. He sat down at the desk to rebook his flight and finish his report.

His laptop was not on the desk. His wallet was in the pocket of his cargo shorts, which he found crumpled under the bed. No money seemed to be missing. His phone was under a chair and his passport was in the room safe. He checked his briefcase. No laptop. His notes from the inspection were missing. He took four Advil and packed his suitcase.

He supposed he could reconstruct the report. It would be a pain in the ass. He wished he had sent the damn thing in before he went to dinner. At least he still had his wallet and passport.

He slept a good portion of the leg to Detroit. By the time they landed at Dulles he was feeling better. He made nice with the family and thanked Phoebe for the chicken dinner. She was attentive when he fondled her and he rolled himself on top of her.

He made it into the office the next day around ten.

"Jet lag was kicking my ass this morning," he said to April, the office manager.

She gave him a peculiar smile.

"Ed and Eric want to see you. They are in the conference room."

Not only were Ed and Eric in the conference room but so was Lisa from human resources and Harry from security. Alvin the attorney was perched in the corner. David looked at the group and raised his eyebrows. He was starting to worry now.

"What is this about?" began David. He turned to Ed. "I should have my report to you this afternoon."

Eric shook his head. "We are not here about your report on the factory. We are here to talk to you about what happened on Tuesday night in Bangkok."

"I wrote up my report. I was going to send it in after dinner. I had some dinner and took a walk. Stopped in a bar for a drink. That was it."

"Are you sure that was it?" asked Ed.

David looked around the room at the somber faces.

"Well, I think someone broke into my hotel room. My laptop and notes were missing when I woke up."

Harry pushed his iPad towards David. "Have a look at these and tell us if you remember anything else about that night."

David reluctantly pulled the iPad towards him. On it was a series of photos. In the first, David was naked, lying on a bed with a young girl, she could not have been more than ten years old. His eyes were closed and his hands were wrapped in her black hair and his cock was deep in her throat. In the next photo, the girl was spread-eagled and he was on top of her. The third photo was of David with a little boy. He could not look at it and shoved the iPad across the table.

"I was drugged. I don't remember anything from when I sat at the bar after dinner until I woke up the next afternoon in my room. I would never do anything like this. This is not me."

He realized he was pleading with them but he went on.

"The factory would fail any FDA inspection. It is a potential shutdown and I told the managers that. They must have set me up and stolen my report. My laptop was missing and my notes but they did not take my money or passport."

"That all may well be true." This came from Alvin. "But it does not matter. The Thai police are demanding reparations from Parlington in exchange for not going public with these photos. They claim to have video as well. And now that the report is missing, we have no way to substantiate what you claim to be the conditions at the factory."

"So I am being blackmailed?" asked David.

"No," said Eric, "we are being blackmailed. If these photos and videos go public, our shareholders will be furious. We will have to send an independent inspector, a team actually, out to that factory."

It was Lisa's turn. "David, we are terminating you for cause, effective immediately. You have to appreciate our position here. What you did violates both company ethics policies and international law. You are lucky that you were not arrested in Bangkok. I suppose they still might be able to pursue charges but they are much more interested in our paying them off."

"Are you going to pay them off?" asked David.

"We have not made a decision on that," said Alvin. "We have no obligation to you here. Our obligation is to our shareholders."

Harry spoke up. "I'm going to escort you to your office so you can pack up your personal things."

"Wait a minute," said David. "What about my stock options and my health insurance?"

"Your stock options will be cashed in at today's price. You have the option of continuing your health coverage under COBRA, at your expense. All paperwork will be mailed to you."

Annie thrust a stack of papers at him. "Please sign where I have marked."

"I'm not signing a goddamn thing." David stood up. "You can all go to hell."

"Let's go, David." Harry took David by the elbow. David shook him off.

"Don't make this worse for yourself." Harry's arm clamped down on David's elbow again, this time with an iron grip. He guided David towards the door. With his free arm, David grabbed a book off the shelf and smashed it into a picture on the wall. The glass shattered.

"Just box up his personal stuff and deliver it to his house." Eric's voice was resigned. He and David had gone drinking many times, had played golf together. "Let's get him out of the building."

The corridor to the front office seemed very long. The office was silent; not even the phones were ringing. Eric and Harry rode down the elevator with David and walked him to his car. David handed over his parking pass and company access badge. He knew all his company accounts were already deleted.

David went to a hotel off of Route 28. On the way, he had stopped at an ABC store and got a bottle of gin, the expensive stuff. He texted Phoebe and told her that he had to go up to New York City unexpectedly. Then he drank himself into a stupor.

On the Friday morning after he was fired, after two days of drinking, very little of which he actually remembered, David woke up with shaky hands. He ordered a large breakfast and washed it down with several glasses of orange juice, four Advil and a lot of coffee. He went over to Dulles Town Center and bought a new laptop. He sat in the food court to check his email. Bangkoknites69 had sent him the same photos he had seen on the iPad.

His phone chirped with a new text message. "How do you like those photos?"

David grimaced. "Who are you and what do you want?"

"I can make those photos go away."

He thought about that. He figured he could not make things any worse.

"How?" he responded.

"Look to your right, at the table closest to Auntie Anne's."

A blond woman in a sundress was sitting at the table. She raised her hand and wiggled her fingers at him.

He made his way over to her and sat down. "What do you want?"

"I can make all this go away."

"Look, I just got fired. How much is this going to cost me?"

"I don't want your money. I want to do business with you."

He stared at her. "You a company headhunter or something?"

She threw back her head and laughed. She had nice white teeth and smooth skin. She re-crossed her legs.

"Do you know how much money I just made from those photos of you? Your company rolled over like a bitch in heat." David just stared at her.

She went on. "Listen, there is all kinds of money to be made in matters of indiscretion. You can double or even triple sell in some cases. I could get you for some good coin to keep me from sending those to your wife. Your wife might even pay me to keep from sending those shots to her job. She's an attorney, right?"

"I don't care about her. So, you are a professional porn agent and blackmailer? That's novel."

She laughed again, this time reaching out to touch his arm.

"For a guy in a tough spot, you have some spunk. I like that. I really think we could work well together."

She stood up.

"Come on. Let's take a walk. I want to show you some more of my work."

They walked through the mall. She stopped at a candy vending machine and got a large red lollypop. She was wearing high heeled sandals and her long legs were toned. She unwrapped the lollipop and put it into her mouth.

"I just love these things."

She sucked at the lollipop and switched it from one side of her mouth to the other. David felt himself stiffen.

"My portfolio is in my room at the Marriott. I have a large MAC with great video quality. Want to come up and check it out?"

The woman had photo and video of him violating children. What more could she possibly do to him? He shrugged and followed her into the elevator. She pushed her sunglasses on the top of her head and ran her fingers through her blond hair. He wondered if her snatch matched. Her eyes flicked to the bulge in his jeans. She smiled.

She opened the door to her suite. No sooner was the door closed she had untied the halter top of her sundress and let it fall to the floor. She wore only a black thong. She left her sandals on and walked over to the desk to power on the computer.

"I started out on the other side of the camera. Can't say it wasn't fun but there is so much more to be made in this business than for posing for crotch shots and low grade video."

She started with a slide show. Women with men, women with women, men with men. The photos were high quality for sure, looked like they had been taken in a studio.

"I know, much better quality than the ones of you. There was limited time and the lighting was terrible in the back room of that bar in Bangkok. Plus, my client there was not interested in art. They just wanted the cash from your company."

"It was the managers of that factory, wasn't it?" She smiled.

"Most of my clients are high-rollers, interested in quality art, sometimes some personal time with the subject. It is all consensual of course."

David wondered about the children who had been photographed with him and how consensual that had been. Of course, he hadn't consented either.

She moved on to video, again, high quality. "Sometimes I do sound, sometimes not. Depends what the client wants."

"So what do you want from me?"

"I need a partner here in the states looking for subjects. I am overseas all the time with my clients. I can't keep up with the demand."

He could not believe he was even considering this. But, his dismissal from Parlington had vastly limited his career options. He was certainly not going to hang around the house with Phoebe and the kids.

"Tell you what. Do a job with me and see how you like it. Get a sense of the money and the game. You won't regret it." He nodded slowly.

She smiled. "Good. I have a potential job down in Virginia Beach. Couple of college gals looking to make some extra money. Let's celebrate."

She walked over to the refrigerator. Her ass sure looked fine.

"Gin, right? Tanqueray alright?"

She did not wait for him to answer, just mixed him his drink and poured herself a glass of white wine. He watched her bend over to put the tonic water back into the refrigerator. She looked over her shoulder.

"Like the scenery?"

She brought him his drink. They clinked glasses.

"So, what would you like to watch?"

"I'd like to see you in a movie." He winked at her.

"Oh that stuff is all so old. How about a live demonstration?"

She got on all fours and smiled at him over her shoulder, running her tongue over her lips. Next she rolled onto her back and parted her legs. Yes indeed she was blond down there. David studied her appreciatively. She licked her fingers and began to play with herself. She returned her fingers to her mouth and sucked greedily. She moaned.

David could not contain himself. He unbuckled his jeans. He was throbbing. She crawled over to him and flicked her tongue along his inner thigh. He pulled her to her feet and stepped out of his pants. She kissed him, hard and he could taste her. He picked her up and thrust into her. She groaned. He carried her into the living room and sat her on a barstool. She wrapped her legs around him and urged him faster. He came quickly.

She was not through though. She led him to the bed and lay down, face down. This time he lasted longer. He grabbed her hair and fucked her from behind as deeply and as hard as he could. Her body shuddered with each stroke. She screamed when she came and he reached under her and stroked her clit.

He texted Phoebe that he had been delayed in New York another day.

"So," David asked later that evening. "What is your name?"

"Annette. Annette Henderson".

• • •

David and Annette's first job involved two college girls. Annette had a condo right off the beach and it was set up for video and still shots. The second bathroom had been converted into a darkroom. Annette explained about the darkroom. It was used for situations where discretion required non-digital material. The girls were anxious to make money and cooperative with all manner of poses and activities. Shooting took two days. Annette paid them $500 each.

"How do we make money off this gig?" David asked. They were sitting in the hot tub on her balcony. "Those are nice videos, but they are not worth that much. What kind of profit are we talking about here?"

First of all, Annette explained, the end customer wants more than the video. He wants a personal visit with the girls. "I can get twenty-five thousand easy, plus all travel expenses."

"But the girls are not going to work for free."

"I arrange for them to 'win' a vacation. We escort them to the location and turn them over to the customer. Then we start sending the photos and videos to the girls' parents."

"Kidnap them? Demand a ransom?"

"Don't be so dramatic. Nothing like that. Just get the parents to cough up a little coin to keep those photos off the internet. After all, they have careers to consider."

"And what about the girls? What happens when they meet the end customer?"

"Some money, some baubles and, with a little chemical help, they keep the customer happy." Customer pays us the big fee and we kick a bit back to them. Everyone's a winner, babe."

She poured him another glass of champagne. Her hands found him under the water. The next morning, he could not recall the rest of the night but he was sure it was fantastic.

Spring break in Brazil. All expenses paid. What college kid could resist that? Bambi and Brandi, their video names, had Ecuadorian passports when the boarded the plane to Rio. David and Annette were traveling on the same flight but in first class. David had never flown first class with Parlington. Company policy had not allowed it, even if you had enough miles.

Annette rented a car and they drove to a private villa an hour or so outside of Rio. On the beach, fully stocked bar. She told David to leave their suitcases in the car. They would have their own villa. This place was for the girls to meet the customer. First she needed to settle them in. She shooed David out to the beach with a drink and busied herself with the girls. From his lounge chair, he watched a limo pull up to the villa. The man who stepped out was in his fifties, heavyset and balding. A few minutes later, Annette came out and sat down next to him.

"It is going great. They are getting acquainted. Wait until you see our place. It is just up the road."

It was just up the road and it was great. What was ever greater was Annette's thong bathing suit. Not that she had it on for much of that week.

David was half in the bag for the return flight. At one point, he asked Annette where Bambi and Brandi were. She told him that they had decided to stay another week. They had gotten along so well with the customer, and he was, of course, paying well. She motioned the flight attendant for another drink and he forgot all about Bambi and Brandi.

• • •

Annette Peterson had been born Anabel Portillo in Gainesville, Florida. Her mother was a stripper in a joint frequented by migrant workers and long haul truck drivers. She never knew quite how she got the last name Portillo. Her mother had turned tricks on the side. Her father might have been Mexican or maybe the Portillo guy was someone she tried to squeeze child support out of by pinning paternity on a one night stand. Either way, Annette never met the guy. She spent the first fourteen years of her life in ramshackle trailers, sometimes with her grandmother, and even for a time in the backseat of an el Camino.

She had hated her mother since as far back as she could remember. The boozy giggle, the smoker's cough. Hours of boredom punctuated by the humiliation of the girls in the various school she sporadically attended staring at her thrift shop clothes. Figuring out when to stay out of the way of her mother's boyfriends who leered at her when her mother was passed out on the couch.

Her mother Glory wound up dead behind a dumpster. Annette imagined that the police in Harrisonburg, Virginia, would not work too hard to figure out who slit the throat of a two-bit hooker.

Annette was placed in foster care. She had not been to school regularly, so she was enrolled in an alternative high school. Her foster mother managed to get her up to grade level. Annette was not stupid.

Another foster child, a teenaged boy, had begun sneaking into Annette's room at night. After several nights of being fondled, she took a razor from her foster father's shaving kit and waited for the boy. When he tried to pull off her pajamas, she slashed his cheek with the razor.

The boy never told their foster parents who had cut him. He never bothered Annette again but she was pretty sure she heard him going into the bedroom across the hall from hers to visit the foster parents' twelve year old daughter.

One night she stopped him in the hall, razor in hand.

"If you are going to bother her you have to pay me first."

He stared at her. She held out her hand.

"Twenty bucks. Or I tell her parents."

Annette made a lot of money that year. To be fair, she gave some of it to the girl. It was the least she could do. She was practical. Sex and money made the world go round. Annette meant to be on the money end of the deal.

She went to community college in Texas and then transferred to the University of Texas at Austin. She majored in finance and paid her way through school by running an escort service. There were plenty of co-eds who were happy to sell themselves to older businessmen and professional athletes. She was not sure who she had more contempt for, the whores or the men they serviced. She kept those feelings to herself and ran a discrete and profitable business. But she wanted more.

One evening, a man with an Australian accent contacted her to arrange for some company. He apologized for the short notice but he had just gotten into town and was very stressed from his business meetings. She arranged for Carmen to meet him for dinner and drinks. Carmen was a lithe brunette with a lovely southern accent.

Daniel Carmichael was in his late forties. Greying and tanned, he took over the room immediately. His green eyes were piercing, his handshake firm and hands calloused. He smiled when he saw Carmen and tipped her generously at the end of the evening. He called Annette the next morning. She assumed he wanted to see Carmen again and told him she would arrange for it.

No, he told her. He wanted to take her to dinner instead. Not an escort thing, he assured her, but rather a business proposition. She was intrigued but cautious.

Over margaritas, he explained that he had a business in southeast

Asia. His was a high end escort business catering to the exotic and unusual. Most of his clients were European and Australian. His employees were exclusively Thai and Malaysian. A marriage of her business with his would round out his available resources.

She was dubious. Her girls were college students for the most part, and would not want to go overseas. What about spring break or summer vacation he had asked. She made no promises but told him she would talk to her girls.

First, he told her, he wanted to take her to see Thailand. She had raised her eyebrows at this. He hastened to assure her that there was no obligation and that she would find her accommodations private and comfortable.

True to his word, Daniel flew her first class to Phuket. She stayed in a suite at a beachfront hotel. He arranged for tours of the local sights, Phang Nga Bay and Wat Chalong, and met her for dinner each evening. His business was located on a private island just off the coast. Guests arrived via motorboat or private helicopter. While his clients had some peculiar fetishes, they paid well and, from what Annette could see, the girls and boys who worked for Daniel were treated well.

The idea is, he had explained, to get a clear sense of the client's particular tastes and then offer a variety of choices. Whet their appetite and then charge a premium. By the end of the week, she had agreed to provide a couple of her girls. She knew exactly who. Samantha and Tatiana, both tall and blond and in particularly dire financial straits.

She came back to Thailand in May with Samantha, Tatiana and Deirdra. She stayed for a week to be sure that the girls were comfortable and Daniel was paying them as promised. Her finders' fee, of course, had been provided in advance.

When the fall semester at the university rolled around, only Samantha returned. She assured Annette that the summer had been wonderful but asked to be taken off the payroll for the fall semester, citing too heavy a course load. Daniel told her that Tatiana and Deirdra had decided to stay and work for the next year. He deposited a second finders' fee into the bank account she had opened in Bangkok. She was not going to argue with that. She had plans of her own for that money.

• • •

Annette and Daniel had a good working relationship. Several times a year, he would visit her in Austin and place his orders. She was selective; she had never had a complaint from Daniel. To the contrary, he always assured her that his clients were very pleased with her girls. Sometimes the girls would chose to stay on in Thailand but many returned after summer break and continued to work for her.

The one that troubled her was Deirdra. She had never returned to Texas and none of the girls who did had seen her. She asked Daniel at one point about her and he had shrugged. Perhaps she had taken off on her own, or had gone to live with her client. In fact, he said after thinking for a moment, he had not seen that client again either. No, he would not ask around. He was adamant. His business depended upon discretion.

One morning in July she received a phone call. The voice on the other end was tearful and identified herself as Deirdra's mother. When Annette assured the woman that she most certainly had the wrong number, the woman became hysterical, threatening to expose her for what she was. Annette quickly hung up.

She ran her business out of a high rise apartment overlooking Austin. It was a elegantly appointed place, with floor to ceiling windows. She maintained a website for a catering business and the apartment had a huge, gourmet kitchen. The girls wore catering uniforms when they came and went from the building. Although they might meet her clients at the apartment, they never left with a client. Instead, they were transported via the catering van to their assignments. She kept a close watch on her girls, monitoring for any signs of strain or instability. She would not hesitate to let a girl go who became unsuitable. She was of course, generous with the termination bonuses and provided any kind of needed healthcare.

A day later, Annette was working at her desk in the bedroom when there was a knock on the door. She was not expecting any of the girls or clients until the evening. A glance into the peephole showed two uniformed Austin City police officers. She considered not answering, or going out onto the roof deck and down the emergency stairs. That would not help in the end, so she opened the door. They displayed their badges and asked to come in. She offered them coffee but they declined. They explained that they were investigating a complaint that she was running an escort service out of the apartment.

She had smiled ruefully and invited them to look around. Hers was a catering business, her employees were college students who helped transport and serve food at various parties and functions around the city. They were welcome to look at her books, talk to her clients.

Did she have a Deirdra Stevens working for her? The younger officer, with short blond hair and freckled forearms had asked this. No she did not. She had never heard the name.

"That's interesting."

This was from the other officer, a female with dark hair in a pixie cut. Annette thought she had a client that might fancy this woman.

"We talked to a couple of your former employees yesterday."

She looked down at her notes.

"Sarah Jones and Melissa Alvarez. They said that Deirdra used to work with you but that she had gone overseas. Does that jog your memory?"

Annette paused. "I think I employed a Deirdra, but her last name was Atkins. She quit a while back. I would have to double check my records though."

"Have you been to Thailand recently?" asked the blond cop.

"Yes, last spring. Have you been? It is lovely."

"Looks from customs records that you have made quite a few trips to Thailand in the last year or so. Want to tell us why?"

Annette smiled. "It is a man, of course. I have a friend, a businessman, who lives there. I go to visit him."

The pixie haired woman stood up.

"Please stand up and put your hands behind your back."

Annette stared at her.

"I want my lawyer."

"You can call your attorney when we get to the station. Now stand up."

Annette complied and looked at the floor as the blond haired one read her her rights. She looked straight ahead as they marched her through the lobby. The usually discrete security guard watched curiously. She was quite certain the entire building would know within the hour that she had been arrested.

She was booked on a variety of charges, including managing a house of ill repute, if you could believe that term still existed, and tax evasion. The federal kidnapping charge was the most worrisome, at least according to Frederick Knowles III, her attorney. He did not think it would stick though, given that her alleged victim had willingly left the country prior to her kidnapping. He rambled on about jurisdictional issues.

Bail was set at a half million dollars. She was considered a fight risk, given her recent trips outside the country. Her accounts had been frozen, so there was no way to post anyway. She spent several days in the Austin City Jail. Her charges apparently gave her some credibility with the other inmates. That and the fact that she punched a woman who propositioned her and knocked the woman out cold. Her years with Gloria and in foster care had given her a steely reserve. On the third day, after a lunch involving lumpy white potatoes, equally lumpy meatloaf and corn, one of the matrons told her she had a visitor.

Daniel was waiting in the visitor's room. She wondered how he had found out about her predicament. She had not called him. She had heard nothing from her attorney. She assumed Knowles had figured out that she had no money to pay him.

"I will see that your bail is posted. It should be in the next day or so. You will have to surrender your passport. That will not be a problem though."

Daniel smiled. Annette knew there would be a price for this. Daniel was all about business. She supposed he had a degree of exposure here as well.

Two days later, her bail was posted. She picked up her belongings and stepped out of the Austin City Jail. A limousine pulled up. Daniel was in the back seat. She settled back into the leather seat. She longed for a shower and a good night's sleep in her own bed.

That was not to be. Daniel handed her a manila envelope. Inside were a passport and a wad of cash. His driver would take her into Mexico and she would fly out of Ciudad Juarez to Mexico City where she would stay overnight. Her final destination was Brazil. He would see her there in a week or two, and they would discuss the nature of their partnership.

Annette could have deluded herself into thinking that she had a choice. That she could go back to her life in Austin, fight the charges against her, maybe set up her business elsewhere in another location. Her girls by now had scattered to the four winds. David Carmichael was not a man to say no to. Not that she did not think that, in the end, she would be more powerful, but for now, he had the upper hand. What he did not know, she smiled inwardly, was that she had been placed a good portion of her earnings off-shore, had been doing so for a few years.

Actual objects of wealth meant little to her. Unlike other people who had grown up in poverty, she did not cling to clothing, or jewelry or furniture or houses. As long as she had money, she had power. The knowledge of that power was enough; she needed no one to recognize, no symbol to flaunt. She assured Daniel that she understood why she should not go back to her home, shrugged off his apology at the loss of her things.

There was no one to call, no one to say goodbye to. Annette had no ability, or need, to connect to anyone. That had stopped when Glory had started letting her johns have a turn with her when she was six, in exchange for those DumDum lollipops. Glory was paid for their use of her body, and with a lot more than lollipops. Her grandmother had only been interested in the money she might make from fostering her granddaughter, which proved not worth the scrutiny from the child welfare officers who insisted that Annette be taken to the doctor, that she go to school regularly.

Yes, Annette had learned it was money, particularly money derived from the sale of sex, that made the world right, gave her the power she so deeply deserved. Unlike her mother, she was quick to assure herself, she made sure that her subjects were compensated. It was only right.

She dozed on and off between Austin and El Paso. The border crossing was without incident and the limo dropped her at the airport in Ciudad Juarez. The flight to Mexico City was delayed a hour but otherwise uneventful. Annette finally started to relax when she reached her hotel room in el Zocalo. She slept for eighteen hours and awoke ravenous. She ate a large lunch in the hotel restaurant and then wandered around for a few hours with the tourists.

The streets were teeming. The restaurants and museums were busy. She sipped an expresso at an outdoor cafe and marveled at how easy it was to lose oneself in the world. Commerce was everywhere. She watched several drug deals take place in the midst of oblivious tourists. It was easy to spot the sex trade, from the young girls on the park benches to the more elegant call girls on the arms of the well-heeled older gentlemen. It was a wonder it was still illegal in so many parts of the world; it was as much of the fabric of society as banking or farming.

A driver took her to a beach condo outside of Rio. It was well stocked. She spent the first week exploring the town, bought a few necessaries and sat on the beach. She was restless by the second week and bored beyond belief by the third. She knew that Daniel was testing her, letting her know how dependent she was on him. Although there was a computer and a phone in the condo, she did not use them, as much as she wanted to reassure herself that her off-shore accounts were untouched. She had to assume Daniel was monitoring both. Why give him anything to be curious about?

There were movies to watch and books to read. She joined a yoga studio. It seemed to help with her restlessness. Looking around the studio at the barely clothed young students, she considered starting her business up again. There were plenty of potential employees. Patience, she told herself. She had no idea what the local climate was or who her competition might be.

Daniel showed up after a month. The concierge announced his arrival and she buzzed him up. As always, he was cordial. She thanked him for the accommodations and assured him that she had been keeping busy. He apologized for the delayed arrival; he had new business to attend to in the middle east. He would explain over dinner.

They ate at a seafood restaurant looking out at the ocean. Daniel ordered a bottle of champagne. Annette had never been much of a drinker; she had seen firsthand where it had gotten Glory. Besides, she liked to remain in control. She sipped politely though, and made sure she ate enough to absorb what she drank.

His new client was a consortium of property developers in Amman. They liked to entertain, both among themselves and with their clients. He had to admit, these folks turned his stomach a bit but the money was unbelievable. You see, he had told her, their taste is strictly the underage. Both boys and girls. Although they could procure their own entertainment locally, they were willing to pay top dollar for non-Arab subjects. As much as a hundred thousand.

Annette raised an eyebrow.

"How can you really swing underage? I mean, it is a far cry from a college student who knows what she is getting into, is willing to get on the plane."

"You are a product of the foster care system, right?"

She had never told him anything about her past. She was not surprised that he knew this; Daniel Carmichael researched everything. She nodded.

"How closely are the kids in that system tracked? All it takes is the cooperation of a foster parent, or maybe an older kid or even a teacher. Sometimes, the kid gets released to a relative for a visit, never returns. There are all kinds of scenarios. A little money goes a long way. Or sometimes, it is the dirt we have on the person that gets them to cooperate."

"What is my role here?"

"Not much different from what you have been doing. The only difference is the extra layer of working the person who gives you access to the subject. A bit more research. Certainly a higher risk. But the payoff is significant."

"But I am a fugitive."

He brushed that off.

"We keep you overseas for a while. I make the Deirdre situation go away. You have a new identity. You work small cities, nowhere near anywhere you have lived before."

She told Daniel that she would consider it overnight. They both knew what her decision would be but for some reason, she felt compelled to show a certain hesitation, maybe a hint of moral misgiving. She had no such feelings; she found such sentiments curious. Annette attached herself to no one. She saw little need for that. She hated the reliance on Daniel that the new arrangement was creating. She assured herself that she would correct that. She just needed to be patient, to find his weak point.

Chapter Eight

Phoebe

On the way home on Saturday afternoon Phoebe received a call from a volunteer with the animal shelter. Phoebe scheduled the home inspection for the following afternoon. She disabled the alarm. The house was quiet and nothing seemed amiss. Eileen begged to go to the mall with her friends and Phoebe relented. Kendall and Damien played Assassin's Creed. Phoebe sipped wine and made spaghetti with meatballs. The first fireflies of the season danced in the yard. They studied the photos of the puppy and talked about names for him. Damien favored Magnet. He said the puppy had stuck to them the whole time they had visited him.

Phoebe ran twelve miles the next morning, breathing in the spring time air and admiring the varying colors of the azaleas blooming in the neighborhood. She flipped pancakes and fried bacon, sipping coffee and diet coke. She cajoled the kids out of bed for breakfast and then set them to chores, sweeping the front porch and making sure the back yard was neat.

The volunteer turned out to be a middle aged couple who were devoted to rescuing pit bulls. They examined the house and the back yard and asked all kinds of questions of the kids about how they intended to help with the puppy. They seemed pleased with Phoebe's history of rescuing various dogs and cats.

"His name is Magnet," said Damien.

"You will hear from the county within a day or two. Everything looks good to us." Phoebe and the kids waved goodbye from the porch.

Later that evening, the landline rang. They rarely answered or used this line but it was Sunday night. Phoebe studied the caller ID. It was not an 800 or 888 number but the area code was not familiar.

"May I speak to Mrs. Rivers?" The voice was male and official sounding.

"Speaking," said Phoebe, certain that she was about to hear some sort of survey or political pitch.

"This is Philip Jones from the Franklin County Mental Health Unit. I need to speak to you about David Rivers. Is he your husband?"

"Yes, he is," replied Phoebe.

"We have him in protective custody and sedated. We found him Friday morning wandering down Route 24 just south of Rocky Mount. It took a while to identify him because he had no ID on him. We were able to match his prints though."

"Is he hurt? What happened to him?"

Phoebe stepped out of the kids' earshot into the laundry room.

"He has some bumps and bruises but nothing serious. He was covered in blood but it does not seem to be his. He is not coherent though. We have had to keep him heavily medicated. He keeps screaming about someone hurting his children."

Phoebe felt ice flow through her veins.

"What do I need to do?"

"First off, I am glad we found you. If you can give us the name of his physician, that would be a good start. Also some insurance information. We can't release him, obviously, but we may be able to transfer him up to Fairfax."

Phoebe gave him Dr. Jacobson's contact information and read him the insurance ID and group numbers. She wondered vaguely if they even had insurance, if David did not work anymore, but, she had taken the kids to the doctor in the last year, and there had been no obvious problem with the insurance card she had provided. She would worry about that later.

Monday morning. She put the kids on the school buses and went to the office. On the way, she left a message for Detective Nichols. She closed the door and sat at her desk. She supposed she should be more concerned about David but the only concern she could muster today was for herself, and for why David would be so worried about the kids. Sure, he loved them but he had always left the day to day worrying and fretting to her.

She left a message for Dr. Jacobson. Something about what Philip Jones had said bothered her. Why would David's prints be in a database? Maybe when he had coached Eileen's softball team a few years ago they had taken prints, just to make sure a criminal or child predator was not working with the kids. The phone rang.

"Oh, good, Dr. Jacobson, thank you for calling back so promptly."

"Well, Phoebe, this is awkward. I am afraid I cannot tell you very much about David, other than that he is in the mental health unit in Franklin county."

"Well, why not? I am his wife."

"It seems that when David was last in here for his annual physical and he filled out privacy forms, he did not authorize us to speak to you about his medical condition."

"What? Why would he do that?"

"He has listed as his emergency contact an Annette Peterson. He also listed her as the policyholder for his insurance information."

Phoebe digested that for a moment. "Well, can you at least tell me if he is safe? Did you talk to the doctor at the Mental Health Unit?"

"I think he is in good hands. I am sorry I cannot tell you anything further."

"Is he being transferred up to Fairfax? He is the father of my children; I need to know."

Phoebe cringed at the pleading tone she heard in her own voice.

"I am so sorry, Phoebe. I just cannot tell you anything more."

She looked out her office window as a police cruiser rolled up to the curb. Phoebe's heart sank. Detective Nichols climbed out of the car. She stepped into the reception area. His grey eyes were serious.

"My buddy at the lake tells me they found your husband down in

Franklin County."

They were behind closed doors in her office. She filled him in on what she had discovered about David not allowing her access to his medical information and about his purchase of the beach house with this Annette Peterson

"Alright, now let's assume that your husband is fooling around, maybe planning on leaving you. This still does not explain the dog. Does he have some sort of grudge against you? Or, maybe it is a medical thing. Does he have any history of depression or psychotic episodes? Any family history?"

Phoebe considered this. She had met David at a concert at what was then called Nissan Pavilion. Carlos Santana and Steve Winwood. 1990. She had tucked her hair into her baseball cap and darted into the men's room when the women's bathroom line was ridiculously long. He had been washing his hands when she emerged from the stall and he met her eyes in the mirror, raising his eyebrows. She had laughed ruefully and shrugged, saying that she did not want to miss any of the concert waiting in line to pee.

He followed her out of the bathroom and to the beer line. They had gotten to talking about other concerts and he walked her back to where her friends were sitting on the lawn. He introduced himself and then went off to his seat under the pavilion. Before the evening ended though, he was back to give her his number.

It was not love at first sight. They had dated off and on for a year, until his mother had died unexpectedly. When he came back from Indiana, he was much more serious. It was losing his mom, he told her, he had come to realize that life was very short and meant to be enjoyed to its fullest. It was at this point that she began to fall in love with him.

"Phoebe? Did you hear me? Any history of mental illness?" Detective Nichols jolted her back from the memory of the early David.

"Not that I know of." She thought for a moment. "Well, I think he is sometimes depressed, has some unresolved family issues. I never met his mom and I don't know what she died from. He is estranged from his dad. Some sort of falling out when he did not want to join the family business, insurance I think. We get Christmas cards from his dad and once he came out to meet the kids but I don't know him at all."

"What about his siblings?" asked Detective Nichols.

"He doesn't have any," replied Phoebe. She hesitated a moment. "At least he has never mentioned any to me. I just assumed he did not have any."

He looked down at his hands, considering his fingernails, which were clean and clipped short.

"Phoebe, something is just not adding up here. Are you sure you have told me everything?"

How could she tell him anything more? Not without implicating herself in two murders and calling into question her sanity, neither of which seemed like a good idea at the moment, what with her now being a single parent with an institutionalized, possibly delusional, estranged husband.

"I can't think of anything," she said. "I do wish I knew more about this Annette, and why David left his job."

"Well," he said. "How about things on the financial front? Everything seem normal?"

A good question, she thought to herself. David handled the major finances: the mortgage, the credit cards. They had no car payments anymore. He monitored their investments and watched the 401K accounts and the kids' 529 plans. He did everything on line, scoffing at her love of paper checks and check book register. She had a household account for day to day stuff, groceries, gas, clothing, kids' activities. She was pretty sure that part of her salary went into the household account and part went into the overall pot. She supposed though, her heart sinking, that she would have no idea if anything were really amiss. It had been years since she had seen a paper bill or account statement.

"I guess so," she said. "David handles most of that stuff. I should probably contact the bank and the credit card companies. I suppose I need to get some sort of power of attorney to manage this stuff, particularly since he is hospitalized, incapacitated, at least temporarily."

Phoebe cringed inwardly. Attorneys were famous for not having their affairs in order, not having wills or guardians appointed for their children. She was no different, though she would not admit it to the detective. Even worse, she had absolutely no idea what their financial picture was. It was not deliberate ignorance, she told herself. She simply trusted him and concerned herself with the children and their affairs, their day to day lives.

"You are a damn fool," her inner self scolded, "worse than the clients you have mocked for not knowing their bottom line."

After she walked the detective to his car Phoebe went back into her office and called her bank. She confirmed that her household account had the balance her checkbook reflected, about $2500. The bank manager told her that the last six months reflected deposits of $750 each week, the money coming from a savings account that was linked to the household account. The balance in that account was approximately $12,000. She took down those account numbers. She relaxed a bit.

Next, she dug into her paper files and found the name and phone number for her 401K. As she had expected, those funds were intact, with regular deposits coming directly from her paycheck. She realized she did not know where David's 401K was held and that it was unlikely that she could access that information, at least not without a power of attorney.

What about the other bills, the mortgage and utilities? She was pretty sure that he paid those on-line. She also wanted to check on the kids' college funds. He had set those up and they might be in his name alone. Her heart sank when she called and asked about the 529 accounts. They had been closed out the year before. That bastard. She was going to get to the bottom of this if she had to go down to that mental hospital and drag it out of him.

"I am sorry, Mrs. Rivers," said Philip Jones when he answered her call. "Mr. Rivers is no longer at our facility."

"Was he discharged or was he transferred?" asked Phoebe.

"I cannot provide you with any further information. Our privacy policies prevent...."

Phoebe cut him off. "I don't meant be rude here but my children and I may be in danger. You yourself told me that he was convinced something was going to happen to them. I can't begin to tell you the strange things that have happened over the past week. I just need to know where he is." A sob caught in her throat.

"I understand," said Jones, "but I need a court order to give you any further information. Mr. Rivers did not authorize us to release any information to you."

She called Trooper Weyson. He listened quietly as she explained her predicament.

"Let me see what I can do," he said finally. "I do have an active investigation into the incident with the dog and he is certainly a suspect."

• • •

Phoebe sat at her desk. It was almost time for the kids to come home from school and she had done nothing in the way of actual work. She told herself that she would work on a couple of cases when the kids went to bed.

In what she was sure would be a useless attempt to distract herself, she logged into Facebook. She had started an account in the way she supposed many mothers did: as a means of monitoring the kids' on-line activities. While it had provided a few opportunities to explain to the girls what might not be appropriate for posting, she had found herself reconnecting to people she had not heard from or even thought about in years. Elementary and high school friends, long lost cousins. She even joined a couple of closed groups, mostly devoted to running, in particular, to training for races. The girls had stopped using Facebook for the most part, and were now more active on other social networks, like Snapchat, Twitter and Tumblr.

She paused for a minute. Maybe all the social networking had contributed to her isolation. Most of her friends were virtual. No wonder she felt so alone now. She brushed aside her self-pity.

She had a message from one of her regular training partners, Moises.

"Have you fallen off the face of the earth? Tried texting you but radio silence. Haven't seen you on the trails. Everything ok?" A smiley emoticon followed.

Phoebe responded with Kendall's phone number, explaining that her own phone had taken a fatal plunge into the toilet (blushing emoticon inserted) and that she was a bit behind in her training for the hundred miler and might not try it after all.

Moises must have been on-line. He wrote back at once. "Don't you dare quit now! Taking tomorrow morning off. Wanna run on the Bull Run Trail?"

She wrote back. "See you at eight in the marina parking lot."

The rest of the evening was uneventful, save for the Phoebe's ongoing worry about where David was, which she kept to herself after tamping it down with a valium, and the receipt of a phone call from the county adoption coordinator. Phoebe's announcement to the kids that Magnet would be joining the family as soon as she could show proof of a fenced backyard was met with squeals of joy.

●   ●   ●

Phoebe parked at the marina. She pulled out her camelback as she powered up her wrist Garmin. Moises got out of his Subaru and hugged her.

"Girl, you are too skinny. Got to get some muscle on those legs if you are going to survive the rocks in the mountains."

She smiled. Moises was a bit of a worrywart. She would tease him that he was channeling his inner abuela. In his fifties, he had come to the United States as a teenaged political refugee from war-torn El Salvador. He had told her once, on a long training run, that two of his sisters had died during the war and that their father had disappeared. He had never married and still lived with his mother, Carmen, in a townhouse in Chantilly. Carmen often sent along homemade snacks for their training runs.

Moises studied her face.

"Is that a bruise?" he asked, touching her cheek.

"It's nothing," she replied, "bumped into a door."

"I see," was his only comment.

The morning was warm for April. The trail was awash in tiny bluebells. Delighted, Phoebe asked Moises to take a picture and send it to her.

"How did you drown your phone?" he asked. "It had a great camera. I hope you backed up all those photos."

"It fell in the toilet," she said with what she hoped passed for an embarrassed shrug. Moises raised one eyebrow but said nothing.

"Eileen says my photos are in the cloud, whatever that really means."

They fell into an easy pace heading south. The creek next to the trail was full and the rushing water soothing. A blue heron sighting was cause for another photo stop. They passed a few other runners and a dog walker coming in the opposite direction and exchanged greetings.

About five miles into the run, another runner overtook them. In an unusual lack of trail etiquette he passed them on the right, without a warning. He had on a black t-shirt and running tights and seeing him appear out of the corner of her right eye caused Phoebe to start violently, stifling a scream. The runner continued wordlessly, iPod blaring. Phoebe stumbled and Moises caught her elbow to keep her from falling.

"Ok, Phoebe, let's walk for a minute." He frowned at her. "Girl, you are trembling. What on earth is going on with you?"

The earnest concern in his voice made her eyes well up.

"You know the ultra-runners' creed, Phoebe. What is said on the trail, stays on the trail."

"Oh, Moe, I wish I could tell you. You would think I was crazy if I did."

"What could possibly be that bad? If I had to guess, somebody or something scared you, or hurt you badly. You are a tough nut, Phoebe, but you are not fooling me here."

"It's a long story," she said. "Promise me that you won't run away from me, or have me locked up." She tried to force her lips into a smile.

"Hey we have nothing but miles to do here. And a lot of what you will be doing during that hundred miler will be walking. So let's just walk and talk."

"It started on the night I did my overnight run," she started. "Or, rather, tried to do my overnight run. I was raped."

Once she started to talk it was as if the words could not pour from her fast enough. Moises listened gravely, wincing when she described the attack, cursing softly in Spanish from time to time. She told him everything she remembered from the attack, her sudden rescue by Petrel and the killing of white glove man and mustache man.

She told him about returning to the site of the attack to collect her running tights and finding the knife. He nodded when she described how she discarded the knife and stared off into the distance when she told him about what she read in the newspaper on the microfiche.

"I assume you did not report the attack?" he asked.

"How could I?" Phoebe was almost hyperventilating. "I killed someone! Besides, who would believe my story about Petrel? They would lock me up."

"Have you said anything at all to David?" he asked when she finally paused for breath and a long pull at her camelback.

"No," she said.

"Why not?" asked Moises. "He is your husband. He should know."

"I don't know," said Phoebe. "I was afraid he would be mad at me for leaving the kids alone to run. You know he doesn't really get the ultra-running thing. I guess I was afraid, and ashamed."

"Well you should not be ashamed," said Moises. "It was not your fault and you should not be afraid of your husband. I am surprised you were able to hide it from him."

"Funny thing is," she answered, "he acted totally normal, even when he saw my face, which looked much worse than it does now. He bought my lame story about walking into a door. Of course, now that he has disappeared…"

Moises stopped abruptly.

"Disappeared? What do you mean?"

She told him about the trip to the lake and poor Roxie and the beach house and Annette. She finished with the phone calls with Franklin County Mental Health Unit and with chagrin, told him about the money missing from the kids' 529 plans. She left out only the episodes at the Civil War field hospital, the graveyard in the woods at the lake and Great Dismal Swamp. Moises would really think she had lost it if she went into all that. She figured he had enough to process already.

"I just wish I could find out more about Annette and I just want to know where David is and if he is alright. I can deal with what all this means for our marriage later. Actually, I don't care if he is even alright."

"Phoebe," he said. "I think you are in very real danger. I don't know why or from whom. I just know. Someone raped you, probably meant to kill you. Your dog was taken out of your cabin while you and your children slept and was murdered, probably by David and maybe this woman. David shows up in a mental hospital and it turns out he quit his job a year ago, or was fired. And you have missing money." He shook his head.

She explained about changing the locks and installing the alarm, the planned gun purchase and Magnet.

"That is all fine," he responded. "And, even if the police are aware of David they don't know the whole story, understandably." He hastened to reassure her. "I am going to keep an eye on you, stay in your house, at least until David turns up and we have some more information."

Phoebe began to protest but he cut her off.

"It is the least I can do," he said firmly.

"Are you sure you don't think I have lost my mind?"

"You are the sanest person I know, Flaca."

She had to admit that it was cathartic to have told part of her story and a relief to know that she was not alone in her fear. And it was so nice not to have been scolded for her role in any of it.

They were hiking up a fairly steep hill, eyes on the ground to avoid tripping on the ever present rocks and tree roots. As they crested the hill, Phoebe suddenly felt light headed and, thinking she was dehydrated, reached into the pocket of her camelback for an electrolyte tablet. She glanced back at Moises; he looked pale and was sipping from his water bottle.

"It must be hotter than I thought," she said.

Her vision narrowed suddenly and she was looking through the trees ahead at a circle of sky. She took a few more steps and felt a slide, more like a shift. She was looking at a woman sitting on a log. The trail was much wider here, marred with hoof prints and horse manure. Here we go again, Phoebe thought to herself. I guess I am just going to have to accept these appearances.

Sorel. It was Sorel sitting on the log; her chin was on her chest and she appeared to have dozed off. Her skirt was dusty and Phoebe's running shoes on her feet were tattered. She awoke with a shriek and clutched a bundle to her chest. Her shoulders relaxed only slightly when she recognized Phoebe.

"Sorel? Are you alright?"

"Yes, ma'am. Jest tired is all. Been walking nights and hiding and trying to sleep during the day. I heard gunshots and hollering and the train whistle this morning from over yonder." She pointed north. "So I just up and run as much as I could. Set down here to rest a moment."

"Are you hungry? Thirsty?"

Phoebe offered Sorel the tube from her camelback which Sorel eyed with more than a little suspicion.

"Go ahead. It's clean water."

Phoebe pulled a packet of peanut butter crackers from the camelback pocket and handed it to Sorel. Sorel rubbed a dirty finger over the cellophane wrapper.

"Here," said Phoebe. "Let me open it for you."

Phoebe considered the surroundings. They were a mile or two north of Fountainhead, which was some five or so miles from where the Occoquan River widened below the town of Occoquan, where Tommy's friend had said there was a Union garrison and field hospital. Hopefully, she explained to Sorel, there was only another day or two of travel.

She dug into the pockets of her camelback and gave Sorel the rest of her snacks, an extra pair of socks and a space blanket she had saved from a race and kept in case of a sudden change in weather or injury. Sorel watched silently as Phoebe demonstrated how to wrap up in the blanket. Phoebe turned to look for Moises, half expecting him not to be there. He was curled on the ground, apparently asleep. She relieved him of him mother's care package and a can of Coke. Sorel wrapped all these items carefully into her bundle, dusted off her skirt and stood up.

"I'd best keep a-movin'. Daylight makes me scairt."

Sorel looked at Moises.

"Keep him close now, ya hear? He a good man. No telling what might happen to a lady on her own."

Sorel melted into the underbrush. Phoebe sat down next to Moises. Her eyelids felt heavy. She closed them briefly. Moises sneezed and when Phoebe opened her eyes, the trail looked normal again. Moises sat up and looked at her, puzzled.

"What happened? Did we decide to take a nap?"

While napping during an overnight run was expected, a daytime sleep break understandably struck Moises as odd. He reached into his backpack.

"Where is my Coke? And my food?"

He shook his head as if to clear it.

"I had the weirdest dream. You gave my food away to a black lady in a long skirt. She was sitting right over there. And she had running shoes on."

Phoebe stood up. She briefly considered sharing this ghost with Moises but she bit back the words. She had so few friends, why scare off the one she had just unburdened herself to.

Instead she said: "I needed some caffeine. Have some of my water if you want. Should we head back?"

She consulted her Garmin. "We have done about twelve."

Moises hauled himself to his feet.

"I did not realize we went so far. Guess I am not going to work at all today."

Conversation on the northbound leg was light, as if the heavy discussion on the way down needed a counterbalance. They gossiped about other runners in their trail running group. The day grew steadily warmer and they stopped several times to pour creek water on their heads. By two that afternoon, they were back at their cars Moises looked unexpectedly weary. He hugged her goodbye.

"I will come by after dinner. Do me a favor, keep me from worrying and text me every hour or so. I love you, girl, and I don't want anything more to happen to you or your beautiful kids."

Phoebe followed his car back to Route 123 and onto the parkway. She waved as he continued north and she turned off on Route 29. A Long's Fence truck was parked in her driveway. She rounded the corner to the backyard and was pleased to see that the work was almost done. The wood looked fresh and new. The latches were sturdy. While she understood the rescue's requirement for a fenced yard, she thought it rather a waste of money.

None of their dogs was ever let out alone and she did not intend to let Magnet roam the yard unaccompanied. Her neighbors had a hound that they left outside for hours. The poor thing would chase squirrels in vain and howl for attention. Besides, it was easier to walk the dog on a leash and pick up poop. Saved stepping in it in the yard too.

Phoebe took a couple of photos of the fence to email to the rescue volunteer and went inside to shower. Sitting in front of her work computer to finish some research, she heard the high school bus pull up at the stop outside the house. She got up to greet Eileen but the willowy teen was not walking up the sidewalk. Had she stayed after and forgotten to tell her? She texted her but got no response. That was unusual but the high school had notoriously bad reception. Eileen was convinced that the administration blocked the signal.

She prepared a roast chicken and scrubbed potatoes. Asparagus would complete the meal, she thought absently. The middle school bus deposited Kendall, talking a mile a minute about a party she had been invited to and the outfit she wanted to wear, which, of course, would require a trip to the mall. Damien's bus arrived some thirty minutes later but it was not until the high school late bus passed without stopping that Phoebe began to worry in earnest.

She tried the high school but the administrative office was closed, as was the transportation office. Besides, the school did not keep track of how the students came and went from school, nor did a parent have to sign a student in or out. A note or a fax requesting early dismissal would permit a student to wait outside to be picked up.

She paced up and down on the porch. While she knew most of Eileen's friends, she did not have phone numbers for any of them. The numbers for the few parents she did know had been on her drowned cell phone. She really needed to try to recover that contact information. There was one classmate who lived up the street. She looked that number up in the neighborhood phone list she had in the kitchen drawer and left a message for the boy's mother.

While she did not think that the Fairfax County police would take a missing person's report so soon, she called Detective Nichols. He picked up on the second ring. When she finished telling him that Eileen was missing he simply said "I am leaving now," and hung up. That unnerved her further.

"You have called her friends, checked to see if anything was out of the ordinary?" he asked immediately upon coming into the kitchen. "How has she been the last couple of days?"

"I have made some calls, left some messages," Phoebe said, knowing this was a bit of an exaggeration. "She has been ok, a bit upset about Roxie of course."

"Does she have any medical issues?" he asked.

"She does take medication for anxiety. Every evening. It helps. Not sure if it just the act of taking the medicine or the medicine itself but it works…"

She trailed off, looking up towards the cabinet where the bottle of Lexapro was, picturing Eileen's panic if she could not take her medicine.

"Has she ever run away before or been out of touch?"

"Never. For a teenager, she is a bit of a homebody. She always checks in with me, tells me she loves me."

Phoebe's voice caught and she clasped her arms around her, gripping her elbows to stop the trembling. She could not the bear the thought of her daughter hurt or scared or worse.

Kendall's phone chirped. Moises. "You, ok, girl?"

She texted back. "No. Eileen missing."

"On my way," was his immediate response.

Detective Nichols made another note and looked up.

"I wish we knew where your husband was. I am going to lean on Franklin County a bit." His phone rang.

"Talk to me," he barked. He listened for a moment and then walked outside to continue his conversation.

Moises' Subaru pulled into the driveway and he ran up the

walkway. Phoebe collapsed into him.

"I don't even know where to begin to look for her." Desperation crept into her voice.

He clasped her shoulders firmly and looked into her eyes. "We are going to find her. That I promise you."

Outside the window, Detective Nichols was gesturing with one hand as he talked. He ended the call and came back inside.

"Let's sit down," he said. "David was released to Annette Peterson two days ago. They gave an address in Virginia Beach. I ran records on both Annette and David. I am waiting for credit checks and a response from the FBI."

Nichols consulted his notes.

"David had a DUI in Henrico County October 13, 2013. Dismissed due to medical issue. He filed an assault claim against Annette Peterson January 17, 2014 but withdrew charges. City of Virginia Beach investigated but closed file due to lack of evidence."

He flipped the next page, which was labeled Annette Peterson. "Possible aliases Anna Peters and Arlene Paris per fingerprints. Booked on suspicion of moneylaundering and running a brothel in Texas but it looks like she was never prosecuted."

Moises turned to Detective Nichols. "I really think this whole family is in danger. Shouldn't they be in protective custody?"

"For starters, I am posting officers here twenty-four seven until this is resolved," the detective said. "I don't want Mrs. Rivers to leave here though, in case Eileen comes home or makes contact."

Or, Phoebe thought, in case someone makes a ransom demand. She nodded.

"And," continued Nichols, "since we are dealing with a possible kidnapping, an Amber Alert is going out. I will need a recent photo. And, the FBI may join the investigation."

Phoebe pointed to the screensaver on her work computer. The sun-kissed, smiling family looked like strangers. She emailed the photo to Detective Nichols, who after conferring with the officers in an unmarked car outside, went back to the station.

"Let's get these kids some dinner," Moises said. "And you need to eat too, Flaca. Keep your strength up."

He bustled around the kitchen.

What to tell the other kids? Phoebe did not want to scare them but she could not stand the thought of them getting on the school bus the next morning, watching the doors close behind them. They ate on the porch. Phoebe kept looking at Eileen's chair, occupied by Moises at the moment, who, bless his heart, was encouraging the kids to eat and told them that he would make brownies with them after dinner. Phoebe managed to eat a few bites and then pushed the rest of the meal around her plate.

Once the dishes were cleared away, Phoebe sat down with Damien and Kendall and explained, as gently as she could, that Eileen was missing and that the police were looking very hard to find her.

"What do you mean, missing?" demanded Kendall.

"Was she kidnapped?" asked Damien in a very small voice.

Phoebe explained that Eileen had not come home from school and that they were not sure where she was.

"The car outside is a police car, here to help look for Eileen and keep us all safe. I think we will all stay home tomorrow, so we can be here for Eileen."

"I wish we had Magnet already," said Damien.

"Hopefully, we will get him in another day or two," said Phoebe, although the notion of a new dog to housebreak and train on top of everything else seemed like not the best idea. The aroma of brownies soon filled the kitchen and Kendall and Damien were temporarily distracted.

The doorbell rang. Phoebe opened the door to her neighbor, Maya Roberts, mother of Eileen's classmate, Julien. Julien, slightly overweight with wire-rimmed glasses, stood next to his mother. Phoebe ushered them into the family room and explained that Eileen was missing, hadn't come home on the bus.

Julien did not have any classes with Eileen but he had seen her eating lunch in the cafeteria around noon.

"What classes does she have after lunch?" he asked.

"Spanish and algebra," answered Phoebe.

Julien began texting, thumbs moving in that frenzied pattern that only people born after 1999 seemed to be able to do. The age of texting and video games.

"Ok, she was in Spanish class," Julien reported after a minute or two.

Another bout of furious thumb movements and he added: "She was called to the office during algebra and did not come back before the bell rang."

He pulled out his iPad. "Mrs. Rivers, can I post something? She if anyone saw her in the office or after?"

Phoebe nodded her consent. Julien logged into Facebook and posted as his status: "Did anyone see Eileen Rivers in the school office this afternoon? This is very important. Life or death."

Next he tweeted. "Has anyone seen Eileen Rivers? Please retweet and use #findeileenrivers." A similar message went onto Tumblir. Finally he took a photo of Phoebe's screensaver and posted it to Instagram.

As Julien monitored his feeds, Phoebe smiled at Maya.

"What did we ever do before social media?"

Within fifteen minutes, Julien had established from a teacher's aide who had been picking up paperwork in the office that a man meeting David's description had signed Phoebe out of school. Phoebe's friend Sarah reported that Phoebe had left the building with David and another student leaving early for a dermatologist appointment had seen Phoebe and David getting into a truck.

A recent grad who was a substitute bus driver reported that while waiting at a light he saw Phoebe in the back seat of a truck driven by a blond woman. Lastly, Eileen's boyfriend (Phoebe did not know she had one), Joseph, had gotten a text from Eileen saying her dad had picked her up because her mom had been in an accident. Joseph had texted her back.

Her only response had been "something is not right here."

That had been a little before three and she had not answered her phone or responded to any texts since then.

Phoebe called Detective Nichols and relayed what they had learned. He asked to speak to Maya and then Julien. Both listened and then nodded, agreeing to let the FBI monitor Julien's phone and iPad.

Julien and Maya left around ten. Phoebe coaxed Kendall and

Damien into bed. She sat in the living room with Moises, who handed her a cup of chamomile tea.

"You need to try to rest, Flaca. They have the Amber Alert out, and they are watching that boy's computer. Things will be better tomorrow, I promise."

Moises settled down on the couch in the living room. Under the pillow and blanket Phoebe brought him, he placed a Glock. Nobody was going to get past him, he thought grimly.

Phoebe found both Kendall and Damien in her bed. She made no effort to move them, just slid between them and tried to sleep with one hand on each child. Her dreams were dark and she woke multiple times, each time hoping that she was just waking from a nightmare. The car parked outside the house was a constant reminder that it was not a nightmare. Her daughter was missing and each hour that went by, their chances of finding her safe diminished.

She gave up on sleeping before dawn and tiptoed downstairs. Moises was already up, padding about the kitchen. He handed her a cup of coffee and stirred a pot of oatmeal. She picked listlessly at the cereal and he frowned at her.

"Ever the abuela," she said, trying to smile at him.

Detective Nichols arrived, speaking first to the officers in the car and then coming into the kitchen.

There had been several reports of David's truck on 1-95 headed south last evening. The truck was found, abandoned, in a Costco parking lot in Fredericksburg. Officers searching the truck had found Eileen's cellphone in bushes nearby. It had been smashed. A surveillance camera on the back of the store had recorded David, Eileen and a blond woman walking east in the direction of the Costco gas station.

Around one in the morning, a woman at a light on Rt 15 just east of Fredericksburg had been approached by a blond woman, who threatened her with a gun and ordered her out of the car. The woman drove off in her Camry. The Amber Alert was updated with the Camry's information but there had been no sightings reported since.

Chapter Nine

David and Annette

For a time, David reveled in his double life. He was smugly satisfied that he was fooling the world. His wife and neighbors assumed he was still working at Parlington, making overseas trips to inspect factories. If he wasn't in Phuket or South America on a job for Annette, he was at the house he had purchased with Annette in Virginia Beach. Of course, he had had to cash in his 401K account to pay his half. Annette wanted everything done in cash. She had assured him that he would make the money back and more. She did pay him for the work but it never seemed like quite enough to cover the expenses of maintaining appearances at the house in Fairfax.

Always, though, in the back of his mind were those photos and the video of him in Thailand. If he were thinking clearly, which was becoming a rarity, he would admit to himself that he did not quite trust her, even as much as he enjoyed her. Who knows who she would send those videos and photos to if he didn't do what she asked of him. He really only cared about his family finding out; he had no work colleagues anymore. Most of his friends had been from work, golf and tennis buddies, neighbors with whom he would go to happy hour or smoke a cigar on the back porch. None of them had reached out to him in months.

He grew increasingly more irritable at home. The mundane details of family life numbed him. The kids' voices grated on his nerves. Phoebe's inquiries about his work enraged him and he discouraged them by snapping at her or answering in monosyllables. He began to fantasize about being rid of them, being done with that life.

One day, he mentioned to Annette that he thought he might get divorced.

"Seriously? Do you know how much that is going to cost you? And just because you get divorced does not mean that you stop paying. You will still be sucked into their lives."

She went on to tell him that a divorce would clearly highlight that he was no longer employed and raise questions about his source of income. He would jeopardize their whole operation. He supposed she was right.

"Look, if you really want to be done with them, there are better ways."

He did not quite like the sound of that. But, she made a convincing argument about how much tax free money he could net in life insurance if he went about this the right way. Phoebe had two policies: one from her job that would yield $250,000 and that million dollar policy she had insisted on buying when a man who lived in their neighborhood had died in a car crash and left nothing to his wife, who was a stay at home mom.

Wait a second, he had told Annette. I don't want to be stuck with the kids. Annette had held up her hand. Didn't he think Phoebe's parents would step up to the plate, particularly since now he would have to travel more to make ends meet, being a single parent?

The trick was, to make it look like a random event. Phoebe put herself out there alone, running at all hours. Lone women running sometimes met with unfortunate events.

And so David found himself, one rainy evening in April, stalking his wife. Annette must have suspected he lacked the nerve to act alone. She assigned a dark complexioned man with a mustache to help him. He gave his name as Tony but David was sure that was not his name.

Tony did not say much. He drove the red pick-up truck. He glowered at the rain and the mist when they parked the truck in the driveway of a house David knew to be unoccupied. Tony climbed out of the truck and lit a cigarette. Annette had insisted that David wear the ridiculous-looking white gloves. To prevent fingerprints and all. It seemed surreal.

David took a swig of gin from the flask in his pocket. He needed a solid buzz to go with the pill Annette had given him an hour before. As much as he did not feel anything about Phoebe, killing someone was bad business. He pulled the hoodie down over his face and made his voice as deep as he could. The fear in his wife's voice was apparent. He was surprised that raping her was so arousing. He was looking forward to watching Tony have his turn. The burly man must have been anxious to force himself on her.

Phoebe grunted. David saw stars and felt blood on the side of his face. Phoebe must have hit him. She was struggling now. Tony put his foot on her chest. David's head exploded with pain. Someone hit him on the other side of his head. He stumbled back and fell to his knees, hands on his temples. He felt a boot connect with the back of his head. He began to black out. Dimly, he saw another figure in the clearing. Phoebe was standing up now, plunging a knife into Tony's back.

David came to with a stinging slap to his face.

"Goddamn fool," Annette hissed. "Help me with him."

Tony was slumped on the ground. David grabbed his legs and Annette his arms and together they dragged the lifeless man toward the stream. David waited with the corpse, huddled below the level of the road while Annette went to get the truck. She opened the side door and they hauled Tony into the back seat. Annette threw a blanket over him. As they drove out of the neighborhood, David noticed a light in the woods where they had been.

"This is bad."

Annette was fuming. "She must have called the cops."

"Some guy showed up. He gave her a knife."

Annette glared at him. "I did not see any sign of another person. Can't believe that the two of you could not handle her."

Some very distant part of David was suddenly proud of Phoebe but the thought was fleeting.

They drove through the night and into the next morning, north on

17 and eventually onto the New York State Thruway. Annette took an exit just north of Watertown and drove some twenty miles into the wilderness. David dozed. His head ached. Maybe he had a concussion. When he mentioned it to Annette she scoffed at him.

Annette stopped the truck and unlocked a metal gate. They drove into what looked to David like an abandoned quarry. Annette backed the truck up to an enormous pit. It made David dizzy to look into it. She pushed the seats down and shoved Tony's body, which had stiffened, toward the back of the truck.

"Come on David, help me. Pull him out and toss him down into the pit."

David inched around the back of the truck. He tugged at the corpse. It was like Tony was resisting being discarded. Tony's arm caught on something. David stumbled and caught himself. He envisioned falling like a rag doll into the pit. He suspected Annette would not care if he went over the side. Tony's body fell end to end and then disappeared out of his line of vision.

David did not remember much of the drive back to Virginia. He felt fuzzy, like his mind was wrapped in cotton and his words were slow. He woke up once, in a motel he thought. Annette was talking on her phone. When she saw him watching her, she stepped out of the room.

●　●　●

Annette had gone to South America a day or two after their trip north to dump Tony's body. David stayed behind in Virginia Beach. He was hazy on the details of the trip north, and when he really thought about it, he had been foggy on a lot of details for the last few months. He did drink a fair amount, probably too much, but he normally felt clear headed when he was sober.

Maybe it was those pills that doctor had prescribed for hypertension, the ones Annette kept filled for him in the bottle in the medicine cabinet. He looked at the bottle; there were only a couple left. Why not just toss them, see if he felt more like himself without them.

He rattled around Virginia Beach for a day or so. He went out for a few drinks in a bar in Norfolk where Annette and he had found some girls for clients last year. Mostly teenagers of Navy personnel stationed nearby. Pretty girls who were bored and looking for cash. He was not working tonight though, just kicking back. He had a pleasant buzz when he left the place and walked to his truck.

"Fine evening, ain't it?"

He turned. A huge black man had come out of nowhere it seemed. He had on some weird rough shirt open at the neck and his feet were bare. David had been reaching for the door handle of his truck but he clasped at air.

"Can I help you?"

David was suddenly sure he was about to get his ass kicked. He looked around at the parking lot but there were no other cars. Come to think of it, there was nothing but darkness and some trees. Maybe he was dreaming or drunker than he had thought.

The big man shook his head.

"A man that goes after his own family, he as low as the serpent. You got some terrible darkness in you, pure evil."

The man regarded him for a few more seconds and then said: "There are a lot of souls on the other side. You had a part in sending them. They was innocent, babies almost. Lotta blood on your hands for certain."

"What do you want with me?"

David's voice shook with terror. He hoped on some level he was dreaming, that he would wake up soon, in his own bed.

"I have money. Here, take my watch, the keys to my truck."

The giant scoffed. "Don't want no money, nothing from the likes of you. You worse than the slavecatchers we run outta the swamp. If I wanted to, ida kilt you already but that would be too good for you. I be here to mark you for the devil, he gonna be waiting for you. Amos gonna see to that."

It was then that David saw the blade in the man's hand. He moved swiftly, slicing David's left forearm with an x. David howled in pain and clutched at his wound. The blood trickled through his fingers. He took a step backwards and stumbled against the bumper of his truck.

He grabbed wildly at the door handle and lurched into the driver's seat, locking the door against the giant.

There was no need. The giant was gone. The parking lot was back and the bar he had just left lit up the night sky. He felt a powerful need for a drink; gone too was the pleasant buzz that had accompanied him into the parking lot. He drove carefully back to the house, searching the rear view mirror for any sign of the giant but no one followed him.

He finished a bottle of gin but the giant still chased him in his dreams. The next morning, he told himself he must have cut his arm when he was drunk, maybe slicing bread for a sandwich when he got the munchies.

He went back to the family for a few days, pretended he was home from one of his business trips. Annette wanted him to put that GPS tracker on Phoebe's car and play the regular family guy. He thought he handled himself fairly well, although he might have gotten a bit nasty with Phoebe that one night. He was feeling more clear-headed though, and that was good. If it were not for that x shaped scar healing on his left forearm, he would have been quite sure the giant with the knife and the weird warning was just a nightmare. He wore long sleeves to hide the scar from Phoebe, not that she would have noticed anyway. It itched like the devil no matter how much he scratched at it.

Annette texted him one afternoon when he told Phoebe he was in Singapore. He was sitting in Starbucks hoping he would not run into anyone from Parlington. She was home early; things had gone really well in Chile. They met for drinks in Tysons Corner. She kissed him hard on the mouth, surprising him. She had not been very interested in him recently, and he had not been bothered by that; more often than not, he was not able to get aroused anymore. She told him that she had put in an offer on a cute apartment in Santiago; he would just love the area. This was the Annette he enjoyed, the cosmopolitan blond who knew her way around real estate and the soft underbelly of the world of the sexually deviant.

She had booked a room in the Hilton, she said. They had been sitting in a booth and she got up to use the ladies' room. When she returned she slid into the seat next to him and whispered to him that she as ready to go to the hotel. Her hand found his cock under the table and squeezed. She smiled at him as he stiffened quickly.

Annette was not an inhibited woman and that night she was in top form. She even let him fuck her in the ass. On her hands and knees she looked back over her shoulder and urged him on. God, how he loved that. He fell asleep in an exhausted heap.

A few hours later, he heard Annette rustling around. He opened one eye and saw her rifling through his overnight bag. She took his iPad out of the bag and went into the bathroom. She was probably looking at the GPS results from Phoebe's car.

Sure enough, the next afternoon, they drove south in David's truck. They checked into a Super 8 in Roanoke and David called Phoebe to make small talk. No sooner had he asked her how they liked the lake when he realized his mistake.

"Goddamn fool!" hissed Annette when he hung up. "Did she tell you she was going to the lake?"

David shook his head.

"She is going to finger you for sure now. I wish you had had the guts to kill her in the forest."

David remembered when he first realized Annette was a killer. It was early in the morning in Cambodia. They had delivered two preteens, a boy and a girl, to their client, some big wig in the Cambodian military, a few hours before. The hand-off had gone well; both subjects were docile with whatever Annette had kept giving them in their sodas throughout the connecting flights. They were both runaways who had been living on the streets of El Paso for months. No foster care personnel or parents or relatives cared about these two. Really, David had rationalized to himself, they were probably better off in Cambodia. Surely they would eat better and have a roof over their heads on a consistent basis.

David and Annette had a late dinner of rice noodles and a local dry white wine. The restaurant was mellow and the chatter of the other patrons soothing. They had hired a car and driver to take them back to their hotel. A day or two of sightseeing to create a semblance of a tourist visit and they would be on their way back, some fifty grand in Annette's bank account. She would wire the money the next morning from the bank at the hotel to one of her offshore accounts. For now, half of it was strapped to her chest, hidden beneath a figure-enhancing bustier. The other half was in a similar bag hidden under David's khakis.

They paid their bill and left the restaurant. There was light foot and vehicular traffic on the street. The hired car was parked at the curb and they got into the back seat. The driver started the engine and pulled away from the curb. He maneuvered the car into traffic as he asked them if they had enjoyed their meal.

"Oh yes, very much," said Annette absently.

She was looking idly out the window. Probably planning her next big score, David thought.

The driver slowed, almost imperceptibly. From the corner of his eye, David saw two men step out of the shadow of a darkened building. Annette slid her hand inside the large straw purse she always carried in the tropics.

The driver hit the button to unlock the door. The first man opened the front passenger door of the car. A flash of metal and the driver groaned. His head slumped to his chest and David smelled copper. Annette slid swiftly across the bench seat. The man had just settled into the seat and turned to look at the driver. He gasped. Annette reached forward and drew her blade across his throat. His head lolled and he slid to the floor of the car. When David looked outside, the second man had melted away into the shadows.

The car idled in park. Annette opened her door and motioned to David to do the same. She walked casually down the street, holding out her hand to him. A half block ahead was a small bar. They went inside and she ordered two brandies and then excused herself to use the ladies room. When she returned, there was not a trace of blood on her hands or a blond hair out of place.

David was intoxicated with her calm. He kept seeing her practiced, small hands wield the blade. He had never seen anything so bad-ass. He wanted to feast on her power, to bury himself in her deadliness. Annette seemed to sense this. She sucked him off in the cab on the way back to their hotel. They rutted well past dawn and her fingernails left deep scratches on his back and buttocks.

After that, David would have done anything for Annette. Part of it was that she had saved both of them and kept them from being robbed. On some level, he probably feared her as well, knew she would not hesitate to slit his throat if he crossed her. Mostly though, he simply admired her; he could not get enough of her. He saw her as an extension of himself.

Back in the Super 8, Annette was very quiet. David knew she was angry at him. He hated that almost as much as he hated not knowing what she was thinking. She left the room for a few hours, returning with a pizza and a bottle of wine. She seemed calmer and he was relieved. Around ten that evening, she announced that it was time.

He raised an eyebrow at her and followed her to his truck. There was no traffic at all and Route 24 was very dark. The road leading into the park was even darker. She drove for about forty-five minutes and then pulled into the entrance to the State Park. She dug a placard out of her purse and hung it from the rearview mirror. She parked the truck at a campsite with a small tent and a cooler. There were two pop-up trailers at the opposite end of the camping area.

Using a small flashlight, she led him along a wooded trail. Cabin lights winked through the trees. He saw Phoebe's station wagon parked outside one of the cabins. Annette peered into the windows and motioned for David to do the same. He saw the girls sleeping in one room. Damien was in a sleeping bag in the other room.

"Go in and get your son."

David balked. Annette frowned at him. He thought about her knife blade, knew she wouldn't hesitate to use it on him. He approached the door to the cabin and looked inside. The old dog snored on the couch next to Phoebe. The doorknob turned in his hand. He kicked his sneakers off and stepped into the cabin, leaving the door ajar. Roxie opened her eyes, thumped her tail and nestled back in next to Phoebe, who rolled onto her side with her face in the couch cushions.

He padded across the kitchen and opened the door to the room where Damien slept. He slid his son out of the sleeping bag and laid him across his shoulder. He had a brief memory of carrying Damien upstairs after he had fallen asleep on the downstairs couch. It seemed very distant, that good night kiss on his son's cheek, the tucking of the blankets around him, placing his favorite teddy bear on his pillow.

He stepped through the open cabin door. Annette slid out of the shadows and he saw the hypodermic needle plunge quickly into Damien's bare leg. The boy winced and opened his eyes.

"Daddy?"

"Hush, go back to sleep. You had a bad dream." David was whispering.

Damien closed his eyes. Annette gestured towards the path in the woods. David carried Damien along the path. It had gotten darker; the moon must have set. He stumbled against something and nearly fell.

"Idiot," Annette hissed. "Watch where you are going!"

"It might help if you used that flashlight," he retorted. His shin was scraped by something hard. He felt a trickle of blood running into his shoe. He shifted Damien to the opposite shoulder.

Back at the campsite, David placed Damien into the back seat of the truck. The boy was snoring lightly. It had started to mist.

"You stay here. There is plenty of food in the cooler. Gin too. I will be back in a day or two. Keep a low profile and don't go wandering around the park."

That was fine with David. He did not want to know what she was going to do with Damien or where she was going. He did think that it was probably stupid of him to stay in the park. Once Phoebe realized Damien was missing, she would certainly contact the cops, who would search the park and want to talk to anyone who had been around when he was taken. He would go down to the marina and help himself to a boat, make himself scarce before the sun came up. But Annette did not need to know that. He wondered if maybe she was setting him up. Fine. Let her think he was drinking himself into a stupor here, just waiting to be caught.

Annette started the truck and drove slowly out of the campground. She did not put the headlights on so she did not see the little girl and boy in front of her on the road. Instead she heard a soft bump.

Cursing herself for hitting Bambi at the worst possible time, she put the truck in park and got out. Her knife was in her hand in case Bambi needed to be put out of his or her misery. She sucked in her breath when her flashlight beam revealed two small forms crumpled on the road to the side of her truck. She poked at one with her foot.

"You is one wretched excuse for a woman." The voice was a hiss. "Thank the lord you never had children."

Annette looked to her right. The woman was dressed in black, barefoot with a long braid coiled around her head.

"Get up offa the ground you two," said the woman in black.

The crumpled forms rose in unison.

"Take that chile out of that contraption and carry him to the cabin. He will be needing some rest and something to drink. Wrap him up good now."

"Yesum."

The children, or whoever they were, lifted Damien gently out of the truck, wrapped him in a blanket and carried him into the darkness.

Annette stepped forward in protest. The woman in black seized her forearm so hard Annette cried out, dropping the knife.

"Oh, no you don't. This lamb here, you will not harm a hair on his head." The woman's voice was low but the words were firm.

The woman picked up Annette's blade. Annette lunged at her. Her hand seemed to pass right through the woman's arm. She felt a sharp stinging sensation and then blood dripping from her shoulder. The blade flashed again.

"Goddamn you." Annette bit back a scream of pain.

The woman in black smiled in the moonlight.

"No, I been blessed. But God has damned you and now you marked for the devil. You gots a lot of souls you sent to be damned, both living and dead. Your time, it'll come."

The blood dripped steadily from Annette's shoulder. The rain fell harder. Annette tried to step forward to open the door of the truck but her hand grasped at air. She could see the F-150 but somehow, it was not there.

Annette was getting cold. The woman in black did not even look damp. The rain seemed to fall around her, but not touch her. Annette decided that the blood loss and the cold was stopping her from thinking clearly. If she could just get back to the tent she could warm up and figure out what to do next.

"I know what you thinking. Your campsite, it not there now. You here with me, until I decide you can go back to your place."

"Who are you? And what do you want with me?"

"Name is Raven. I mean to stop your evil. And I will."

The older woman nodded firmly.

"Pure evil, it is a rare thing. But I sure nuff know it when I see it."

Annette felt a surge of rage. No one stood in her way, at least not for long. Not even her own mother. Who was this creature in black, who dared to challenge her?

Time passed. Annette pressed her hand against her wounded shoulder, hoping the pressure would stop the bloodflow. She grew colder and wetter standing in the dark staring at Raven. Raven was unmoved by the weather or the passage of the hours. The sky lightened at last. Raven casually walked over to the truck and sunk Annette's blade into each of the tires. The truck settled onto its rims.

"Jesus Christ," muttered Annette.

It might be a ghost truck now but its tires would surely be flat later.

"I will be watching out for that chile. And I will be watching you, you can be sure of dat."

Annette scoffed. Raven disappeared into the woods. Annette looked at her shoulder. It had stopped bleeding but was marked with a deep scar in the shape of an x. She should probably have stitches and an antibiotic.

Annette unzipped the tent flap. David was not inside. His clothes were gone and so was the cooler with ice and food. She cursed softly. The medication she had him taking should have ensured that he slept hard and long.

She texted him: "where R U?"

There was no response. She felt the rage building, the white hot anger that she had used to her advantage yet had fought her entire life. She willed herself to be patient and listened for any sound of a search being mounted for a missing boy, anything out of ordinary on an early morning in April on a lake in Virginia.

The morning stretched into the afternoon. There were no sirens, no inquiries around the campground. She smelled coffee and bacon and heard children shouting and playing. She had texted David a few more times but he did not respond. Mid-afternoon, she ventured out of her tent and used the campground shower. She hated the mildew smell of the place, the dirty tile floor. It reminded her of all the campgrounds she had lived in with Glory.

She dressed in hiking boots and shorts and went looking for the truck. She started on the trail that led from the campground to the cabins. She paused to look at a small graveyard. Maybe that stone with the lamb on the top of it was what she had smashed her shin into the night before. She paused in the grove behind the cabin where Phoebe was staying. The little boy was walking the dog. He stopped at one point to kiss the mutt's grey face. It reminded her of the stupid dog in the campground in Nebraska and the rage surged again.

Annette stayed in the shadows and watched the station wagon pull away, Phoebe at the wheel. She walked into the clearing by the cabin. She heard the dog barking and she wished she had her knife. She continued down the road away from the cabin, in the direction of the park entrance. The F-150 was in the parking lot at the Visitor's Center, placard hanging from the rearview, all four tires intact. The doors were unlocked and the key was in the ignition. She got in and drove back to the Super 8.

She took a shower so hot that the steam fogged the entire room. Her shoulder throbbed. She took a couple of Advil and two Bactrim. The scars looked angry red.

Her cell phone chirped.

David had responded: "At the campsite."

She did not answer. Let him stew a while. She had come to detest David. He was so clingy and he lacked backbone. She had had to browbeat him into signing the paperwork for the life insurance policies for his kids. Finally, a reminder of the video and photos from Thailand had done the trick. He had these occasional, annoying pangs of guilt, despite the drugs and alcohol she made available to him to dull his memory. She would be done with him at some point but for now, she needed his access to those kids. Three white kids for her clients' pleasure and then a fatal fire or car crash to collect on the policies. Of course, Phoebe would need to be out of the way.

Annette returned to the tent after midnight. She had stopped at the Walmart and picked up a new knife, a hunting blade. David was snoring.

She shook him awake and hissed: "I told you to stay here!"

He blinked at her. His eyes were clear and still.

"You take me for a fool. Why would I stay here when you and I both know that when they searched this park for my son, I would be the obvious suspect." He paused and took a deep breath. "I saw him with Phoebe and the other kids at the beach this afternoon. How did he get away from you? I know you didn't just let him go."

"Idiot! You let them see you?"

Annette fought to contain herself. She dug her fingernails into her palms.

David scoffed. "Of course not. I borrowed a pontoon boat this morning and watched the park."

He looked at her more closely and switched on his flashlight.

"What happened to your arm?"

He reached for her forearm but she stepped back, guarding her bandaged limb.

"Nothing. I fell in the dark and bruised it on a rock."

The scar on David's arm began to itch.

"Let's go."

She opened the tent flap and stepped out. David did not move.

Annette poked her head back inside the tent.

"I mean it."

She had a gun in her hand and used it to motion towards the woods. David got up and followed her onto the trail.

"You are going to get that old dog out of the cabin."

"What the hell?"

David stopped. Annette pointed the gun at him. He shrugged and followed her up the trail towards the cabin. He wondered when Annette had become such a bitch. Maybe she had always been one.

When they got to the cabin, Annette pointed towards a window that was slightly open at the top.

"Go in there."

Her face was grim. He thought about protesting but instead resolved to be clear of her as soon as he could. He was tired of being bossed around and the threat of the video had paled. He was not even certain she had a video and besides, who would even care about it now? She would implicate herself.

He eased the window open and hoisted himself into the small room where Kendall and Eileen slept. The door creaked slightly as he opened it but not enough to wake anyone, including Roxie. He put his hand under her nose and patted her head. She opened one eye and her tail thumped. He took her leash off the kitchen chair and snapped it onto her collar. She clambered obligingly off the couch and followed him out the door. He locked the flimsy lock behind him.

Annette took the leash out of his hand and led them into the woods. Roxie moved slowly, sniffing at the bushes. When they reached a spot overlooking a cove, Annette stopped. She drew her knife out and handed it to David.

"Kill the dog."

David recoiled. Annette waved the gun at him.

"Why?" he asked.

Roxie sat down. She was panting.

"Because I want to see if you have any guts at all."

"Annette, please. She is just an old dog. What does she have to do with anything?"

Annette cocked the gun.

"I can't believe this shit. You are going to shoot me because I won't kill an old dog that sleeps all day? You are a crazy bitch."

Annette slapped him. He laughed. She put the gun to his temple. Roxie looked up at them. Annette grabbed his hand and slashed at Roxie's throat. A howl was cut short and arterial blood sprayed. Annette stepped out of the stream but David was soaked. He shrieked.

"Shut up."

Annette still had the gun in her hand. She shook her head in disgust.

"Wait for her to bleed out and then drag her down to the marina. Nice little surprise for the early morning boaters."

David was silent. He would go along with this but he was done with her. He tried to avoid getting any more blood on him as he pulled the carcass through the woods.

Annette made him sit on a plastic bag in the passenger seat of his truck. He was surprised when she drove out of the park without stopping at the campsite. She turned left and headed south away from Roanoke. He felt a stinging sensation in his left thigh and looked down to see a hypodermic needle.

"Hey! What are you doing?"

His vision blurred and he slumped.

Annette drove south for another ten miles. She pulled into the parking lot of an ice cream shop. She shook David awake enough to get him out of the truck. He staggered over to the steps of the shop and sat down. As she drove away, he shouted after her.

• • •

Annette's first kill had been a small dog that was following her home from one of the many schools she had attended. It was a stray. Annette had a half cheese sandwich that she had fished out of the cafeteria garbage can when the lunch monitor's back was turned. She put the sandwich in her tattered backpack. The dog could smell it she was sure.

Her home at that point was a tent in a KOA just outside a shabby little Iowa town off Interstate 80. It was late spring and the days were getting longer and hotter. The campground had two types of people: travelers spending the night on an eastbound or westbound journey and poor folks who either worked in the corn fields, turned tricks or otherwise hustled. She knew that eventually Glory would be kicked out of the campground, either because she would fail to pay the fees or the local child and welfare people would start nosing around and realize she was leaving her nine year old daughter alone all night.

The dog was a brown and white mutt with matted hair. She fed it a piece of bread crust and it kept following her. Annette was tired because the night before Glory had made her wait outside the tent on the playground while she entertained several clients in the tent. She had dozed on and off on the top of the slide. She had washed up in the campground bathroom before school. A woman gave her an odd look as she used the air dryer to get the dew off her clothing, the same clothing she had worn to school the day before. Annette did not particularly like school but she liked even less to spend the day at the campground, either listening to Glory snore or trying to entertain herself outside the tent.

The mutt reminded her of her mother. She loathed her mother. Her cigarette cough and bad dye job. The way she would do almost anything for food or money or drugs. The dog trotted along behind her. Just like her mother chasing some gross guy who might pay her for a blow job or share his coke.

Her mother was sleeping inside on the cot. Glory smelled of booze and a trickle of blood had crusted under her nose. Either she had been snorting or one of her clients had roughed her up. Annette rummaged under her own sleeping bag for the kitchen knife she had stolen from one of the other campsites a few nights earlier. The dog was sitting outside the tent.

Annette whistled and the dog pricked up its ears. It followed her hopefully into the underbrush at the side of their campsite. Annette walked deeper into the wooded area. When she was out of sight of any other tents or trailers she sat down. The dog sat next to her. She studied the dog, and then the knife. It would not do to have a lot of noise. She could not stand the sound of pleading or whimpering. Without hesitation, she grabbed the dog's ears and lifted its head, exposing its throat, furry and white.

She jammed the knife into the dog's throat and yanked it right and left. The dog's eyes widened, its body stiffened. She was not expecting the gush of warm blood on her hands and face. It even splashed her t-shirt. Her slippery hands clutched the dog's ears and the dog slumped to the ground. Its legs twitched a few times and then it was still.

She looked at the fur, matted now with both mud and blood. A new feeling washed over her. She could not have said, at nine years old, what it was, but when she looked back at her childhood, she recalled this moment as the moment when she finally was in control. She smiled in satisfaction.

She dragged the dog deeper into the underbrush and covered it with leaves and branches. No one would care to look for a stray. Sticking to the outskirts of the campground, she looked at the pop-up trailers and tents. She found a clean t-shirt hanging from a clothes-line. She pulled it over her head. It was large enough to cover the blood stains on her jeans. She worked her way over to the laundry room next to the campground office. It was deserted. She found a dryer full of clean clothes and selected a pair of walking shorts. A little big but they would do. She discarded her bloody jeans and blouse near an underpass close to Route 80.

Glory was still sleeping in the tent. Annette rifled through the pocket of the slacks Glory had tossed under the cot and was rewarded with a ten dollar bill. More than enough for the bacon cheeseburger at the diner in town. She slept soundly that night, not noticing when Glory staggered though the tent flaps before dawn, trailed by a man in a cowboy shirt who recoiled when he saw the child sleeping in the corner of the tent. The man threw a twenty at Glory and disappeared.

For a year or two after she killed the stray dog in Nebraska, Annette carried the knife with her everywhere. She used it once on a cat begging for food outside a shelter. She would sharpen it regularly, and sometime imagined slicing into one of Glory's customers, picturing warm red blood pulsating from a throat. The images calmed her.

Glory tended to head south in the colder months but the winter of 1990, when Annette turned fourteen, was different. Glory shacked up with the manager of a truck stop off of interstate 81, just south of Harrisonburg, Virginia. She and Annette had a room in the hotel adjacent to the truck stop.

Alvin was a disgusting fellow by anyone except Glory's standards. He was unkempt, with a beer belly. Glory's needs were simple: a six pack or two a night and a warm place to sleep. Annette slept most nights in the lobby of the hotel on a tattered couch. The woman who waitressed overnight at the truck stop would cook her breakfast and drop her at the school in town. Annette stayed out of Glory's way as much as she could. She knew it was just a matter of time before Alvin would figure out that Glory was turning tricks while he was at work.

One afternoon after school, Annette let herself into Glory's room. She planned to wash the few pieces of clothing that she had. Glory was sitting on the bed sporting a blackened eye and a split lip. Annette studied her mother but said nothing, waiting for the inevitable announcement that they would be moving on.

"Honey, I want to talk to you about something."

Annette hated being called Honey. It was mockery of what should have been a term of endearment. Annette waited.

"We are going to Atlanta. I have a job lined up there and you can work too."

"Let me guess," retorted Annette. "Good old Al figured out you were banging truckers on the side and knocked you around. Now we are getting kicked out. Shocker."

"This?" Glory pointed at her face. "This is nothing. I just fell down. No, Al has found me a job with a friend of his in Georgia. His friend is coming tonight and he wants to meet you."

Glory got up off the bed and opened the closet.

"Look at the pretty outfit I got for you to wear when you meet him." She held up a garish green dress. "You can even wear some of my lipstick."

"Give me a break." Annette sneered. "You are pimping me out. I got news for you. I am not going anywhere with you."

Annette gathered the rest of her clothes and left the room, slamming the door for good measure.

Annette watched the clothes spinning in the front loader. Her thoughts churned. She considered all the Dum-Dum lollipops she had been given in exchange for letting Glory's friends touch her, take photos of her, do unspeakable things to her. Glory certainly had other ideas now. Annette thumbed the blade in her pocket. All those nights sleeping in hotel lobbies and parking garages and on playgrounds, all the different schools. The snickers from the other kids at her clothing and the stale food fished out of dumpsters.

She switched her clothes to the dryer. Glory was calling her. She ducked into the utility room adjacent to the laundry room and switched off the light. She watched through the crack in the door as Glory tottered into view on her red stilettos and huffed away when she saw the laundry room was empty.

After a few minutes, Annette let herself out of the utility room. She could smell the Charlie perfume in the hallway. Glory must be headed into town. She stepped into the lobby and saw the headlights on Al's car switch on. Too late. Glory had spotted her.

Glory stormed out of the Pinto and grabbed Annette by the arm. Fingernails dug into Annette's flesh.

"You are coming with me," she hissed. "I promised Jim that he would meet you tonight. Get in the car. You can put on the dress as I drive."

Annette could have easily fought Glory off and run into the woods behind the truck stop. Glory would get a few drinks in her and forget about Jim. But Annette was tired. She smiled at Glory and got into the back seat of the Pinto. Glory drove into Harrisonburg and pulled into a strip mall. It was dark now and Glory disappeared into an ABC store. She emerged a few minutes later and got back into the car, taking a few pulls at the bottle of Southern Comfort.

"Mom, pull around the back of the store. I don't want anyone to see me changing in the car."

Glory sighed but obliged, parking beside a dumpster. Annette went through the motions of changing her clothes. Glory fiddled with the radio. Annette stood on the back seat, as if to pull on the black fish net stockings Glory wanted her to wear. She eased the knife out of her pocket. Glory took another pull on the bottle.

Annette reached forward, as if to embrace Glory. She placed her left arm across Glory's chest and with her right hand, dragged the blade across Glory's throat. Glory's eyes bulged in terror in the rearview mirror and Annette smiled placidly. Blood gushed from the ruined throat.

Glory died in a matter of minutes with a final gurgle. Annette sat quietly in the backseat to be sure no one else was in the area. She opened the backdoor and eased out. She wrapped her hands in the green dress and opened the driver's door to pull Glory out by her feet. Glory's head hit the asphalt with a satisfying thud. Annette dragged the body behind the dumpster and threw the green dress on top of her. She wiped the blade on the hem of the dress. She left the keys in the ignition of the Pinto.

After she helped herself to the cash in Glory's purse, she walked several miles to a 7/11 where she used the pay phone to call a cab. She went back to the motel and slept soundly. For the next two days, she ate at the truck stop and went to school. On the third day, the police connected her to the body behind the dumpster. Al's car had been stolen from the parking lot with Glory's ID in it and was found two days later in North Carolina.

Annette tried to look sad for the social services lady who processed her into foster care. She thought she was pretty convincing.

Chapter Ten

Eileen

Eileen's throat was very dry and her head ached. She opened her eyes to near darkness. She was lying on a couch in what could be a basement. Gingerly, she pushed herself up to a seated position. A wave of nausea washed over her and she put her head between her knees, just as her mom would have her do when she was overwhelmed by anxiety. After a moment of deep breathing, she was able to look around the room.

The floor was carpeted and there was a single, low table to the right of the couch. The place had a vaguely musty smell and faint light came in from two narrow windows to her left. She eased up to standing and tried each of the four doors in the room.

One was a closet with three shelves. Beach towels, some deflated floaties and a couple of pairs of flip flops. Another door opened to a half bathroom. She drank greedily, scooping up water with both hands. She flipped the light switch. Nothing. She looked up; the bulb was missing from the single socket.

The other two doors were locked. She knocked on both. One seemed thicker and had two locks. Must be to outside, she told herself. She dragged the table over to the window. Not tall enough to see outside. She added two of the couch cushions and standing on tip toes, was able to see outside.

The door to the outside appeared to be under a porch or a deck. What she could see of the ground was sandy. Beyond the overhang the sun was out. She glanced down to check the time but her watch was missing. What time was it? For that matter, she thought, what day was it?

Her stomach rumbled. She tried to remember when she had last eaten. Definitely the tuna fish her mom had made for her lunch. She had eaten it in the cafeteria, before her dad had come to sign her out of school.

That had seemed weird for sure. Her dad had never even been to Fairfax High School. He was nice enough and at least he did not get on her case like some of her friends' fathers did. But, he left everything to her mom and never really seemed interested in what she did or thought. Besides, he was always traveling for work.

A family emergency was the reason he gave the school secretary for signing her out. On the way out of the building he had told her that her mom had been in an accident and that they needed to get to the hospital. That had made her scared and anxious. She climbed into the back of his truck, only realizing once the engine started that her dad was not driving. A lady in a brown sweater with a blond ponytail was behind the wheel.

"Who are you?" she had asked.

"A friend of your dad," had been the response. "Name is Annette."

"What happened to mom? Where is she and is she going to be alright?"

There was no response. She texted Joseph.

"My dad just picked me up. He said that my mom had an accident. But something is not right."

Her father reached around and pulled the phone out of her hand.

"I will take that now," he said, his voice wooden.

She stared at him but he just turned back around and took the battery out of her phone. They were on Route 50 East at a light. He opened his window and let the battery slip out of his fingers.

Eileen sank back into her seat. They were close to Fairfax Hospital now but Annette pulled onto 495 South, passing the exit with the blue hospital symbol. Traffic was heavy; rush hour had begun.

"Where are we going?" asked Eileen.

She looked to her father. His head was slumped against the window and his mouth was open. He began to snore.

"What is going on?" she directed towards Annette, voice rising as panic set in.

"Best that you just keep quiet," was the only response.

Eileen tried to do the breathing exercises that her therapist had taught her to help ward off an anxiety attack. She willed herself to be calm, told herself that the Lexapro she had taken the night before was still working.

She studied her father more closely. His hair was messy and he looked like he hadn't shaved in a couple of days. The truck was too warm and the windows were up. She pressed the button to put her window down but Annette must have the child safety locks on.

"I think I am going to be sick," Eileen announced.

Annette looked at her in the rearview window, her eyes blue and calm. She handed Eileen a plastic bag.

"Use this if you need to throw up."

The truck inched along in the heavy traffic. The clock on the dashboard read five-thirteen. Her mom, she assumed that the story about the accident had been a lie, must be worried by now. Eileen should have been home by two-forty. Even if she had taken the late bus by five. She hoped that Joseph was worried enough by her last text, and her lack of further contact, to let someone know.

She pushed panic down again. She father was still out cold, drool dribbling from the side of his mouth. Annette drove on, silently.

At two minutes after seven, Annette got off 95 South and pulled into a McDonalds. She shook David awake and handed him a gun. She looked at Eileen.

"Please don't try anything. He will hurt you if you do."

Annette got out of the car and walked into McDonalds.

Eileen looked at her father. He looked confused and sad.

"Dad," she asked. "What is going on here? Where are we going? And what is wrong with you?"

He returned her gaze but his eyes were unsteady.

"I don't want to hurt you, any of you. Just listen to her and do as she says."

"Dad, please, let me out of the car."

Her dad looked away.

"Do you have a phone? Daddy, listen to me."

David reached for his hip where his iPhone normally rested in its case. He seemed puzzled not to find it. His eyes drifted closed.

Eileen tried the door, frantic. She began to climb over the seat on the driver's side when Annette reappeared.

"Don't even think about it," said Annette, handing her a white paper bag.

She shook David awake, with a roughness that made Eileen wince.

"Next time I will have to tie you up when we make a stop," said Annette in a pleasant tone.

Annette started the truck.

It was McDonalds, a cheeseburger and a vanilla milkshake, that she had eaten last. Eileen peered out the window where a little brown bird pecked at the sand. She tried to remember what had happened after the cheeseburger but there was nothing there.

Surely, her mom had reported her missing by now. Her mom must be frantic. Eileen never liked to worry her mother, always checked in with her each morning after she got to school. Maybe they had issued one of those Amber Alerts. People had seen her getting into her dad's truck.

She thought of Damien and Kendall and was suddenly awash in homesickness. The next time she saw that little boy, she would kiss his face over and over, even if his nose was runny. She would never, ever, tell Kendall again that she was too busy to play with stuffed animals. Her eyes welled with tears as she watched the little bird. She envied its freedom.

The window. It was not one that could be opened and closed, merely intended to let in some ambient light. Maybe she could break it, wrap her arm in a beach towel. She would have to stand the couch on one end and stand up on it. She eyed the window. It looked too small for even her thin frame to fit through. What if someone heard her break it? Maybe she should listen for a bit, see if she heard anything.

The house, she assumed it was a house, above her was quiet. No sound of footsteps or water running, no doors opening and closing. She thought she heard a car outside once or twice, but it seemed distant. Her heart began to pound, her mind raced. What if she had been forgotten, left to die? What if she never saw her mom again? What if that Annette came back and did something awful? She recalled the story of a woman who had been locked inside a California garage, imprisoned, a sexual slave for decades. She gritted her teeth, told herself to be calm, to think.

She went into the bathroom and urinated. She debated flushing and decided that the noise would not matter. If whoever put her here was upstairs, they would not care. If someone else was up there perhaps the sound would alert them and they would rescue her. Her flush seemed to go unnoticed.

Under the bathroom sink were an extra roll of toilet paper and a scrubbing brush. Tucked behind the sink pipe, she almost missed a glade candle, lavender scented, wick unlit. She pulled it out, hoping she might find some way to light it, to stave off the darkness that was descending rapidly. The lower shelf of the cabinet held two bars of soap and a frayed toothbrush. God knew what it had been used to scrub, she thought. The top shelf at first seemed to be empty but as she ran her hand along it for a second time, she felt a thin metal object. A pair of tweezers. She tucked them into the front pocket of her skinny jeans.

She opened the closet. In addition to the beach towels, deflated beach balls and floaties and the flip flops, which still had sand on them, she found a bucket and a plastic shovel. Inside the bucket, was a child's flashlight shaped like Spiderman. Damien would love such a toy. To her surprise, it worked, although the beam was dim. She put it in her sports bra.

When she pulled the beach towels off the shelf, she saw a metal box, about a foot wide and maybe eighteen inches high. It had a little door. She opened it. It reminded her of the box in their garage that her mom would fiddle with when the vacuum cleaner made some of the lights in the house flick off. What did she call it? A fuse breaker box?

She studied the switches. Most were flipped to the right but several were in the opposite position. What the heck. She began to flip those to the right. She heard something start to hum outside. Maybe the heat or the AC. She flipped the last two and at first, nothing. Then, the florescent light over the mirror in the bathroom started to flicker. Good. At least she would not be spending the night in complete darkness.

Her next task was to drag the couch over beneath the windows. It was fairly heavy and she realized quickly that her original plan to stand it on one end was flawed. The armrest protruded too far to the side and the couch would never balance in that position. She removed two of the couch cushions and placed them on the top of the table, which she then placed on the third cushion, centered on the couch. Balancing carefully, she peered out the window.

Car headlights swept the sand beneath the overhang. She froze. An engine cut off. She jumped off the table and yanked the couch back towards the center of the room, scattering the cushions in the process. She scrambled to flip the three switches back to their original positions. She heard a door open and shut and footsteps directly overhead. She crammed the towels and beach items back into the closet and tossed herself onto the couch. As the footsteps descended she assumed a dejected posture and sank back onto the couch, pulling her knees to her chest.

Annette unlocked the door, her figure backlit by the light above the stairs. She looked more severe today, a black baseball cap was on her head and what looked like a rain coat covered most of her slim torso. In her hand was a white bag. Eileen's stomach growled as she smelled French fries.

"Brought you some food," said Annette. "Also, your medication. Your dad says you take Lexapro. You should take one of these. Keep things calm."

Annette held out a small bottle.

Eileen did not respond. She made no move to accept the food or the pill, just hugged her knees more closely to her chest.

"Don't make this more difficult than it needs to be," Annette told her.

"Where is my father? Why am I here?"

"He is resting. Not feeling well. You are here because we need you."

"What is wrong with him? And what do you want from me?" Eileen was practically shouting now.

"That is enough," said Annette.

She put the food and the medication down on the table.

"I don't care if you eat but I want you to take that pill. Last thing I need right now is one of your famous panic attacks."

Eileen flushed with shame. So her dad had ratted her out. Did he really think she had panic attacks on purpose, like she was trying to manipulate him? She had overheard him say something like that to her mom once, after she had had a particularly bad episode, before her mom had taken her to a therapist, and when talk therapy had not alleviated her symptoms, to a shrink for medication.

"I don't need that pill," she said.

"You will take it," Annette said in a conversational tone.

She drew the gun out of the pocket of her raincoat.

Eileen grabbed the bottle and shook out a pill. It was not the same shape as the pill she normally took. She put it in her mouth, took a sip of her milkshake and swallowed visibly.

"Good girl," said Annette. "Eat up."

Annette closed the door and the lock clicked on the other side. Footsteps ascended the stairs.

Eileen spit into her hand. Most of the pill was still there, awash in milkshake. She rinsed her hand and mouth in the sink. She looked at the food. Normally, her mom did not let them eat fast food more than once a week and now she had a steady diet of it. She took a big bite of the Burger King chicken sandwich and chewed once. It had a tinny taste. She stopped in mid chew and spit into her napkin.

What if Annette had drugged her? After all, that was what serial killers and sexual sadists did. She had seen it on Dexter and Criminal Minds. And, she reminded herself, she had no memory of how she had gotten into this room, no memory since she had eaten the McDonalds in the car. As hungry as she was, she was not going to eat anything from Annette.

She broke up the food into small pieces and let them dissolve in the toilet. Then she poured the rest of the milkshake into the bowel and flushed. She used the Spiderman flashlight to be sure there was no trace of the food.

She lay down on the couch. Annette, or someone, walked overhead. Briefly, she heard raised voices. Maybe her dad? There there was silence for some time. It was full dark outside. The footsteps came down the stairs again. She closed her eyes and rolled onto her side, feigning deep sleep and not responding to a hard shake on her shoulder. After what seemed like hours, she heard the door lock and the footsteps fade back up the stairs. A moment later, a car started and pulled away.

It was now or never. Annette thought she was down for the count, knocked out for hours. She dragged the couch back to its spot under the window. She took the scrub brush out from under the sink and wrapped her hand in one of the beach towels. Holding the brush she thought of what it had scrubbed and then shoved that image away. She began to bang at the window.

The glass was pretty strong and the banging seemed incredibly loud. After swatting the window a half dozen times she paused to see if there were any indications that her efforts had been heard. Nothing. The glass was intact. She began to weep in frustration.

Chapter Eleven

Phoebe

Moises was at the sink, washing the breakfast dishes and the cutting board he had used to chop vegetables for something he was putting into the crockpot.

"I need to go to Virginia Beach," she said. "That has to be where they took my baby."

"Flaca, you need to let the police do their job. Don't you think they are already there looking for this woman and searching that house she and David have there?"

Phoebe sighed in frustration.

Detective Nichols knocked on the door. From his face, Phoebe could tell there was no news of Eileen.

"Fredericksburg PD searched David's truck again. They found this bag in the trunk, stuffed under the spare tire. I thought we could look through it together, see if anything clicks."

He put a black duffel bag, medium sized, onto the table. Its contents were typical David. Scraps of paper, scrawled notes, candy wrappers, match books and receipts for gas and food, mostly in Fairfax but a few in Virginia Beach and Charlottesville. She grabbed one receipt.

"Here is one from a McDonald's in Bedford."

"Yes," said Detective Nichols.

He studied the receipt.

"Puts him near the lake the day your dog was killed. Probably two people, from the order. A Big Mac Meal, a salad and two drinks."

"David would never order a salad," Phoebe mused.

Detective Nichols pulled out a black hooded sweatshirt. Phoebe stared at it. At the bottom of the bag was a pair of white gloves.

"I don't recognize that stuff," she said at last.

"Well the lab is running tests. The gloves have some sort of stain on them, might be blood."

Phoebe half listened as Detective Nichols told them that the Amber Alert was still in effect and included a photo of David.

"Also the surveillance tape at the Costco had some coverage. Looks like the female walked away from the truck and came back with a Toyota Camry about an hour later. Let me show you."

He pulled out his iPad and a grainy black and white tape played. Phoebe's heart lurched as she watched David lift Eileen out of the back of the truck and place her in the backseat of the Camry. Her daughter's head lolled to one side. The time on the tape showed thirteen minutes after ten.

"I know it is hard to watch, Flaca," said Moises. "But it shows she is alive and gives the police another vehicle to track."

"It looks like she was drugged." Phoebe moaned. "My baby, god what is happening to her?"

Moises put his arm around her shoulder.

Nichols left and Moises turned back to his work in the kitchen. Phoebe watched as he unwrapped a package of chicken thighs and placed them in the crockpot.

"That man who raped me," she said at last. "He was wearing a black hoodie and he had those awful white gloves on."

But the white gloved man had not been David. She knew David. Surely she would have known if he had hurt her, touched her in that vile way. Maybe he had hired someone else to hurt her?

"What about the other guy?" asked Moises. "What did he look like? Do you remember anything that he said?"

"What does that matter!" cried Phoebe. "They are dead. I think I helped kill them."

Moises insisted that she think carefully about both men, try to write down descriptions of what they had been wearing, how they acted, anything they said. She tried to compose herself and picked up a pen.

"Does David smoke?" Moises asked suddenly. "Why would he have matches in that bag?"

"Just cigars every now and then. He collects useless crap. There are matches in all his dresser drawers upstairs too."

Phoebe was suddenly blinded by rage at David. Not just for this affair, or whatever he had with this Annette person, but for all the years of messiness and absenteeism, his mediocrity and lack of interest in the details of their life and family. And that he would touch a hair on their daughter's head. If she found that he was involved in any way with her rape or the killing of Roxie, well there was no telling what she might do.

She forced herself away from that train of thought. She grabbed several contractor sized garbage bags from the garage and went upstairs.

She started with his closet. Typical of David, clothing was shoved randomly into drawers. Suits and jackets, too many for any one person to ever use, were hung not only in his closet but in the hall closet and the closet in Damien's room. Her first instinct was to haul everything to the dump. She resisted and settled for trashing anything she was sure did not fit him, and picking through every scrap of paper he had.

She set aside any receipts or paperwork that showed David had been outside of the immediate Fairfax area. Not surprisingly, there was plenty of evidence of his presence in Virginia Beach, dating back to 2010. At the bottom of what she could only refer to as a drawer devoted to ratty underwear and unmatched socks, she found an envelope with the Parlington logo on it, marked "Confidential". The letter was dated August 3, 2010.

"Dear Mr. Rivers:
This letter constitutes formal notice of your termination from Parlington, effective immediately. Your termination is due to your

breach of ethical obligations and conduct unbecoming an officer of Parlington. Be advised that Parlington reserves the right to proceed against you in a court of law in this matter. You may wish to seek legal counsel in this matter. Upon conclusion of our investigation, we may choose to return your personal effects to you. You are hereby barred from Parlington property. We remind you of your obligation under your employment agreement not to contact any Parlington clients upon termination of your employment."

He must really take her for a fool, a naive feckless wife. All this stuff right in her own bedroom, some of it for years.

She emptied out the remaining dresser drawers, filling three garbage bags in the process. The suits and jackets were going to Goodwill. Most of them had not been worn for at least decade. First though, she checked all the pockets. In the inside breast pocket of a brown jacket that looked exactly like the other three brown jackets hung in various closets, two of which still had price tags on them, she found a receipt from a Seth Dellany, MD, dated February 22, 2011.

She filled the back of the station wagon with the suits and jackets and hauled the trash bags to the curb. The officers in the car parked in front of the house watched her curiously. Moises' chicken was smelling very good. She felt a pang of guilt at her ability to feel hunger even in the face of a missing child. She peeked into the TV room where Kendall and Damien were watching Sponge Bob.

Seth Dellany, according to Google, was an oncologist in Norfolk. The website for the practice with which he seemed to be affiliated claimed to provide comprehensive care for patients with cancer and blood disorders. She put the receipts from Dr. Dellany and those from Virginia Beach into an envelope which she placed on top of her yellow legal pad.

Phoebe stepped onto the porch, thinking that some fresh air would help her think. The new fence gleamed in the afternoon sun. Daffodils dotted the backyard. She would pick a few to put in a vase on the kitchen table. She reached down for a particularly pretty yellow flower and felt a twinge in her neck. She turned her head from side to side to release the crick. Her vision slid along the fence, which shimmered for a moment and then disappeared.

Startled, Phoebe sat down. She massaged her neck, looking down at the ground. A pair of brown boots came into view. She looked up into Petrel's face. He regarded her quietly. She swallowed a couple of times. It was way past time to get to the bottom of this, her inner voice scolded.

"Petrel," she began. "I need to talk to you about the other night. Can you please tell me what really happened. I am so confused."

Petrel extended his hand and helped her to her feet. He led her to the log cabin. There was no one inside. She imagined that the speakeasy would be open in the evenings. They sat at the rough-hewn bar. A teakettle whistled and Petrel brewed two mugs of tea.

"What do you remember?" he asked.

"I was running and two men attacked me. One raped me and hit me, the other meant to do the same. I was sure they were going to kill me. Then, out of nowhere, you appeared. I think you knocked out the one who raped me and I took your knife and stabbed the one with the mustache."

"Those men were federals, looking for my sill. They meant to shut me down. I saw them fall on you, like a pair of wolves. I done what needed to be done." Petrel explained all this in a calm voice.

"But did we kill them both?" persisted Phoebe. "I read in the newspaper that one died, stabbed to death, but what about the other one?"

Petrel shook his head.

"Not sure about him. The sheriff found the one. Maybe the animals got to the other or he come to and drug himself off."

"Are you in trouble for this? I hate to think of you in trouble for saving me."

Petrel smiled. "No more trouble than normal. Jest the cat and mouse came with the federals chasing moonshine. But you," his eyes turned serious, "you need to watch yourself. I think you know that."

"My daughter, my daughter has been taken. I think it was by her father. And somehow, I think he was involved in the attack on me."

Petrel thought a moment.

"Those federals were from down past Virginia Beach. Back Bay area, if I recollect. They are after the rum shipments that come in at the river mouth off the ocean. For some reason they got sent up here for a spell, maybe tracking the hootch coming up from Franklin county. But those two, they aren't just federals. There has been some talk of them taking children, selling them off to farms or worse. Two young girls from Fairfax went missing a week before I found you. They haven't been seen since."

Phoebe sipped at her tea. Mid afternoon sunlight streamed in through the cracks in the log walls. She stood up and thanked Petrel. As she stepped down from the stone stoop, she felt the familiar vision slide. She closed her eyes and sat down. Moises was calling her, asking her what she was doing sitting on the ground. She picked up the scattered yellow flowers and went into the house.

Detective Nichols was back. The house on Eastern Shore Road had been thoroughly searched and there was no sign of Eileen although it was evident that David and Annette used the house and had clothing and belongings stored there. There had been no pings on Eileen's cell phone since the text reported by Joseph. The Amber Alert was still in effect. The police guard would remain at the house.

And what am I supposed to do, thought Phoebe to herself as she thanked Detective Nichols. Just sit in the house guarding my kids? She obviously could not tell Detective Nichols what she had learned from Petrel or about her attack. How could she explain having the information without implicating herself? Was there even such a thing as an anonymous tip anymore? She supposed if she could even find a pay phone, she might place a call.

What she did do was tell Detective Nichols about the receipt from Dr. Dellany. He made a note of it.

"I know this is hard, Mrs. Rivers," said the detective. "All these bits of information will add up to something. We will get a break. I am sure of that."

Chapter Twelve

Eileen

Eileen wiped her nose on the sleeve of her hoodie. Get a grip, she told herself. You still have some time before Annette comes back with more drugged fast food. She did not think she would ever eat McDonalds again. She stood up and something in her front pocket poked her. The tweezers.

She studied the locks on the outside door and the one that led upstairs. She wondered if she could use the tweezers to pick the lock. Or maybe she could break down the door with the table, if she used it like a battering ram, like cops had done on an episode of CSI New York to get to a child trapped inside with a psychopath. She took out the Spiderman flashlight and played it over the door, tapping on the door to see if any spot sounded hollow.

The beam shone on the door hinges. There were two. She trained the light on the lower one. Maybe she could use the tweezers to pull the bolt up. She grunted with effort as she tried to grasp the top of the bolt. Sweat dripped off her fingers. The bolt did not budge. She squeezed the pincers together, thinking maybe she could wedge the narrow part under the bolt and use the flashlight like a hammer to force the bolt out of its slot.

After several attempts, all she had managed was to bend the

tweezers slightly. She sank back onto the couch. She thought about her mom and her brother and sister and the rage began to build. She had done nothing to deserve this and she was goddamed if she was going to just sit here cowering and waiting for Annette to come back. What was her dad even doing with Annette? What could they possibly need her for, except maybe, it suddenly occurred to her, to somehow torture her mom. Could her dad be having an affair with that horrible woman?

She felt a panic attack coming on. If she let it get a grip on her, she would be useless. She tried instead to summon all the anger she could.

She flipped the table over and stood in the center of it. She grabbed one of the legs and using all her weight, she pushed against it. Nothing. Then she slid the table across the rug and wedged two of the table legs under the couch, standing the table on its end. She yanked the table towards her and was rewarded by a cracking sound. She began to bang on the doors with the table leg, alternating between the inner and outer ones. She punctuated the banging with calls for help.

She paused for breath. A footfall overhead. Faltering. She continued to bang and yell. The footsteps were coming down the stairs. She pulled the tweezers out of her pocket and cupped them in her right hand. The left hand, clutching the table leg, was behind her.

"Be quiet."

It was her father.

"Daddy?" she pleaded. "Please let me out of here."

She banged harder on the interior door and continued to shout.

"Shut up," he growled, "or I will come in there and shut you up."

"Please, I am having a panic attack. I can't stay in here."

She began screaming at the top of her lungs.

She heard the lock turn. She stepped back towards the bathroom. The door opened and her father stepped gingerly into the room peering into the darkness. He was wearing only boxer shorts and one sock. She crossed to the couch and crouched down, as if she was sitting. She dropped her head down and let her hair fall into her face peering up through her hair to watch him.

"Eileen. You must keep quiet. If she comes back and hears you, there will be trouble."

He approached the couch where she pretended to cower. That was what he and Annette wanted, for her to be a sniveling little baby. He had left the door open behind her and she could see the stairs. He extended a hand towards her, bending his knees as he did. She drove the tweezers as hard as she could into his right thigh. He shouted in surprise and clutched at his leg.

She sprang up and he grabbed for her hoodie. She switched the table leg into her right hand as she wheeled around and brought the table leg as hard as she could against his left knee. He howled and let go of her sweatshirt. She flung herself through the door. Almost as an afterthought, she turned around and slammed the door behind her. She turned the deadbolt and raced up the stairs. He was yelling her name.

The stairs led directly into a small kitchen with a yellowed linoleum floor. She glanced around, wondering if she should search the house, see if there was a phone. Her overwhelming need to get out of the house took over and she sprinted out of the kitchen into a dank living room. A single lamp was on, revealing the front door. She reached down to unplug the lamp and burst outside. She breathed a silent thanks to Mr. Kudson, her track coach, who had insisted that the girls on the team practice fighting off a larger attacker.

The night air had a distinctly salty smell. She breathed deeply and dove into some scrubs at the edge of the dirt driveway. There she looked around. The house where she had been imprisoned was a small one, more of a cabin really, at the end of a dirt road. There were no lights or other houses in sight. A dirt road led away from the cabin. There was some moonlight but it was not bright.

She crawled out of the bushes and began to walk down the dirt road. There was a chill in the air and she shivered. She broke into a slow jog. She was grateful that she had on her Keds rather than the Dansco clogs she normally wore to school. She studied the horizon ahead. There was a faint light but she was not sure whether it was civilization or dawn breaking. She had no clue which direction was which.

She saw two pinpricks of light ahead. Headlights. She sprinted to the right, desperate for cover. She tucked herself behind a grove of scrub pines, burrowing into the sand. She was almost afraid to look at the car but she forced herself. The headlights got closer. The car was traveling slowly on the dirt road. She shivered in fear but the car did not stop. It had to be Annette. She had not passed another house since she had left the cabin. Maybe her father had even been able to call Annette, and had told her that Eileen had escaped. She jumped to her feet and raced for the road. It was only a matter of minutes before Annette started searching for her. She needed a better place to hide.

Her feet struck wood. A wooden bridge. She veered off the road to look beneath it. Her feet slid on a patch of mud and she skidded down the embankment, barely stopping herself from slipping into the river that eased by.

She heard a car engine and froze. The car stopped on the bridge overhead.

"Eileen," called Annette, "I know you are down there. Don't make me shoot you."

Eileen heard a faint splash in the water. She looked in the direction of the sound. A hand touched hers. She bit back a scream. The hand was tiny, smaller than Damien's, and it tugged on hers. She let herself be led into the water, wincing at the cold. The water deepened quickly and she could feel the current tugging at her legs. A second hand, stronger, clasped her other hand.

"Just float," came a whisper. "Duck your head under water as much as you can."

Eileen obeyed. The water carried them along. She continued to hold hands with two people who she could not see. She could hear Annette shouting her name but her voice grew more distant.

After a while, Eileen had no idea how long, the larger hand pulled her towards the riverbank and the three clambered out. She sank to the ground. The sky was pink overhead. She studied her companions. One was a little boy, no more than four, with a mass of curly hair. The other was a young woman, maybe a year or two older than Eileen.

"Thank you," said Eileen. "They would have caught me for sure if you had not helped."

"Do you think they meant to eat you?" asked the little boy.

"Eat me?" Eileen smiled. "Do you mean like monsters?"

"Oh they are monsters for certain," said the young woman. "There is no telling what folks will do when they are hungry."

Eileen stared at them. They were both barefoot, wearing what looked like tattered, homemade clothing. The little boy had on short pants and a muslin shirt, what was left of it. The woman wore a long skirt and a torn blouse. She wore her dark hair in long braids tied with scraps of black velvet.

Dawn was breaking. Eileen looked around her. Nothing but the river, mud flats and scrubby pine. There was no sign of civilization, no roads and no houses. Not even a telephone pole.

"I need to get to a town, find a phone and call my mom. Can you tell me where the nearest town is?"

"There are no towns here," said the young woman. "Just the settlement, and you don't want to go near that place. Those that didn't perish this winter are ruthless."

"They wanted to eat me," piped the little boy. "We runned off."

"Best we can hope for is to meet up with some of the natives. As savage as they might be, they won't eat us and they might even let us live with them." The young woman spoke in a matter of fact tone.

Eileen was quite sure she was dreaming, or perhaps even suffering from some sort of anxiety and stress induced hallucination. It was as if some characters from her American history textbook had come alive out of the pages. She shook her head and pinched herself. The little boy and the young woman were still there. And Eileen was still sitting on a muddy riverbank. Her feet were bare. She must have lost her Keds during the time in the river.

She felt light-headed. She supposed it was from lack of sleep and food. She stood up, but got so dizzy that she immediately sat back down and put her head between her knees. She gulped at the air. She smelled exhaust. She looked for her companions but she was alone on the riverbank. She heard a car and winced. She was too tired and dizzy to run. She looked towards the sound and watched a car pass by on the road above the river bank. It did not stop.

She heard another engine, but it did not sound like a car. She looked at the river and saw a motorboat putting along towards her. An elderly man was at the Evinrude engine and he was looking right at her. He raised a hand. Reflexively, she returned the greeting. There were several fishing poles and a tackle box visible. He drew near.

"You alright, young lady?"

He had a weatherworn face and wore a soiled baseball cap but his eyes behind his gold wire-rimmed glasses were grey and kind. The boat drew closer.

"Where are your shoes? And what are you doing there in the mud?"

She looked at him mutely. He studied her face more closely.

"Are you cold?" he said. "I have some tea and some crackers here. The missus, she always sends me off with something to nibble on."

He cut the engine off and the boat glided towards the riverbank. He stepped out and drew the rope on the bow with him, wrapping it around a boulder. He wore docksiders and khaki pants with a flannel shirt. He offered her a thermos.

She drank the warm sweet tea and offered him a wan smile. She found her voice at last.

"Do you have a phone?" she asked. "I need to call my mom."

He drew out an iPhone. "Let's see if I have service out here. It can be spotty."

He handed her the phone.

With shaking hands she dialed her mom's cell phone, and then hit Cancel. What was Kendall's phone number? She waited for her memory to click on. When it did she looked down to see the No Service message.

"No service here," she said. "Is there a town nearby?"

"If you like, I can take you up to the marina. There is a pay phone there."

He helped her into the boat and settled her onto the middle seat. He handed her a sleeve of saltines. As the skiff pulled away from the riverbank, she stuffed three of the crackers into her mouth.

"Been a while since you ate, no."

It wasn't a question. She just nodded and grabbed more crackers.

"Did you escape your father and that woman he was with?"

Eileen gaped at him.

"I saw the Amber Alert two days ago. Said that you might have been in the Virginia Beach area. You are Eileen, right?"

She blinked at him.

"Oh excuse my manners, my name is Henry Williams."

He extended his hand. She shook it. It was a warm, firm grip.

"I am Eileen Rivers. My dad kidnapped me from school. I really need to talk to my mom."

She ducked her head to hide the tears that threatened to spill down her cheeks.

Henry smiled gently. He touched her shoulder.

"Don't worry. We will get you back to your mom."

"My dad, there is something wrong with him. That lady he is with, Annette, she is just horrible. I don't know why he is listening to her."

The boat churned up the river. The water was wider here and Eileen saw more boats and a parking lot. She was suddenly seized with fear and threw herself into the bottom of the boat, hiding her face.

"What if they are here, waiting for me? What if they told the police I ran away from them?"

Henry slowed the boat. He patted her back.

"I don't have to stop here at the marina. We can go upriver another mile or so. A friend of mine has a place there. She has a land-line. We can call your mother from there. I am sure she will be so happy to hear from you."

Henry looked up at the marina. Continuing to speak in a quiet voice he said, "Stay just as you are. There are three or four police cars at the dock. Not sure why but let's just keep going."

Eileen opened her eyes and looked up at him. He raised a hand in greeting to someone on shore. She tried to make herself as small and still as possible. The water pulsed beneath her as Henry sped up.

A few minutes passed. Eileen could hardly breathe. She was gripped with terror and fatigue and the ever-present anxiety.

"It's ok. You can sit up now. We are out of sight of the marina. My friend's place is just a few minutes ahead."

Eileen watched the riverbank slip by. The sun was up now and the water looked peaceful. A blue heron stood on one leg in the shallows as the passed by. Around the next bend in the river was a wooden dock. A solitary figure with a fishing pole was at the far end. They drew closer and the figure raised a hand to them. Henry slowed the motor and now that they were near Eileen saw that it was a woman dressed in jeans and a windbreaker.

"Hi, Edith. Fish biting?" said Henry as the woman caught the bowline that Henry tossed to her.

She wrapped it around a piling.

"Oh I caught a couple perch but they were too small," replied Edith.

She smiled at Eileen. Her grey hair was long and loose, hanging down to her waist.

"This is my friend, Eileen. She needs to use your phone. No service out here."

"Of course. Y'all want some coffee? I made a coffee cake earlier. Couldn't sleep."

Edith ushered them into her yellow kitchen. A blue parakeet squawked in its cage and a fat cat swished its tail as it perched on the kitchen table.

"Scat Tobias!" said Edith. "Leave Bluebell alone."

Tobias eased down from the kitchen table and wrapped himself around Eileen's feet. His purr was audible. Eileen reached down to pet him and he swatted playfully at her hand.

"Most folks, he either bites or runs away from," said Edith. "Ornery old thing."

Edith smiled affectionately at the tomcat and gestured at the black landline on the wall next to the kitchen table.

"Go ahead. I have unlimited nationwide. Verizon gave me a deal I could not refuse. I hate a cell phone but this one, it works all the time."

Eileen sank into one of the chair at the table and reached for the phone. She picked it up and breathed a sigh of relief at the dial tone. Tremulously, she dialed Kendall's cell number.

Phoebe was in the kitchen, drinking coffee. Moises had made some muffins earlier and she was picking halfheartedly at the blueberries in one of them. Kendall's phone was in its holster on her waistband. It chirped and she grabbed at it. An unfamiliar area code.

"Hello?"

"Mommy?"

"Oh baby," Phoebe cried. "Where are you? Are you alright?"

Moises hopped down from the stool where he was perched and

crossed to her, catching her shoulders and leaning into the phone.

"I am ok. I am not exactly sure where I am. I am at Edith's house with Henry and Tobias."

"Who is Henry?" asked Phoebe.

Eileen handed the phone to Henry, who explained where he had found Eileen and gave Phoebe the address in Scott's Landing. She looks pretty good, he reassured Phoebe. Just a bit hungry but we will give her some breakfast.

Edith gestured wildly at Henry and pointed at a black and white TV on the counter. The sound was turned down but Henry got the gist. He stood in front of the TV so that Eileen would not see it.

"I think it best if you come and get her," said Henry. "Don't involve the police. There is some confusion down here right now. We can fill you in when you get here."

Phoebe hung up the phone and turned to Moises. "Can you please stay with Kendall and Damien?"

He looked at her, puzzled. She filled him in on what Henry had told her. He frowned.

"Don't you think you should at least let Detective Nichols know that she has been found?"

"Let me go and get her. Figure out why Henry says not to involve the police. I will keep in touch with you, check in every hour. Please keep the kids inside."

She gave Moises a hug and a kiss on his leathery cheek. She pulled the wagon out of the driveway and stopped to roll down her window. The two cops in the car looked at her.

"Just going to get some groceries," she said. "Should be back in an hour or two. Do you need anything? Coffee or a sandwich?"

The officers demurred and she drove sedately out of the cul-de-sac. She plugged the address Henry had given her into her GPS and headed south on the Parkway and then onto 95 South. Her GPS said four hours and twenty minutes to Scott's Landing. She willed herself not to go more than five miles over the speed limit.

She fiddled with the radio. WTOP promised an update into the case of missing Eileen Rivers. She waited impatiently through several commercials, the traffic and the weather report, and the lead story on a downed helicopter in Afghanistan.

"WTOP brings you an update on the case of missing sixteen year old Eileen Rivers. Rivers disappeared two days ago, presumably taken from Fairfax High School by her father, David, and a woman who was later identified as Annette Peterson. Early this morning, Virginia Beach police responded to an anonymous tip and found David Rivers at an undisclosed location near Virginia Beach. Emergency personnel, who asked not to be identified because they were not authorized to speak to reporters, indicated that Mr. Rivers had been injured and was taken into custody. The manhunt continues for the two women."

Phoebe supposed she should be concerned but the news that her husband was injured and in custody was a relief. So much for notifying the next of kin first. She was two hours into her journey when the phone rang. It was Moises.

"Detective Nichols was here. I told him that you went grocery shopping. He said to call him when you get back, he has some news he wants to tell you in person."

Phoebe explained to Moises what she had heard on the radio.

"I will call him when I have Eileen with me," she said. "Not before."

Moises sighed but did not argue.

"Just be careful, Flaca. Keep in touch."

She pulled into the driveway of a small cottage. An older woman opened the door to her. Eileen sprang up from the kitchen table and flung herself into her mother's arms. Her shoulders shook.

"I was so scared, Mom. I never thought I would see you again."

"This young gal has a lot of grit."

Phoebe looked up at an elderly man with kind, grey eyes.

"She will tell you all about it but she managed to escape those two, busted out of the house and floated down the river to get away from them. I found her on the riverbank. I recognized her from the Amber Alert."

Phoebe shook his hand.

"You must be Henry. Thank you so much for helping us. And you too, Edith. We are so grateful."

"Come Eileen, let me get you some shoes and socks. You look

about my size, maybe a seven?"

Edit led Eileen out of the kitchen.

"I heard the radio reports," said Phoebe. "Please tell me why you did not want me to contact the police."

Henry grimaced.

"That woman who calls herself Annette Peterson, I am pretty sure she is connected to Congressman Davis. Add to that, I am none too crazy about the sheriff here, he's been known to take kickbacks, and I figure you are better off getting her out of the county and then letting your law enforcement know you have your girl."

Phoebe absorbed all that. She nodded in agreement. Eileen reappeared in a pair of leather sandals and grey sweatpants with a long sleeved t-shirt. Edith handed her a plastic bag with her wet jeans and sweatshirt. Phoebe bundled Eileen into the car and hugged Edith and Henry.

"Drive safe, now," said Henry.

Edith raised a hand as they pulled out of the driveway. Eileen was asleep within minutes. As eager as Phoebe was to hear what had happened, she knew her child needed to rest. She stroked her dark hair away from her cheek and Eileen sank deeper into her seat.

Once she had cleared Norfolk, Phoebe called Moises to let him know they were on their way home.

"You'd better call Nichols," he said. "I don't think he is buying the grocery store tale anymore."

Phoebe called the Detective. He listened quietly as she explained her journey.

"Alright," he said at last. "I will meet you at your house in a couple of hours. Try not to make any stops. I am going to call my friend in Fredericksburg to meet you on 95 and escort you in. You probably won't notice him. He will be in an unmarked car."

Phoebe obeyed Nichols, only stopping for gas when she was sure the wagon was running on fumes. She pulled into a drive through McDonalds. Eileen stirred when Phoebe asked her if she was hungry. Eileen gave her a funny look.

"Mom, please don't EVER make me eat fast food again."

Phoebe cast a worried glance at her eldest child. Eileen's brow was furrowed and her hands were clenched.

"Not even a milkshake?" Phoebe asked gently.

Tears began to roll down Eileen's pale cheeks. Phoebe pulled into a parking spot and took Eileen into her arms. She stroked her daughter's hair.

"Honey, I know you went through something terrible. You don't have to talk about it until you are ready."

Eileen gave one heaving sigh and looked up at her mother.

"I don't understand why, Mommy. Why would Daddy want to hurt me? He got me out of school by really scaring me. He told me you were in an accident and that we had to get to the hospital. I was so worried until I realized her was probably lying."

Phoebe shook her head.

"I have no idea sweet pea. We are going to sort this out together, whatever it takes."

She started the car.

"Would you mind terribly if I had a coffee from McDonald's? I am awfully tired and we have another two hours until we get home."

Eileen gave her a wan smile.

"Ok, Mom."

They passed Richmond and got onto 95 North. Eileen spoke up suddenly.

"I don't want Damien or Kendall to know all of this. I don't want them to think badly of Daddy or to be scared. Part of me wants to just hate him, but, Mom, I think there is something really wrong with him. I am not sure he is himself."

Eileen explained about David falling asleep in the car and his unkempt appearance. Phoebe hesitated for a beat and then told Eileen about the calls she had received from the Franklin County Mental Health Unit and finally, about the receipt she had found from the oncologist in Norfolk. Eileen listened and then nodded.

"It is like that lady, Annette, has some sort of weird control over him. He does everything she tells him to do, even when it seems like he doesn't want to."

As they passed through the Springfield exchange, Phoebe called Detective Nichols. He answered at once, his tone brusque.

"I have Eileen with me," she said. "We will be home in thirty minutes."

"I hope you have a good reason for not keeping me in the loop," he replied.

The detective's car was parked in front of the house. Kendall and Damien bounded out of the house and hurled themselves at Eileen. Eileen closed her eyes as she clutched at Kendall's hands and buried her face in Damien's neck. Moises smiled gently from the porch and Nichols looked coolly at Phoebe.

"Kendall and Damien, why don't you fix Eileen a bubble bath?" suggested Eileen.

"Wait a second now," said Nichols. "We need to make sure that we don't destroy any evidence."

Phoebe's heart lurched. She had not even let her mind go there. Eileen had not said anything about anyone touching or hurting her.

"Eileen," said Nichols in a tone much gentler than the one he had used with Phoebe. "I have someone inside who I would like you to talk to. She is really helpful when someone has gone through a stressful experience. Why don't you come and sit with Marion for a little while?"

Eileen hesitated and looked at Phoebe. "Go ahead, honey," Phoebe reassured Eileen. "I think it is a good idea."

Marion looked barely out of high school. She had close cropped red hair and an ring in her nose. She smiled at Eileen and ushered her into the TV room. Phoebe started to follow her but Nichols stopped her.

"Best that we let Marion talk to her first. She can give us an idea of whether we need to screen her for physical trauma as well as emotional."

Moises busied himself with the younger kids, bringing out the blender and fruit to make smoothies. Phoebe explained to Nichols about the phone call from Henry and his warning not to involve the police. She told him as much as she knew about how Henry found Eileen and how they came to be at Edith's house.

"I kept the radio off in the car on the way home," she finished. "I understand that something has happened with David but I just did not want to her to hear anything until I knew for sure. Henry and Edith said that David had been taken into custody with injuries."

"Yes, that's right. We don't have an update on his condition but we were told that he was in surgery."

Phoebe began to respond when the door to the TV room opened. Marion came out and drew Phoebe and Nichols outside.

"I am concerned that she does not have a memory of a good portion of the time she was missing. She was very likely drugged. I would like to run bloodwork and a sexual assault kit on her."

Phoebe felt sick.

"Can I be with her please? And does this have to be done at a hospital? She just got home, she has anxiety." Her voice trailed off.

"We can run it here. I just need a nurse to do the exam and I can witness. You can be with her as well."

"It's ok, Mom," Eileen said. "I understand why it has to be done. I really don't know if anything happened to me. I don't think so, but I was really knocked out."

Eileen looked resolute and suddenly very adult. Phoebe felt a pang at this display of dignity. She caressed Eileen's cheek.

The nurse, a rotund woman of undetermined age, arrived about ten minutes later and introduced herself as Eva. Phoebe and Marion took her upstairs to Phoebe's room. Eva carefully examined Eileen, taking a photo of a bruise on her back. When Eileen took off Edith's grey sweatpants, her right thigh showed bruises that looked like fingermarks. Eva took scrapings from under Eileen's fingernails and swabbed her mouth.

When it came time for the internal examination, Eileen clutched Phoebe's hand and squeezed her eyes shut. Phoebe put her face next to her daughter's and remembered, it seemed a lifetime ago, staring into her child's eyes to distract her from a shot at the pediatrician. Eileen winced and Phoebe soothed her. Never had Phoebe known such helplessness and rage.

"Finished," said Eva, giving Eileen a kind smile and squeezing her shoulder.

"Go ahead and take that bubble bath. It'll make you feel better."

Eileen disappeared into Phoebe's bathroom and the comfort of the sunken tub. Phoebe looked questioningly at Eva.

"I won't know for sure until we run the lab tests but in addition to the bruising on her leg and back, she looks like may have experienced some vaginal trauma."

Phoebe swayed and Marion caught her arm, easing her down onto the loveseat next to the bed.

"Probably would be a good idea to get her the morning after pill and maybe an antibiotic. And a follow-up to check for venereal disease."

All of which, Phoebe thought to herself, she could have used for herself a week or so ago. Eva packed up the evidence kit and made her way downstairs with Marion.

Phoebe's head reeled. She knocked on the bathroom door and Eileen called her in. Phoebe peeked in at her surrounded by mounds of bubbles.

"I think Damien put half the bottle in here," smiled Eileen. "Mom, please don't look so worried. I am home now. Whatever happened, it happened. Can we have Chipotle for dinner?"

Phoebe nodded in agreement and blew her a kiss. Nichols was downstairs.

"How is she holding up?" he asked.

"Asking for Chipotle. I am waiting for the other shoe to drop though. She is prone to anxiety attacks, take medication for it."

Nichols explained that he was leaving two officers outside, at least until the situation with David had been sorted out and Annette apprehended. He seemed confident that both were imminent, a confidence that Phoebe did not share, although she nodded her approval.

"Phoebe," said Nichols. "May I call you Phoebe?"

"Sure," she said.

"Phoebe, are you sure you are telling me everything? I keep coming back to the why here. What's David's motivation and what's the connection to Annette? You must know something."

If I told you what I do know, it would only raise more questions and you would think me insane, or lock me up for murder, she thought to herself.

"I wish I knew. It's like my husband is a complete stranger."

How could you live with a man for nineteen years and not have a clue? Was it that she had gotten so used to him that she just assumed he was what he appeared to be, a rather hapless, uninvolved man? No one had a perfect marriage certainly but how could she have been such a poor judge of character? He had never truly mean, although he could certainly be insensitive and unkind. She could not say that they had been close or, she hated the expression, soul mates or best friends. Maybe co-parents or partners but the past few days confirmed that she clearly lacked all insight into his psyche.

"Don't be so hard on yourself, Flaca."

Moises was folding laundry. She looked up at him.

"I am being completely unfair to you," she said. "You have a job, and your mom to look after and I have taken up so much of your time. Mind you, I am forever grateful, but I know you have your own life."

"Stop. I am here because I want to be. I am not going to leave you alone at a time like this. My mom is fine. She is watching her novelas with her neighbor. And I have plenty of use or lose leave."

Phoebe exhaled. She had considered calling her own mother, a woman of seventy-five who doted on her grandchildren but who would be terrified at the events of the past few days, even an abridged version. As much as the kids would love to see her, she would be adding to her burden by having to explain the situation and then reassure her own mother. She wondered at how she had become so isolated. Certainly having busy children and a job claimed a lot of energy but when had she stopped having friends? She wasn't even sure. Her shoulders slumped and she felt like there was a million pounds around her neck, pulling her down to the ground.

The kids attacked the Chipotle, much to Moises' chagrin.

"That is not real food," he protested and insisted on making a large tomato and basil salad laced with mozzarella.

Phoebe watched her brood, she never ever tired of listening to their banter. Today, she could not tear her eyes away from them.

The kids were in the TV room, playing yet another round of Walking Dead. Phoebe sat down to her computer. She logged into her email, first her personal and then work. She marked what seemed to be junk mail and then noticed that she had received jpeg files from what looked like the same sender at both her home and work addresses. She looked again. The subject line for both was "Daughter." She wondered if she should contact Nichols before she opened them but she went ahead and clicked anyway.

What she saw she would never forget. Eileen, at least she was pretty sure it was Eileen, after all, a mother would know her own child, was wearing a black hood. She was on her back and naked, on a mattress. Her legs were spread it a grotesque fashion and the naked lower half of a man's body was posed next to her. His penis was large and engorged. The next photo showed a young woman on her stomach. A woman's hands were spreading her buttocks and what appeared to be the same penis was inserted into her rectum. In the final picture, the black hood had been removed. It was clearly Eileen. Her eyes were closed and the penis was in her mouth. This photo had a caption: "Wait until you see the movies!"

Phoebe felt the salad and Chipotle rising in her throat. She ran into the bathroom and vomited. When there was nothing left in her stomach, she rinsed her mouth and washed her hands. Her palms were sweaty. When she looked in the bathroom mirror, her eyes were stark in her chalky face. She willed herself to be calm and checked on the kids. They were watching a movie and sitting close together. Moises was upstairs, doing some laundry it seemed from the sound of the washing machine on the spin cycle.

She went back into the kitchen and faced her computers. The screens had locked while she was in the bathroom and she entered her passwords. She picked up her cell to call Nichols, to ask how she should send him this information. She had left the email open, at least she thought she had, but nothing was on the screens. She opened her new mail. Nothing from VABTCH9874@yahoo.com. She checked her old mail and then the deleted and spam folders. Nothing on either computer.

Her AOL instant messenger blinked. "Like those crotch shots?" appeared along with a smiley face. It closed out before she could see who it was from.

A new message appeared on her Facebook account. "Film at 11."

Phoebe shut down both computers. Kendall's phone chirped with a new text message. "Daughter got some of what you got."

Phoebe deleted this one and then cursed her stupidity. While she was not terribly tech savvy, she assumed there would be a way to retrieve all of these messages. With growing horror, she realized that somehow, her attack and her daughter's abductors, were connected.

There was no way she could explain that last message to Nichols even if she could retrieve them. She poured herself a glass of wine and pulled out her yellow legal pad. The first item on her "to do" list was to get the morning after pill and antibiotics for Eileen. She left a message for Dr. Sayers. There would be no need for Sayers to file any kind of report; Phoebe made clear that the assault was the subject of a police investigation.

The kids were laughing in the other room. She knew that Eileen's euphoria at being home might wear off and be replaced by panic, or even worse, Eileen would start to recall her ordeal. Eileen had shown remarkable poise so far, but she was still a child. It would be wise to keep her home from school a day or two. She could always get her assignments via email. The school counselor had proven in the past to be reasonable.

She needed a new cell phone and number, and while she was at it, new phones and numbers for Kendall and Eileen.

The next item was trickier. What to tell the kids about David and the circumstances of Eileen's disappearance and homecoming? The simplest, and probably still fairly accurate, explanation was that he was sick and not thinking clearly. Of course this would necessitate a stern warning about not getting into any car with David or communicating with him.

She was avoiding the last item. The David and Annette problem. She broke it down into parts. 1) Find out where David was and his condition. 2) Figure out the connection between David and Annette and those awful photos. 3) Determine the connection between her rape and David and Annette. 4) Figure out if she had actually killed the white glove man. 5) How to put an end to all of this madness. She felt oddly better for writing her list. The mental activity kept her from screaming at least.

Kendall's phone buzzed with Nichols' number.

"David is out of surgery. He had a minor stab wound to his left thigh and it looked like someone took his baseball bat to his right knee. That part, we know Phoebe did. He was also shot in the arm. That we do not think Phoebe did. She had no gunshot residue on her hands."

"Is he going to live?" asked Phoebe, half hoping the answer was no.

"He is stable. We have a police guard on him and will question him when the anesthesia and pain meds wear off."

"I don't suppose I can talk to him."

"No reason you can't. I can call down to Norfolk Trauma and let the police guard there know that you may come in to see him."

"Are they going to arrest him, take him into custody after he is released?"

"Doesn't look like he is going anywhere anytime soon. Once we interview him and finish processing the house, the prosecutor will decide on charges."

Phoebe thanked Nichols and hung up. As exhausted as she was, she did not think that she could sleep. She debated taking an Ambien and decided against it. Eileen might need her during the night. Moises was dozing on the couch. It was time to get these kids into bed.

Damien, she discovered when she went up to tuck them all in, had curled up in Eileen's bed, along with a collection of Pillow Pets.

"Leave him be, Mom," protested Eileen when Phoebe stooped to pick him up and cart him off to his own room.

"I don't mind him here."

Phoebe kissed them both and turned out the light. Kendall had her iPad hidden under her blanket, probably chatting with her friends or posting to Facebook.

A horrid thought occurred to her. What if those terrible images appeared on the girls' computers? It was one thing to change a cell number but quite another to ban them from social media. What if those photos went viral? The damage to Eileen would be incredible.

"Give me that iPad, sweetie. I don't want you on it any more tonight."

Kendall pouted. Phoebe shushed her and assured her that this was not a punishment. She was worried because her computer had been hacked and she wanted to be sure that the devices in the house were free of viruses.

She went back into Eileen's room but it was too late. Eileen's face was illuminated by the light from her iPad. She tried to hide what she was looking at from Phoebe but her stricken expression gave it away.

"Mom," she said. "I think this is me."

The photo of the girl being violated anally had been sent to Eileen via Facebook message. Phoebe took the iPad out of Eileen's hands and pulled Eileen to her.

"Let's go into my room. I want to let Damien sleep."

Eileen allowed herself to be led down the hall. They sat together on the loveseat in Phoebe's room. Phoebe told Eileen about the photos that had been sent to her computers, only to disappear.

"I guess it was because of the obscene content," said Eileen. "Whoever sent them to me does not want to be reported. I bet that message was deleted from my Facebook too."

She was detached, like she was discussing someone else.

"Anyway, I blocked the person. They can't tag me or post anything about me now."

"Who was the message from?"

"VABTCHGRL or something like that. Why is this happening?"

"I have stopped asking why, honey. The only thing I want is for this to stop."

Phoebe explained that she was going to Norfolk in the morning, to try to talk to David. Eileen nodded woodenly. Phoebe wondered if maybe whatever drug had been used on Eileen was still in her system.

A few minutes later, Eileen yawned and stood up. Phoebe hugged her again and watched her pad down the hall to her room.

●　●　●

Eileen figured she was in some sort of shock. She thought she ought to be more upset but all she felt was the comfort of Damien's sleeping body curled into her blankets. She kissed his hair and smelled his dirty little boy smell. She closed her eyes and slept.

She dreamed of the little boy and his mother. They were running through the woods. Angry shouts rang out. She could feel their fear, smell terror in the sweat that ran down both their faces. The woods were damp and mosquitos whined. Tree roots caught at their bare feet. The little boy gripped his mother's hand but he stumbled. She scooped him up in her arms and ran on blindly. They were exhausted and the men were getting closer. Hungry men with clubs. Eileen knew she had to help them.

Eileen woke with a start. The alarm clock said three minutes past two. Damien snored softly. She was very thirsty and eased herself into the bathroom for a glass of water. She looked out onto the backyard.

Why could she not remember what had really happened to her in that awful house? Maybe she needed to be hypnotized or revisit the scene. That always seemed to work in the movies.

She heard her mother stirring.

"Are you all right, sweetie?" Phoebe whispered.

"I am fine, Mom, just thirsty. Go back to sleep. You need rest."

Eileen hated the worry she had seen etched in her mother's face. She tried to fall back to sleep but all she could see were those pictures. Even if it was not her, and she was pretty sure it was because the carpet she had seen in the corner looked a lot like the one it the basement dungeon, those pictures were starting to make her very angry. She glanced at her little brother and imagined what it would be like if something like that happened to him. She could understand the sickness of a sexual predator but for a younger child it would be so much worse.

She was clenching her jaw and clutching the comforter in her fists. The odd sorrow she had felt for her father in the basement was now a hot rage. He had failed her. She fumed until dawn light came in her window.

Phoebe got up at six and went for a four mile run. After coffee and a shower, she called the high school attendance line to report that Eileen would be absent. She made pancakes and bacon and wrote an email to the elementary and middle schools prohibiting them from releasing the kids to David, or anyone other than her or Moises. She called Dr. Sayers and left a message requesting the morning after pill and an antibiotic. She warned the kids that their father was ill and not to go anywhere with him. Eileen reminded them of how David had tricked her into thinking their mom was hurt.

Kendall was uncharacteristically quiet and Damien wide-eyed. With some misgivings, Phoebe put them on their respective school buses. Kendall was mortified at being kissed good-bye in plain view of a bus filled with middle schoolers.

There was a wrinkle at the Verizon store. Her American Express was declined when she tried to use it to pay for three new cell phones. She shrugged and used the MasterCard that was in her name only.

Moises had packed sandwiches and drinks into a small cooler. Phoebe told him she expected to return around dinnertime. He kissed her on both cheeks and told her to be careful. She looked for Eileen to tell her goodbye but the bathroom door was closed and the shower was running. Eileen was famous for her lengthy showers. Phoebe smiled at the steam coming out from under the door.

She was on the road before ten. A half hour into the ride, she turned down the radio that was blaring classic rock and dialed Eileen's new cell. The phone rang once and then cut off mid ring. The next time she tried, it went to voicemail. She called Moises who reported that the shower was still running.

"Bang on the door and tell her to call me," Phoebe said and laughed.

Moises was the one who called back, voice concerned, to tell her that the shower had been running but Eileen was nowhere to be found. Phoebe pulled off at the next exit and shut the wagon off. She sent Eileen a text and was rewarded by a nearly instant buzz. She got out of the car and opened the hatchback. Roxie's blanket was still back here. It had a distinct bump under it. She snatched it up, revealing Eileen.

"What the hell do you think you are doing?"

"I am going with you. I need to understand what happened to me."

Eileen was resolute. Phoebe opened her mouth to object but relented.

"Well then get into the front seat and buckle your seatbelt. And call Moises before he has a stroke."

Eileen grinned and scampered around the car to commandeer the radio.

Norfolk Trauma Center was a sprawling complex with a helicopter pad on the roof. When they asked for passes to visit David Rivers, the pink-jacketed volunteer asked them to wait in the lobby. In a few minutes, a police officer appeared and took them to the second floor. A second officer was sitting outside the room.

David was propped up in bed staring at a muted TV. His thigh and knee were bandaged as was his arm. His eyes followed them as they entered the room.

"How are you feeling?" asked Phoebe, although she could care less how he felt. In fact, she would like to tear off his bandages. He shrugged.

"Got a bad infection from whatever your daughter stabbed me with."

"You owe me an explanation, Daddy," said Eileen.

David remained silent.

"I don't care who this woman Annette is," said Phoebe. David said nothing.

"And I could give a shit if you have been having an affair and buying houses with her and that you got fired from your job. What I want to know is how you would hurt your own child. And why in the world did you kill Roxie?"

Eileen started at Phoebe and then whirled on David.

"You killed our dog?"

Somehow this revelation hit Eileen more powerfully than her abduction, probable assault and the obscene photos.

"I hate you. You are the worst scum of the earth. What did that dog do to you? What did any of us do to you?"

David stared out the window. Phoebe put her arm around Eileen, who had begun to weep with anger. Phoebe looked over her shoulder at David. He was grinning. Phoebe led Eileen out of the room and sat her down in the chair next to the officer.

"Wait here honey. I am going to talk to him some more."

Phoebe returned to the room.

"I hope they throw the book at you. I don't care what happens to you and I don't really care why you did any of this. It is going to stop."

She paused. He stared at her coldly.

"I have only one question for you. Did you hire someone to rape me, try to kill me?"

He leered at her. His mask had slipped.

"Well now, it is impossible to rape your own wife."

Phoebe crossed the room in two steps and slapped his face as hard as she could. He grunted and recoiled.

The police officer opened the door.

"Is everything ok?"

David's face wore a flaming handprint. Eileen peered around the officer.

"We are leaving," announced Phoebe.

She put her arm around Eileen and guided her to the elevator.

"Mom," said Eileen with unmistakable glee, "Did you smack him?"

"Yes I did. I let my temper get the best of me."

"Give me a break." Eileen rolled her eyes. "He totally had that coming. Do you think he will get raped in prison? Don't other prisoners hate child abusers?"

"I don't know," said Phoebe. She opened the car door. "Let's eat our lunch."

Chapter Thirteen

David and Annette

David's mouth was cotton. He could not move his arms or legs. When he opened his eyes, he saw bars on the one window in the room. He was wearing a blue hospital gown and there was an IV in his right arm. The door opened and a nurse bustled in.

"Ah, awake at last."

He opened his mouth to ask how he had gotten there but his throat was so dry that only a feeble croak came out. The nurse poured him a cup of water and held it to his lips.

"Covered in blood and full of all kinds of drugs. Didn't seem to be your blood though. You must have had yourself quite a party. Did you walk away from your car or did you piss someone off so much that they dumped you out there on 24?"

David had no idea. He shrugged.

"We called your wife when you were admitted. She gave us the name of your doctor up there in Fairfax. We can call her and have her come down here to get you once we are sure you are down from whatever it is you took. The police will probably want to interview you too."

"No, not wife. Don't call her."

The nurse blinked.

"Ok, then, who do you want us to call?"

David gave her Annette's number. The nurse released his arms and legs from the restraints and brought him some soup and crackers. He got out of bed and moved around unsteadily for a few steps to get to and from the bathroom. Then he crawled under the thin blanket and went back to sleep.

He next opened his eyes to Annette's voice.

"How are you feeling, sweetheart? I was so worried about you. How did you get so far from the campground?"

She was putting on quite a show for the nurse.

"He was camping and fishing up at the State Park with some buddies. They woke up on Wednesday and he was gone. They tied one on pretty good on Tuesday night."

Annette shook her head at him and smiled.

"Last time I let you out with those clowns."

David tried to look sheepish. "Sorry, honey. I guess we got a little over the top. Trying to be frat boys with high tolerance."

"When can I take him home?" Annette turned to the nurse.

"The doctor has to write up the discharge orders. The police will want to know whose blood was all over you."

"I can explain that," said Annette. "The idiots hit a deer with their car and then tried to butcher it. I know it is not hunting season, but they were not technically hunting."

"Well, he can probably go home in the next day or two," said the nurse.

The nurse refilled his water pitcher and closed the door behind her.

Annette looked at him with hardened eyes. She scratched at her left shoulder.

"I hope you can get yourself under control. We have a lot of ground to make up. We lost a good opportunity here."

David felt slightly sick. He wasn't sure if it was whatever was left of the drugs in his system or the realization that Annette still intended to take his kids and expected him to help. He sighed deeply and closed his eyes. He considered faking being crazy so they would not release him to Annette, but that seemed like too much effort. After a moment, he heard her high heels clicking away.

It was three days later when he signed Eileen out of her high school. David was pretty mellow from whatever was in the pills Annette gave him. He could sense Eileen's anxiety and it made him vaguely sad but his mind drifted and he slept in the car. Annette shook him awake to transfer Eileen from his truck to some other car. He wondered where the car had come from but soon went back to sleep.

They got to the dumpy house in Mitchell's Landing around midnight. Annette made him set up the video equipment in the basement where Eileen was sleeping on the couch. He balked at undressing his daughter. Annette slapped him and he tried to shove her back but she stepped easily out of the way.

"Go upstairs then. I don't need you for this."

She turned her back on him. He stumbled up the stairs, found his high blood pressure medication and got into bed. As he drifted off to sleep he heard the front door open and male voices. He pulled the pillow over his head and slept.

When David woke up late the next morning, he was alone on the main level. He went into the kitchen and saw the locked briefcase Annette used to store video and photos, mostly VHS tapes and photos printed in a darkroom. Nothing went onto a computer unless she wanted it to.

The house was silent. He wondered if Annette had moved Eileen. He hoped he would not have to do anything else with Eileen, or even see her.

Sometimes, when the pills were wearing off, David tried to imagine life without Annette, or life before her. He could not picture either. It had started with admiration and then obsession and then she had crawled right into his brain. Maybe he could just stop taking the pills, just walk away.

He knew though, she would find him. Besides, he rationalized, where would he even go?

He went into the bathroom to take a piss. He looked at himself in the mirror, considered shaving and showering but decided it was too much work. He heard a car outside and a moment later, Annette let herself into the house. She had a bag of fast food in each hand. She did not look at him, just put one of the bags on the counter and disappeared downstairs. David heard her raise her voice briefly once.

Annette came up the basement stairs and grabbed the locked briefcase. She looked at David, patted the briefcase, and smiled.

"Back in business," she said.

Annette opened the front door. She looked at David.

"She should not give you any trouble. Do your best to stay awake and keep an eye on things. I am off to meet our friends and make a delivery. Maybe you should take a shower sometime in the next day or two."

A moment later, a car engine revved and then faded. David ate the greasy cheeseburger and cold fries and tried to watch TV but nothing was keeping him awake. When he next woke, it was full dark and his bladder was about to burst. He stumbled into the bathroom to pee and splashed water on his face. He stepped into the kitchen and heard shouting.

Eileen was screaming and banging at the basement door. He went partway down the stairs and told her to shut up. She only got louder. If Annette showed up, he was going to be in trouble. She must not have given Eileen the right meds. Eileen was claiming to be having one of her attacks. He was getting a headache from that shrieking. It was as bad as when she would wail, relentlessly, as an infant.

He went down the stairs and unlocked the door. She was sitting on the couch, hair hanging in her face. He extended his hand towards her. A sudden, sharp pain in his right quad. He grabbed at his wounded leg. A hard object connected with his left kneecap.

He howled in rage and confusion. Belatedly, he grabbed for her sweatshirt but she slipped out of his reach and slammed the door behind her. The lock turned and her footsteps raced up the stairs and out of the house.

He sat down heavily on the couch. He struggled to clear his mind. Annette was going to be furious. He had no idea where Annette was and no way to contact her.

He did not have to wait long. Gravel crunched as a car pulled up. Panic rose in his throat and he tried to hide himself awkwardly behind the couch.

Doors opened. Footfalls on the stairs. Annette was moving cautiously. She must see that he was not upstairs. She had not called out for him. The door unlocking. A click and then then a different click as she flipped the switch on the circuit breaker and the light in the bathroom flickered on.

He peered around the couch as she moved, slowly, towards the bathroom. He was not used to seeing her with a gun. It was oddly fascinating. He scurried around the couch, hoping to stay out of her line of sight.

Maybe she heard him scrabble at the carpet on his hands and knees, wincing at the pain in both legs. She turned towards whatever she heard, leveling the gun at him. He began to pull himself up. Maybe it was the awkwardness of his movement. Maybe it was because she was really pissed that Eileen was gone. Or maybe it was an accident. But she shot him in the arm and he began to scream.

He slumped to the floor. Hot liquid pooled beneath him. He could hear her on the phone. He could not make out the words. He felt her hypodermic needle in his stomach.

Someone was shaking him, telling him to stay awake. Flashing lights and sirens. An anesthetic smell and the cold glare of lights. A mask over his face. And then, nothing. Until he woke in a hospital bed with his arms restrained and an IV in his foot.

Phoebe came and made a fuss. Eileen babbled at him. He supposed Annette would not be happy that he cottoned to the rape but it was sure worth the look on Phoebe's face, even that slap. His arm with the scar itched. A pair of detectives came to interview him but he refused to speak. Day turned to night. A different police officer looked in on him. He watched TV for a bit and dozed.

The loudspeaker was talking about a Code Blue. There was a rush of activity outside his room. The door opened and Annette was yanking the IV out of his foot and cutting off the restraints.

"Get dressed," she hissed, thrusting sweatpants and a t-shirt at him.

He tossed the hospital gown into the corner and stepped into the flip flops she dropped onto the floor.

She led him out the door. The police officer's chin was on his chest. She yanked him into the stairwell. They were exiting the parking lot in a car he had never seen before when three police cars raced up to the front of the hospital.

And now, David realized, she truly owned him. He was beholden.

Chapter Fourteen

Phoebe

"Can we take a ride to Mitchell's Landing?"

Phoebe thought Eileen's eyes were almost too bright.

"Do you really think that is a good idea?" Phoebe asked Eileen.

"Yes, Mom. I need to see that place again. Maybe it will help me remember."

At Eileen's urging, they parked on the wooden bridge on Pine Road. The water was calmer now than it had been the other night. They ate Moises' turkey club sandwiches and sipped diet vanilla coke. Eileen pointed out the spot where she had plunged into the river.

Eileen pulled Phoebe to her feet to walk along the river's edge. A few minutes into their walk, Eileen spotted something red caught in the water. It was one of her Keds, caught on a rock. She fished it out and shook off the sand. They walked a bit further and then climbed up the cliff onto the road to walk back to the wagon. Eileen paused to tug on a piece of black fabric caught on a bramble. She freed it and smoothed the velvet in her hand before tucking it into the shoe she was carrying.

They drove down Pine Road. The cabin looked smaller and shabbier in the daylight, a tired split level with missing shingles. The only sign of recent activity was a strip of yellow crime scene tape lying on the grass near the front door. Eileen climbed up onto the sagging stoop. The lock had been broken and the knob turned in her hand. She pushed the door open before Phoebe could yank her back. She shook off her mother's hand and surveyed the small kitchen with a dripping faucet and peeling, yellowed linoleum.

"What if she is here?" asked Phoebe in a hoarse whisper.

"How could she be? There is no vehicle here. How would she get here? The nearest road is seven miles away."

The living room was dank and featured stacks of old magazines on the coffee table and in the corners. An overstuffed couch wore a mildewed quilt. Eileen wrinkled her nose.

"Not much of a decorator, is she?" Phoebe shivered.

There were two small bedrooms that shared a bathroom. One had a double bed, the other twin beds. Phoebe recognized a green and yellow windbreaker she had bought for David a few years before. It was balled up on the floor of the closet.

The bathroom cabinet had a prescription bottle for Clozaril labeled "David Peterson." It contained several pills and Phoebe put it in her pocket.

Phoebe began to open the drawers in the bedrooms. They were full of typical David paperwork and pocket litter. She found a large plastic bag in the kitchen and scooped the contents of the drawers into the bag. So much for police investigation. Must be that sheriff connection Henry had talked about. Eileen took a second bag and went through the kitchen cabinets.

Eileen paused at the top of the stairs to the basement. She descended slowly, listening to the thud of her clogs on the wood. The door was off its hinges, the frame battered. There was a metallic odor. She pushed the door open. The light from the two windows was enough to see the dark stain on the carpet. She flicked the light switch in the bathroom. The bulb had been replaced.

Phoebe opened the closet doors and pulled out the beach towels and toys. She hated to think who might have used those items and for what. She ran her hand along each shelf. The second shelf seemed loose. When she wiggled it, it fell to the floor and dislodged a piece of tile at the back of the closet. She moved the tile with her foot, intending to nudge it back into place but it had cracked in half. Underneath was blackness. She knelt for a closer look.

There was a hole in the floor. It held a metal box with a combination lock. Phoebe pulled it out and set it on the floor next to the garbage bags.

The bathroom had drops of dried blood on the floor and in the sink. The shelves in the medicine cabinet were empty. Phoebe pushed on one of the inside panels and it gave, falling back into the wall. A clunk resounded somewhere inside the wall. Eileen handed her the toilet brush and she poked around the inside of the cabinet. The brush caught on something and she tugged. Several pairs of little boys cartoon underwear and two pre-teen sized bras fell into the sink.

They stared at the pile of clothing.

"Maybe we should leave this for the police." said Phoebe.

Eileen shook her head. "They are done here, Mom. I guess Henry and Esther were right about the local law."

Eileen slept a good deal of the way home. Nichols called with the news that Eileen's bloodwork was positive for opiates and Versed. Also, he was sorry to have to tell her that the physical exam had revealed semen in her vagina, anus and mouth. Phoebe's soul felt like it was being suffocated under a wet, woolen blanket. She debated whether she should even tell Eileen the test results.

Eileen stirred in the front seat when Phoebe's phone chirped a second time. They were twenty minutes from home and the rush hour traffic was heavy. The volunteer from the animal shelter told Phoebe that their application for Magnet had been approved and they could come in and pick him up any time before eight that evening.

The next few hours were a blurry scene of puppy comes home to delighted kids. Magnet was a quivering mass of excitement, so much so that he piddled more than once on the kitchen floor. Moises, who was not a big fan of dogs, frowned at him and then got his face thoroughly cleaned by Magnet's tongue when he got down to wipe up the mess. The brown and white puppy raced around the backyard with Kendall and Damien in pursuit. He barked happily at a squirrel and stopped long enough for Eileen to scratch his ears. When he was finally exhausted, he showed true intelligence and selected Moises' lap. Moises sighed in resignation and began to stroke Magnet's fur.

Phoebe took the garbage bags and the strong box out of the wagon and into the garage. She flicked on the light over David's cluttered workbench and began to sort. Takeout menus and mass mailers went into the trash. Receipts for restaurants and gas went into one pile. There were a couple of utility bills.

A boarding pass caught her eye. It was for a flight to Thailand in November 2012 and was issued in the name of Amy Peters. She would double check her 2012 planner but she was pretty sure that David had gone to Bangkok around that time. There was a coaster from a bar in Phuket. She would need to look that up.

There was a wadded up envelope wrapped in duct tape. When she worked the tape off, David's wedding ring rolled out. The one he claimed he had lost a few years ago and she had replaced. This one was a simple gold band. When she had selected it, she had had their anniversary date engraved inside. Even with that date on his hand, David could never remember their anniversary. She yanked her own ring off her finger and threw it into the backyard.

She set the strong box onto the work bench. She tried a few different numbers, birthdays mostly and their ATM PINS. None worked but when she tried their anniversary date, the box popped open.

"Asshole," Phoebe muttered to herself.

Inside the box was a stack of US passports issued to children, ten in total, ranging in age from four to sixteen. They held entry stamps for Thailand, Chile, eastern Europe and one for Brazil. None contained exit stamps. Phoebe had the beginnings of a migraine and a terrible sick feeling in her stomach.

Back inside, Phoebe checked on the kids. She tried not to think of the passports and the little pile of underwear as she picked up discarded clothing from the bathroom floor. She tried to focus on the kids bantering as they bathed and settled in for the night. She walked Magnet a final time and got him into his crate next to her bed. She had a feeling that as soon as he was housebroken, he would be claiming people beds as his own. Provided of course, that he did not chew.

She changed into her pajamas and brushed her teeth. Rinsing, she remembered she needed to call American Express.

"I am sorry, ma'am," said a voice that was probably in India but faking a midwestern accent. "That account is in collection. No further charges can be made until the minimum balance has been paid."

"When was the last payment made?"

According to Fake Accent, the account was over sixty days in arrears, the full balance was $22,032, with a minimum payment due of $731. The last payment was made from a Chevy Chase Bank account. Phoebe wrote it down even though they had never had a Chevy Chase account.

Phoebe awoke at four in the morning to Magnet whimpering. She took him outside and he snuffled happily at the dew soaked grass. There was no way she could go back to sleep. Magnet attacked his puppy chow and she sipped her coffee. He whined at her feet and she picked him up, inhaling puppy and kissing the top of his soft head.

She logged into her computer and steeled herself to research the names on the passports. First, though, she checked her email and Facebook. There was a message notification on Facebook.

"You took something from me. I will get it back."

"Oh, no you won't, bitch," Phoebe muttered.

Her cell phone buzzed. Nichols told her that David had escaped from the hospital. Phoebe felt like she might faint. The walls were closing in on her and her palms were damp with sweat.

"How is that even possible?" asked Phoebe, trying to keep from hyperventilating.

"Happened sometime early this morning. They had only one guard on duty and they found him in the hall outside the room with his throat slit. The nurses were all responding to a code down the hall. Somehow a patient's respirator got disconnected."

Phoebe checked to be sure the police car was still outside. She poured herself another cup of coffee and raised the mug to her lips. A wave of nausea and she barely made it to the bathroom. She vomited a stream of bitter brown fluid.

She took her computer out to the porch and gulped at the fresh air. The stack of passports was haunting her. She made a list of their names and started to search.

Margaret Lewis, age six, had disappeared on a family trip to Poland in February 2013. Security cameras at the hotel in Krakow where she had last been seen showed her leaving the hotel in the company of a woman. Margaret's passport had disappeared from her parents' hotel room safe but those of her parents and younger brother were not taken. The case had been turned over to Interpol and the FBI was involved. Local press speculated that Margaret might have been the victim of a human trafficking ring. Phoebe's hand shook. Her 2013 planner showed that David had been in Poland from 6-13 February 2013.

Selene Martinez, age twelve, had been taken to Brazil in December 2010 presumably by her non-custodial father. Selene's mother had not been able to locate her ex-husband and there were no leads. Phoebe was not sure where her 2010 planner was but she did recall that David had missed Christmas because he was late returning from a trip due to a flight cancellation.

Damien appeared next to her. She jumped and tucked the passports under her laptop.

"What is for breakfast? Do we have school today?"

His pajama top was inside out. She tousled his hair.

"It's Saturday, sweetheart. What about chocolate chip waffles?"

Damien beamed. Magnet jumped off her lap and chased Damien into the backyard. Damien's giggle echoed. Magnet tugged at his pajama bottoms and Damien grabbed at the waistband to keep them from falling down. His Sponge Bob underwear peeked out. She thought about the little pile of underwear in the plastic bag in the garage. She fought the metallic taste in her mouth.

She stood up to start breakfast and had to grab the table to keep from falling. The lightheadedness must be due to the vomiting. She heated up the waffle iron as she made herself a cup of Ramen. Normally, she hated the stuff but the salty noodles were oddly appealing.

Dr. Sayers had Saturday clinic hours. Phoebe took Eileen to be tested for venereal disease. Dr. Sayers was kind and mercifully quick. She promised to call soon. She pulled Phoebe aside and gave her a referral for a counselor.

"Give her a chance to get stuff off her chest without you there. Kids like Eileen, they want to spare mom the details."

Phoebe's eyes welled up and she nodded.

"And, Phoebe, take care of yourself. You look tired and run down. Come back in a few days if you are not able to get some rest."

It was not until after dinner that Phoebe had the chance to look up the other children. Andrew Williams, age seven, failed to return home from a trip to Thailand with his godmother in April 2011. Jason Lee, aged nine, walked away from a foster home in Tennessee in October 2010. Michelle Quinones, age fifteen, was an endangered minor possibly taken from Arizona to Mexico by an older boyfriend in January 2012. Alec Baker, age sixteen, had disappeared from a cruise ship in November 2009. The theory was that he had jumped from the ship as his flip-flops were found on an upper deck.

She could not bring herself to look up the last four. She got the idea. Her husband of nineteen years, who she thought she knew, was somehow involved in the kidnapping and probable exploitation of children. He had all but admitted wanting her dead. He had kidnapped Eileen and allowed her to be raped. How could this be the same man she had married? And she could not tell any of this to Nichols. She was going to have to kill David herself. And Annette too.

The trouble was finding him. She supposed he would come looking for her, or worse, for the kids. She went to look for Moises. He was weeding the garden. She told him that David had escaped from the hospital.

"Flaca," he said. "Let me take the kids to my place for a few days, or at least until they find that loco."

She opened her mouth to protest but he held up his hand.

"Let the police sit outside my townhouse. David does not even know me, much less where I live. But that perro, he stays with you."

It made sense, really and she called Nichols to arrange for a car to watch Moises' townhouse. The kids protested. She did not blame them; she did not want to be away from them either. She explained, as gently as she could, that is was safer for them to be with Moises, since the police did not know where David was.

"I love Daddy," Damien sobbed. "Why would he be dangerous to us?"

"He loves you too, sweetie," soothed Phoebe. She crossed her fingers behind her back. "He has something wrong with his mind."

Eileen scoffed. "He needs to be in jail."

Phoebe gave her a pleading look and Eileen looked away.

Phoebe sent the kids upstairs to get some clothes and toys. Eileen hung back.

"You can't make me go," said Eileen. Her mouth was a grim line.

"I just want to keep you guys safe. Please go with your brother and sister. I need you to do this for me."

Eileen hugged Phoebe and went upstairs.

The house echoed with silence. Phoebe walked Magnet. She smiled at the young officer in the patrol car. The night was warm and her flip flops slapped against the asphalt. She thought she would be unable to sleep alone in the house but she drifted off right away.

A car door shut. Phoebe's eyes popped open. Magnet stirred in his crate. Must be the officer stretching his legs. A faint scratching sound. Squirrels in the attic again.

No, that was from downstairs. She pulled herself into a sitting position and looked out the window. She could not see anyone in the patrol car despite the moonlight. The alarm clock read twelve fifty-two.

The burglar alarm pierced the air. Magnet began to bark, rattling his crate. Phoebe grabbed her cell phone and her mace. Still no movement visible from the patrol car. She let Magnet out of his crate, picked him up and took him into the bathroom. She locked both the bathroom door and the door to the toilet.

The alarm company was supposed to call her to make sure she had not accidentally triggered the alarm. If they could not contact her they called the local police station. But what if the local station waved them off because the patrol car was already there? She called 911. The operator told her to stay in the bathroom. Magnet was drinking out of the toilet.

She heard sirens. There was a brief silence and then a second siren approached. The voice on the phone had stopped sounding officious.

"Stay right there, ma'am. We have another unit on the way and an ambulance."

A few minutes passed and then the operator told her that she would hear a window breaking as the officers entered the house to secure it. Voices and footfalls now, moving from room to room. A knock on the bedroom door and the operator told her to come out of the bathroom.

Detective Nichols was standing in her bedroom. He explained that someone had shot and killed the officer who had been guarding the house. He had been shot at close range, probably the shooter had used a silencer. The alarm had been triggered when the screen on the downstairs bathroom window was removed and an attempt made to open the window. The house was now secure. A search was underway in the neighborhood. The department would move the family to a safe house later in the day. If she wanted she could go to a women's shelter now.

There was no way she was going to a shelter. She asked about the slain man. He was twenty-nine and left behind a newborn son. She blinked back angry tears. She told Nichols she was staying in her home; whoever it was would not be back tonight. The alarm had seen to that. He frowned at her but arranged for two officers to be posted outside. The window the officers had broken was being boarded up for now.

There was no more sleeping tonight. Her phone chirped. "Mom, I heard. Worried about you."

Phoebe smiled sadly. Social media at its worst.

"I am alright. xoxox. Talk in the morning."

She spent the rest of the night on the couch. Magnet was curled up next to her. Around dawn, he began to bark and ran to the sliding glass door. There were three or four deer in the backyard. Phoebe switched off the alarm and opened the slider to the porch. The deer bounded gracefully into the wood. The birds were beginning to stir. Magnet whined.

She closed the slider and put Magnet's leash on him. When she opened the front door, the officers in the car gave her a wave and watched them. She stayed within their view.

She reactivated the alarm as soon as she stepped into the front hall, locking the door firmly behind her. She fed Magnet and glanced into the living room. She was sure that she had closed the slider. She stepped into the living room and saw that the trap door on the porch was open. She had always hated that thing and the expressions it brought to the faces of the plumber and HVAC repairmen who had to use it to access the crawl space under the house. It was a tight space and frequented by spiders and snakes.

Magnet barked once and then howled in pain. Phoebe whirled around and looked straight into David's face. He was pointing a gun at her.

This was not the David she had seen in the hospital bed or the David Eileen had described. This one was clear-eyed and his hands were steady. His pants and shirt were muddied from a night spent in the crawl space.

"Upstairs." He gestured with the gun.

She hesitated and he pistol whipped her. Her head snapped to the side. Magnet growled. She forced herself up the stairs. The muzzle of the gun was pressed into the small of her back. She felt no fear, only anger at David and gratitude for the children's absence.

They went into the master bedroom. He opened the closet door while keeping the gun trained on her.

"Where is all of my stuff?"

"I took it to the dump."

He backhanded her. "Bitch."

He dug out a flannel shirt and a pair of chinos.

"Now, let's go wake up those kids."

"They are not here."

He stared, then advanced on her.

"Go ahead. Hit me. Shoot me. I know you mean to kill me."

"Not before you tell me where the kids are."

"Why? So you can sell them overseas, just like Selene and Andrew and Jason and the rest of those poor children. What is it David, illegal adoptions, child pornography, snuff films?"

"Do you have any idea how much money I can get for a white virgin in the middle east? Or a little boy in Thailand? Seventy five minimum."

She was not sure if he meant dollars or hundreds of thousands of dollars.

"Why, David?"

He grinned. "It's fun, Phoebe. I love the life. I have a huge house in Phuket. Instead of working for that fucking company, traveling coach and staying in rat-hole hotels, I go first class. I can do what I want, fuck who I want and have the best of the best. This is my last trip to the good ole USA for a while. I will escort my field trippers to their new lives, collect my money and chill. Might work a bit on my porn business. You gave me an idea. There has to be some serious coin in snuff."

She had a sudden image of David and his mouse trap obsession. The field mice came into the kitchen each winter. He had a collection of mouse traps which he baited carefully each evening and then inspected with glee in the morning, examining each body with peculiar interest.

"Your own children, David?"

"Look, this is not really personal. You are a bore. All you do is kid stuff and run. You are terrible in the sack, particularly after the treats I have had. Mind you, I won't actually sell our kids, although I might take some videos. I will just collect their life insurance. And yours."

Keep him talking, though Phoebe.

"Who is Annette?"

"She is one crazy freak," laughed David. "The brains behind all this. She finds the customers and gives them a one-two punch. They pay up front for their boy-toy or girl-toy and then she puts the squeeze on them halfway through the deal, sends them some captivating photo or video and gets them to cough up more money, maybe to grease the skids in immigration, pay off the uncle who saw us snatch the kid, whatever. She uses that nasty imagination she has. And when we kick back, let's just say she really does it for me."

He grabbed his crouch, flaunting his erection.

Phoebe felt sick. Maybe this was why she had grown to hate sleeping with David. Maybe some deep subconscious part of her had known how deranged he was. God why hadn't she been more in tune with herself, paid attention rather than numbing herself with frenzied activity, running away from everything that bothered her?

"Well, enough about me. Let's talk about where those kids are."

He slapped her. She screamed, hoping to alert the officers outside the open window. He grabbed her by the ponytail and yanked her into the bathroom. He closed the door and turned on the water in the tub.

"Take off your clothes and get in."

She stood still. He punched her full in the mouth and she felt a tooth break. Blood began to drip onto the black and white tile. He ripped her t-shirt off and savagely grabbed her nipple.

"Skinny cunt. You disgust me."

She cried out and Magnet began to howl in the other room.

"Damn dog."

He cocked the gun. He scratched at his forearm.

"Oh so, you are going to kill him too, just like Roxie?"

"Killing that old mutt was Annette's idea. Just like she made me snatch Damien out of the bedroom. She never did tell me what went wrong with that plan, how he ended up back with you."

He was lost in the memory. Magnet had stopped barking. He rummaged in the medicine cabinet until he found one of his straight edge razors. She had never understood why he liked to use those things. He thumbed the blade fondly.

"You might as well kill me David. Get it over with."

She was taunting him.

"I won't tell you a thing."

He shut the water off. It was steaming, probably hot enough to scald her. She left her sweatpants on and lifted one leg to climb into the tub. She heard the light tone that signaled that the alarm had been disabled. She splashed into the tub to cover the sound. She pulled her knees up to her chest.

David slashed her cheek with the blade. She felt a stinging and the bathwater turned red. There was a light thumping in her ears, her pulse maybe. She focused on the sound as he raised the blade again. It sounded like Magnet's tail thumping against his crate. But he was not in the crate. She ducked her head and her shoulder stung.

"Ready to tell me? If you tell me now I promise they will not suffer."

She considered this and dismissed it but raised her eyes as if to plead with him. He held the blade against her throat. The gun was on the bathroom counter behind him. She watched in the mirror as the bathroom door opened. A hand appeared and quietly slid the gun out of her line of sight.

"Ok, ok. I will tell you. Please don't hurt them."

She was screaming now and trying not to look at the door.

"They are in a shelter. Up in Herndon. If you look in my purse the address is there on a piece of paper."

Phoebe watched as Eileen slipped into the bathroom holding the gun with two hands. It happened in slow motion. Eileen's first shot went wild and shattered the glass shower door. David whirled around wielding the blade. Phoebe lurched out of the tub. The second shot hit him in the thigh. He howled and lunged for Eileen. Eileen raised the gun again but he slapped it out of her hand and slashed the blade across her throat. Eileen's eyes widened and she raised her hand to her throat. The gun skittered across the tile. Phoebe snatched it up and fired into David's back.

Magnet was barking wildly and feet were running up the stairs. David was slumped on the bathroom rug. Phoebe cradled Eileen in her arms. The front of her hoodie was drenched with blood. She looked up at Phoebe.

"Baby, stay with me. Help is coming."

She could hear the officers on the radio, calling for backup and an ambulance.

"Keep your eyes open. Look at me," Phoebe pleaded.

Eileen opened her eyes. Phoebe could see into her soul, see her as a grown woman, see her with her children. Eileen smiled faintly.

Her lips formed the words "I love you too, Mom."

Her eyes closed. There was so much blood.

"No!"

Phoebe was sobbing. She kissed her daughter and stroked her hair. Two paramedics were in the room. One of them asked Phoebe to please let go so they could work on Eileen. Phoebe released her daughter and the medics moved grimly about the room. One of the officers brought Phoebe her bathrobe. David was being zipped into a body bag.

The walls of Phoebe's bedroom would be forever painted with anguish.

• • •

They let Phoebe hold Eileen's body until all warmth was gone from her daughter. The room was silent as the two stretchers were carried out to the waiting ambulances. Phoebe rode with Eileen's body. She watched as the stretcher with her daughter was wheeled down the hall to the morgue. She accepted a valium from one of the ER nurses and closed her eyes as her cheek and shoulder were stitched.

Detective Nichols and Marion took her statement. They told her that the ballistics reports showed that the same gun that killed the officer outside her house killed David. She told them most of what David had told her, leaving out only the rape and the documents in the strong box. This information, she rationalized, would only serve to get her into trouble, maybe get her children taken from her.

Nichols and Marion drove her to Moises' house, stopping once to pick up Magnet. Moises took Magnet from her arms. The guilt and pain on his face was a reflection of her own.

"Flaca," he began. "I am so sorry, she must have taken a cab."

She stroked his cheek and brushed away a tear.

Damien and Kendall swarmed her. Damien wanted to know why her face was bandaged and her arm in a sling. She took a deep, sobbing breath and told them that there had been a terrible accident, that David and Eileen were dead. She swayed, suddenly dizzy. Moises guided her to the sofa and brought her a glass of water. Kendall began to scream and ran from the room.

Damien looked dazed. Phoebe pulled him onto her lap. She could hear Moises talking quietly to Kendall in the kitchen. Kendall's screams became quiet sobs. Phoebe felt her world shrink.

Phoebe went several days without being able to sleep or eat. She paced around Moises' house until he finally called Dr. Sayers and had her come to the house and administer a sedative. Phoebe fought it but she finally slept. When she woke the next day, the crushing sadness and the terrible guilt came rushing at her like a deadly freight train.

She tried her best to be strong. She took Zoloft during the day and a sedative at night. She did not want to upset Damien and Kendall further. They were both pale and tip-toing around Moises' house. After several more days, the kids wanted to go home. Phoebe never wanted to set foot in her house again but she knew that was impractical. She gritted her teeth and took what remained of her family home. She could tell the kids felt better there but it made it even harder for Phoebe to function. She kept seeing David in the kitchen with the gun. Her mind replayed the terrible motion David had made with the knife that had changed her life forever.

The coroner released Eileen's body the next week. Phoebe had her cremated. They were not a religious family; the kids were not baptized. She talked to Damien and Kendall about having a special ceremony to say good bye to Eileen and maybe scattering her ashes. Damien wanted to keep the ashes for a while. Phoebe placed them on the mantel with a candle and fresh flowers from the backyard. Kendall retreated to her room and spent hours on her computer. Damien would play quietly with Magnet, but neither wanted to stray from Phoebe's side.

The police guard was still on the house, although Phoebe supposed it would end eventually. There had been no sign of Annette. She had heard no word on any progress made towards finding the missing children.

David's autopsy took longer and involved exploration of his medical history. His toxicology was positive for Clozaril, a drug used to treat schizophrenia as well as for barbiturates and cocaine. The oncologist in Norfolk had treated him for a blood disorder caused by the Clozaril. The Mental Health Unit in Franklin County had diagnosed him with a psychotic break, possibly due to over or under medication. Phoebe debated what to do with his body. She did not want a ceremony, or to scatter his ashes but the kids might need the closure. They were all seeing a grief counselor. In the end, she had him cremated too. His ashes, she stored in the garage.

She thought a lot about how little she had known David. She had wandered through life with him, not seeing the demons. He had been selfish and distant for sure but weren't most men like that? She knew that she was, in large part, responsible for the tragedy, for burying herself in her children's lives and ignoring that sixth sense, that feeling that something was wrong. It was something she would never forgive herself for. She supposed it was a fitting punishment, this crushing feeling of having utterly failed those who depended upon her the most.

Phoebe closed off her bedroom and bathroom. She slept in Eileen's bed, not changing the sheets or pillowcases for almost two weeks, not wanting to wash away her daughter's scent for fear that she would not be able to remember it. Along with the nearly unbearable sadness and guilt, she was deeply fatigued. She picked at her food and was often sick to her stomach. Moises went back to his townhouse and his mother but he checked in on them regularly. It was Moises who convinced her to go to the doctor, get some bloodwork done and maybe get some prescription vitamins.

She sat in Dr. Sayer's office.

"Well," the doctor began. "You are anemic and have lost a bit of weight. Your vitamin D level is low too. You have been through a terrible ordeal. I am sure you are not eating or sleeping well."

She paused and studied Phoebe's face.

"I will do a physical exam in a moment but I need to tell you that you are pregnant."

Phoebe blinked. "Pregnant? I thought I was menopausal."

"I know this is the last thing you were expecting to hear and maybe more than you want to deal with right now."

Dr. Sayers explained that fertility might be diminished during perimenopause but that it was still possible to get pregnant. The transvaginal ultrasound confirmed a heartbeat. Dr. Sayers estimated her to be about six weeks along.

"You have some time. Don't decide anything right now. Go home and think about it. Take the prenatal vitamins and try to eat a bit better for your own sake."

Three weeks after Eileen and David died, the kids went back to finish the school year. They were reluctant to go. Damien did not want to leave Phoebe alone but she convinced him that Magnet made very good company. The grief counselor who was working with the family told Phoebe that reestablishing normal routines for the kids and particularly reconnecting with their friends was important now. Damien cried when he got on the bus but he seemed more cheerful later that afternoon. Kendall was just quiet, and unreadable.

After six weeks, Phoebe tried to go back to work. Her colleagues were kind and Nancy had put fresh flowers in her office. She had to admit that the distraction helped but she could not focus on her work. It made her feel guilty to know that she was not giving her clients her best but it was a relief to think about anything other than the pain and guilt that haunted her nights.

Phoebe tried to stop taking the medication; they made her feel flat and fuzzy. She started running a bit. Just a few slow miles with Magnet in a vain effort to get those endorphins to kick in and take over and make her forget her sadness. The puppy was growing fast and he was strong. His enthusiasm got her out the door and he made her feel safer.

As she ran she thought about the life now growing inside her. Was this child the product of a brutal rape or had conception been a mutual act between husband and wife? Would he or she carry David's psychotic side? She worried about that for Damien and Kendall as well. Was David's sickness something that had always been a part of him or was it triggered by Annette? She supposed she would never really know.

She came to the conclusion one morning at mile three of the first run of the year where the summer heat and humidity were like a thick blanket, that the circumstances of the conception of the baby did not matter. The issue was only whether she wanted another child. What really, she thought as the sweat trickled off her face, was more pure than the love of a child. Maybe she could make up with this baby for her failure to protect Eileen. No child could ever replace Eileen but maybe there was some reason she was carrying this child.

She stepped into the kitchen and filled Magnet's water bowel. She added a few ice cubes and then poured herself a large glass of water. Each day, her arms ached more for Eileen. She worried that she was hovering over Kendall and Damien but she loved them so much. Maybe this child was something they all needed.

Settling David's estate was proving to be problematic. He had a tremendous amount of debt. He had emptied out his 401K account and somehow taken out a $250,000 line of credit on their house. This she was contesting because he had forged her signature on the loan application. The property in Virginia Beach that he had owned with Annette was heavily mortgaged. He had cancelled his life insurance policy with MetLife, the one they had taken out years ago and which was supposed to be paid directly from their bank account. She applied for his social security. At least that was a little something.

She was angry at him all over again. He had left them with nothing other than what she had in her own 401K account and what she could earn. They would need to move to a smaller house and she would have to work more hours. She had no idea how she would pay for college for the kids. She did not care about the house; the memories it held were too painful anyway. She hoped that it would not be too hard for the kids. Summer was almost here. She would take them on a nice vacation and put the house on the market. Make them part of the adventure of choosing a new home.

She unburdened herself to Moises on a hike at Manassas Battlefield. It had started out as a run but when she told him that she was pregnant, his internal abuela came out and he insisted that they walk the rest of the ten miles. She indulged him. It was hot, even at eight am.

"I won't tell you what to do, Flaca. But I know that you are a great mom. You will love this baby no matter what, maybe even more because of the unknown. Listen to what your heart tells you."

Her hand went unconsciously to her belly, still flat.

"And you would not have to worry about a baby sitter. My mom and I, we will watch the little one."

This made her smile.

"The money is just money and a house is only a home when you make it a home. Don't waste your energy being angry with David. You have so much that is good."

She knew he was right but she was still so sad. She wondered if she were depressed and supposed she must be. If not for Damien and Kendall, she was not sure that she would get up in the morning, or that she would really want to go on living. She found herself reading all the obituaries in the Washington Post and tearing up on the ones of the young people whose parents were listed as those left behind. She was left behind. It was unnatural, unfair to have to bury a child.

She asked the kids where they might like to go for vacation. Damien immediately asked to go back to the lake.

"We can finally go swimming," he explained.

Kendall just shrugged. "I guess that would be cool," the teenager said.

Phoebe was surprised they would want go back there. Phoebe could only think of poor Roxie and Damien missing from the cabin. But, Damien and Kendall had not been told how Roxie had died and Damien just thought he had had an adventure in the woods.

Why not? Anything to make the kids happy. There was no GPS on her car. Detective Nichols had told her the week before that Interpol had tracked Annette into Thailand but that there had been no sign of her since. The house in Virginia Beach had been foreclosed and the house in Mitchell's Landing had belonged to a cousin of Annette who had died the year before. One of the cousin's daughters who lived in California had inherited it. It was now on the market.

They stayed in a different cabin. The park rangers greeted them warmly. Phoebe stopped in to see the vet who had cremated Roxie. She had forgotten to pick up her ashes but the vet had held them for her.

"Sometimes it takes a bit for folks to want to pick them up. Besides, you live a good distance from here. I figured you would be back."

Phoebe thanked him and accepted the small metal box.

The lake was busier than it had been the past spring. There were jet skis and fishing boats. Speedboats and even house boats. Phoebe and Magnet took early morning hikes and then the dog dozed in the cool of the cabin during the heat of the day. The State Park Beach was charming. They spent hours there. There were people to watch and the water was clean and clear. There was an ice cream boat that pulled up to the dock each afternoon. Phoebe sunned in a beach chair and read trashy novels. Her belly was starting to swell.

Phoebe grilled chicken and hamburgers in the evenings, or they went into the marina for pizza and to play at the arcade. Phoebe sipped a glass of merlot as she watched the kids play mini golf. She felt some of the tension start to leave her body and a little of the fog of sadness lift but Eileen was never far from her mind.

It was Friday, the day before they were supposed to leave. Phoebe took Magnet to the trail where the tiny cemetery was. She had avoided this part of the park until now. She sat in the grass next to the gravestone with the lamb on the top. She closed her eyes, suddenly flooded with memories of Eileen. The moment the obstetrician put the tiny blanket wrapped bundle on her chest and she looked into the baby's blue-black eyes. The toddler's delight at wooly bears and jumping in a freshly raked pile of leaves. The kindergarden graduate clutching her diploma.

"It ain't natural to bury a child." Raven spoke quietly. "You never gets used to it. Each morning, you have to remember it all over again. If you gets lucky, you might see them from time to time, beyond what you seen in your memories and dreams."

Phoebe thought that she would give almost anything to see Eileen again. To see her smile, to hear her voice.

"Where did you bury your chile?" Raven asked.

"I haven't yet. I am not very religious. I have her ashes though."

"You needs to put her to rest. That way, you have a place you can come and set with her. This here is a peaceful spot. Nobody will fuss if you was to bury her here. She would have company here with my little lambs."

Raven turned suddenly, transfixed. Phoebe watched as she reached her arms out, smiling.

"My babies. Mama misses you."

Magnet barked. He wagged his tail and licked at the air. He ran in a circle around the graveyard. Raven laughed. Phoebe closed her eyes. She heard small voices in the distance. Magnet barked once more. When Phoebe opened her eyes, she was alone.

Phoebe stood up and dusted off her shorts. Magnet was calm on the walk back to the cabin. Kendall and Damien were stirring. She made breakfast and asked them what they would like to do on the last day. Swimming and ice cream were high on the list.

Damien must have read her mind.

"Can we go see the stones for Elsie and Noah?"

Kendall looked at him and said, "Who?"

Phoebe explained about the little graveyard.

"I like playing with Elsie and Noah," said Damien. "They came to see me last night. I read them a story and we watched Sponge Bob."

"How did they die, Mom?" asked Kendall.

"I think they got sick one winter. Back in those days, they did not have antibiotics or vaccines and a lot of children died of things that we can treat now."

Phoebe packed some fruit and water. They left Magnet in the cool of the cabin. The cemetery was shaded. The insects buzzed and they could hear boats in the distance.

"What would you guys think if we brought Eileen's ashes here?"

Kendall smiled and Damien nodded.

"She would have company here," he said. "And we could come and visit her."

Phoebe stopped at the ranger station on the way to the beach. Angie was on duty. Her eyes widened and filled with tears when Phoebe explained what had happened to Eileen.

"The kids and I would like to bury her here. How would we go about getting permission to bury her in what looks like a family graveyard?"

Angie considered this. "Let me see if I can find out if there is a family member who could grant permission. There is a foundation that places wreathes at Christmas. Maybe they know."

Phoebe gave Angie her phone number.

"Mrs. Rivers," said Angie as they were about to leave, "I am glad that you came back, especially after all that has happened. This is a special place. A good place."

Phoebe smiled. "I know. Thank you."

Chapter Fifteen

Kendall

Phoebe had started to really worry about Kendall. She had always been the quiet one. She loved to read and write and would spend hours playing with her stuffed animals. In the weeks after Eileen's death Phoebe took Kendall's withdrawal as part of the normal grieving process. After a few sessions with the grief counselor, Kendall refused to return. Her glum mood persisted deep into the summer. Kendall began to snap at Damien and even slapped him a few times.

At thirteen, Kendall was a gangly kid with tight curls and a sprinkling of acne. She took to staying up until two or three in the morning and then sleeping until Phoebe woke her up to watch Damien. In the evening, Phoebe had to coax Kendall out of the house to go to the pool. She hated leaving the kids alone so much but she could not afford summer camp. She tried to work from home as much as she could.

Phoebe was struggling, not only emotionally but financially. She had put the house on the market, but things were not moving. She was working full time hours to make ends meet and to qualify for health insurance. She cut off the house phone, in part to save money but mostly to stop listening to calls from David's creditors. She was beginning to show but had not told anyone except Moises. She still slept in Eileen's bed and woke unrested most mornings.

Late in the evening at the end of July, Phoebe heard voices coming from Kendall's bedroom. She rapped on the door and entered. Kendall was sitting on the bed Skyping. Her face was lit by the computer screen and her curly hair was disheveled. She slammed the laptop shut and glared at Phoebe.

"Who are you talking to?" asked Phoebe.

"No one." It was a growl.

"Then why did you shut your computer? Please tell me who you are talking to. It is very late."

"What do you even care? It is not like you talk to me."

Phoebe sighed.

"Honey, of course I care. Please shut off your computer and go to bed."

Kendall reluctantly shut off her computer and slid under the sheet. She turned her back on Phoebe and refused to respond to Phoebe's effort to kiss her goodnight.

Phoebe was used to teenage volatility but not to this hostility and furtiveness. Eileen had certainly been emotional. but she was an open book. God, she missed her child. Eileen could always reach Kendall. Phoebe felt paralyzed in her inability to connect with Kendall.

Kendall waited for a few minutes after her mother left the room. She drew her cell phone out from under her pillow. She had a new text from Howard. Howard loved to talk to her. He made her feel special, important. He had started following her on Instagram last month. He was a junior in high school. She was pretty sure he had been a friend of Eileen. He certainly knew a lot about Eileen. It made him a good listener when she was sad about Eileen. The Skype call this evening was the first time they had talked in person and it had been interrupted by her mother barging into the room. Kendall thought he was very cute.

"U are really pretty." She blushed at the words.

"U are not too bad yourself," she wrote back.

"Get some rest, beautiful." Kendall smiled as she tucked the phone back under her pillow.

Kendall was more cheerful the next morning. She returned

Phoebe's goodbye kiss and sat down to watch Sponge Bob with Damien for the first time in weeks. Phoebe had an afternoon court appearance but she promised to come straight home with Chinese take-out. After dinner, they went to the pool.

Phoebe sat on the steps in the shallow end and watched Damien swim. He was a good swimmer but she liked to keep him close. He coaxed her into the water and she floated next to him.

"Guess what, Mama?"

"What sweetheart?"

"Kendall has a boyfriend. I think she is in love." Damien giggled.

"Really. And why do you think so?"

Phoebe was only half listening. Damien loved to make up stories and he always had the most fanciful dreams.

"Because I saw him. She was talking to him outside today. She made me go inside but I looked out the window. They were holding hands."

Damien now had her full attention.

"He came to our house?"

Damien looked at her.

"Oh no." He was dejected. "I was not apposed to tell you. Howard was going to bring me a treat tomorrow. Now Kendall is going to be in trouble and mad at me and it is all my fault."

"It is alright. You did the right thing by telling me."

Phoebe looked over at Kendall, sprawled in a pool chair, hunched over her phone. Damien and Phoebe splashed around a few more minutes until the lifeguard blew final whistle.

Phoebe waited until Damien was bathed and in bed. He had tried to go to bed without brushing his teeth. She sent him back to the bathroom with a playful swat on his rear. He convinced her to read an extra bedtime story.

It was almost ten when she knocked on Kendall's door. She sat down on Kendall's bed.

Kendall looked up from her phone.

"What, Mom?"

"Please tell me who Howard is and how you met him."

Kendall glared at her. "None of your business."

"It is very much my business. Please answer my question."

"He is just a friend. He follows me on Instagram."

"What do you know about him and how old is he?"

Kendall rolled her eyes. "He's a junior in high school and he's really cool. He actually likes me, thinks I'm interesting."

"Was he here at the house today?"

Kendall glared. "He wasn't IN the house, Mom. We were talking outside."

Phoebe sighed. "Honey, you cannot give our address and your personal information to someone you met on-line. This boy is three or four years older than you and I have never met him or his parents."

"You hate me." The tears were flowing. "You treat me like a baby."

"What you did was not safe. We have talked about internet safety. I expect you to behave responsibly, particularly when you are supposed to be watching your brother."

"That little shit. He told on me. I have to spend my whole day with a six year old so that you can go to work. My friends' moms do fun stuff with them over the summer. Not me. I am stuck here with him."

Phoebe willed herself not to lose her patience. Her teenager was just acting out, not realizing how much her words stung Phoebe.

"Please give me your phone and your computer. When you can show better choices, you may earn them back."

"You are ruining my life!" sobbed Kendall.

She thrust the phone and computer at Phoebe and buried her face in her pillow. She shrank from Phoebe's touch, pushed Phoebe's face away when Phoebe tried to kiss her.

Phoebe went downstairs. Of course, both the phone and computer were password protected. She debated getting the passwords from Kendall but she let it be. Tomorrow was Friday. Maybe some of the tension would dissolve over the weekend.

In the morning, Kendall was quiet but not sulky. She offered to take Damien on a bike ride. He was delighted and raced out to the garage to find his helmet. He filled a water bottle for each of them and stuffed apples into the pockets of his shorts. Phoebe watched as they rode down the driveway together. It was good to see Damien so excited and Kendall engaging him.

She had a brief to file by the end of the day on behalf of a private school that had been sued by the parents of a transgender child for not allowing the child access to restrooms for the gender with which the child identified. The parents also alleged that the school had forced their child to play on the soccer team of birth gender. She actually found the school's actions reprehensible and was having trouble focusing enough to argue against the child.

She sat outside on the porch. The humidity level was bearable. She would make the kids lunch and then take the brief to the office for Nancy to finalize and file. The cicadas hummed in the backyard and Magnet, worn out from their morning run, snored softly at her side. She glanced at her watch and was startled to see it was after one.

She went out to Branch Road with Magnet and looked in both directions. No sign of the kids. She drove slowly down Branch Road towards one of the local parks. It had a small playground and a pond where people would sometimes fish, although she had never seen anyone actually catch a fish there.

She parked in the small lot and walked into the part. Damien was sitting at one of the picnic tables. Magnet bounded up to him, barking happily. Damien's face was dirty and tear-streaked.

"What is wrong, honey?"

"I can't find Kendall. We were playing hide and seek. It was my turn to hide and I just waited and waited and she never found me."

"Where were you hiding?"

"Right over there."

Damien pointed to the other side of the pond. There was a footpath that led around the pond.

"That was a mean trick. I was scared. And when I tried to ride my bike home, it did not work. And I was not quite sure how to get home."

He pointed to his little two-wheeler. Both tires were flat. Kendall's bike was next to his. Its tires were intact.

"Alright." Phoebe stood up and held out her hand. "Let's get you home and cleaned up. I am sure Kendall is around here someplace."

She put Damien's bike in the back of the wagon and looked at the tires. Both had been slit. She could not fit Kendall's into the wagon without removing Damien's car seat. She would come back for it later, or make Kendall ride it home.

Phoebe was not really alarmed. Kendall had shown a mean streak towards Damien lately. She had stormed out of the house on more than one occasion, returning a while later. Phoebe assumed this was more of the same, although she did not like that Damien had been left alone.

She fixed Damien a grilled cheese sandwich and made one for herself, adding some tomato slices to hers. Her appetite had been better the past few days. She loaded the dishwasher and kept one eye out the kitchen window. No sign of Kendall.

She locked and alarmed the house. Kendall knew how to let herself in. She buckled Damien into his booster seat and drove back to the park. Kendall's bike was still there. She put it in the back of the wagon.

Damien read a book in her office while she finished the brief. Nancy would have it messengered to the court to meet the filing deadline. She wished her colleagues a nice weekend and went home. Still no sign of Kendall.

"Damien," she asked. "Did Kendall say anything about Howard today?"

"She was mad at me for telling you about him. She said you could not keep her away from him."

"Was anyone else at the park?" Damien shook his head.

"Did she have a phone with her?" Phoebe asked suddenly.

Damien thought for a moment. "Yes. She was texting."

Phoebe remembered that she had not deactivated Eileen's phone. She was not sure where it was.

• • •

Kendall was at the mall with Howard. They were in the food court, eating soft pretzels. She kept glancing around, hoping that one of her friends from school would see her. Howard was holding her hand across the table. His arms were tanned and muscular and his fingers were rough.

Howard was so nice. He always asked how she was doing and if she needed anything. He listened sympathetically when she told him about her mom taking away her phone and computer. He asked a lot of questions about how her family was doing since her dad and sister died.

"Maybe she does not see that you are growing up. Some moms want to keep their girls little forever. I can tell, though. You are not like most girls your age. More mature. Much more mature."

Kendall blushed. She twirled a curl around her index finger and looked at him from under her lashes. She had put on a bit of mascara this morning. She had also swiped a pink lipstick from her mom. She hoped she had not overdone it.

She felt a little bad about leaving Damien at the park. It did serve him right for telling on her. She hoped that he had not been scared and that he had ridden his bike home. She had been so happy that Howard texted her and asked her to go to the mall. She could not exactly take Damien along.

"I should probably be going," she said to Howard.

"Sure thing."

He got up and stretched and extended his hand to her. They strolled out of the mall to his jeep. He started the engine and cranked up the AC.

"You know, Kendall. I really like you. I feel like we have such a connection."

He touched her cheek and turned her face towards his. He leaned in and kissed her gently on the lips. She kissed him back, hesitant because she had never kissed anyone other than her parents. She was not sure if she was doing it right. Howard seemed to think so. He put his hand on the back of her neck and pulled her closer. His tongue slipped inside her mouth. It was faintly salty. She was glad that she had flossed and brushed before she rode to the park with Damien.

He pulled away and put the jeep into gear.

"I could just kiss you all day but I better get you back to the park."

His hand was on her thigh. It was warm.

She asked him to let her off on a side street near the park. Before she got out of the car, he kissed her again and gave her a package.

"I hope you like this. Open it later."

He drove away and she tucked the package into her backpack. The park was deserted and her bike was missing. She sat on a bench next to the jungle gym and opened the package. Inside was a pink and white teddie with matching underwear. She had never had anything like that. Her mom bought her basic white underwear and bras at Target. She touched the fabric and imagined kissing Howard again.

She trudged home. The two miles felt a lot longer on foot than they did on a bike. No one was home but her bike was outside the garage. She was pretty sure she was going to be in serious trouble. She hid Eileen's cell phone behind some boxes in the garage and went upstairs to take a shower. When she got out, her mother was waiting. The look on her mom's face was not happy.

Phoebe sat across from Kendall at the kitchen table. Kendall's arms were crossed. Damien was practicing his violin upstairs.

"Why did you leave your brother alone in the park?"

"I was tired of taking care of him. I figured he would just ride home and find you."

"How could he ride home if his tires were slashed?" asked Phoebe.

Kendall's eyes were big. "I did not slash his tires."

"Well, someone did. And you left him alone in the park, maybe with a sick person who would slash the tires on a little boy's bike."

Kendall looked at the floor.

"Where did you go, Kendall?"

"Nowhere. I just walked around to think."

Kendall would not meet Phoebe's eyes.

"Kendall, you let both me and Damien down. I trusted you to take care of him and you violated that trust. Even worse, you left him scared and in a potentially dangerous situation. I am going to have to make arrangements for a babysitter for both of you. I can't tell you how disappointed I am in you."

"Whatever." Kendall shrugged. "Can I go to my room now?"

"One more thing. Have you seen Eileen's cell? I need to return it to Verizon."

Kendall shook her head and walked away. Her bedroom door slammed.

Phoebe felt overwhelmed. She was failing her children. She didn't think that Kendall would have any idea how to slash a tire. But maybe something of David was emerging in Kendall.

Kendall sat on her bed and studied the present from Howard. She locked her door and tried it on. She giggled as she looked at herself in the mirror. She swished her hips and looked coyly over her shoulder. Having a boyfriend like Howard was awesome.

• • •

Phoebe's mother arrived on Sunday morning. Rebecca towered over Phoebe but she was not a commanding presence. She was nervous and uncertain and hated to drive in northern Virginia. She had agreed to come and watch the kids for a few weeks. Phoebe always suspected her mother was more than happy to escape Phoebe's father, who since retiring occupied his time critiquing his wife. Rebecca was gentle and patient with the kids and Phoebe was relieved to have another adult in the house. Even Kendall came out of her room and was cheerful.

After a lunch of corn on the cob and chicken Phoebe was sleepy. She tried to hide a yawn but Rebecca shoed her out of the kitchen.

"Go take a nap, Phoebe. I will clean up here and take the kids swimming."

Phoebe did not argue. When she reached the landing on the stairs and turned towards her room, she realized that she was going to have to face her bedroom. Rebecca would be sleeping in Eileen's room. She had not been in her room since Eileen died. Moises had hired and supervised a cleaning crew to remove all traces of that terrible morning. She took a deep breath and opened the door.

Moises had not just had the place cleaned. He had redone the room entirely. The masculine furnishings that David had insisted on, the huge oak dressers and massive desk, were gone. Her bedroom walls were not brown anymore but were instead a light peach. The bedspread and curtains were a delicate floral pattern, lily of the valley and honeysuckle. There was a white vanity and a matching set of dressers. A rocker with a reading lamp was next to the bay window. A small table held photos of the kids. She picked up one she had never seen before. Eileen smiled at Damien who was sitting on his big sister's lap. Moises must have taken that one at his house, right before

Eileen died. Phoebe pressed her lips to the glass.

The broken shower door had been replaced and the bathroom freshly painted. All of David's toiletries were gone and his closet was bare, painted with a fresh coat of white glossy. Moises must have done this when they were at the lake.

She called him. "I can't believe you went through all of this for me. I know you must have thought me ungrateful. This is the first time I have gone into my room since…"

"I know. It is ok. I hope it made it a little easier. Besides, all that heavy dark furniture, it needed to go."

"Thank you, Moises. This is so very nice. I love you."

"I love you too, Flaca."

She hung up after promising to eat and rest. She lay down on her bed and slept.

She dreamed of the man in the Great Dismal Swamp. His leg was no longer bandaged. He was deep in the swamp. The trees were so dense that almost all the sunlight was blocked. He was cutting down a tree. There was a large stack of felled trees. Another man was cutting trees into rough boards and lashing them together.

He sensed her staring at him. He turned around, his bare chest dripped with sweat. He reached for a shirt caught on a low-hanging branch and pulled it over his head. He ducked his head in greeting.

"Thank ya kindly for the potion. It fixed my leg right up."

He pointed at his lower leg where a pink scar glistened.

"I am glad," said Phoebe. "Do you remember what you told me the last time we spoke."

"Yes, m'am. I tole you to beware dat woman. She mean you and your children harm." A shadow passed over his face. "She done got your chile kilt."

Phoebe nodded sadly.

"That is a terrible thing. She pure mean. A woman that hurts a chile belong with the devil."

He mopped at his brow with a rag he pulled from his pant pocket. "Dat woman, she still trouble for you. You took something from her. A man?"

"Yes," answered Phoebe. "He was my husband. I killed him."

He considered that.

"She think he hers. She a vengeful, hateful woman. You might think she gone far away but she close. She watching. She have many ways to see."

"What is your name?" asked Phoebe.

"I go by Amos."

"Do you live in this swamp?" asked Phoebe.

"Was born here. We all maroons. Nobody dare come into the swamp, not even the slave catchers. Too easy to get lost, or the panthers or gators will get you. We take care of our own, don't harm none lest they hurt one of us. Once in a while, we come out of the swamp to take care of evil."

Amos's face creased into a smile. His teeth were very white and his eyes danced.

"You with child. Dat good, it heal you. Don't take on so bout the one you lost. Bury her proper so she can rest."

Phoebe woke to the late afternoon sun streaming in through her new curtain. Peach sunlight dappled the hardwood floor. She wished she could recall more of the dream. The harder she tried to recall Amos, the more faded the memory became.

She could hear Damien and her mother playing in the sandbox under her window. Their voices made her smile. She splashed water on her face and went to check on Kendall. Kendall was just out of the shower and wrapped in a towel. She smiled and returned Phoebe's hug.

When Phoebe left the room, Kendall locked the door and removed Eileen's phone from under her pillow. She went back to taking selfies, some with her new lingerie and several with no clothing. Howard had really loved the ones she sent last night and had asked for more, maybe some close-ups. He said she looked really pretty and that he could not wait to see his girl again. She had to admit, thinking about Howard looking at the photos gave her a warm feeling somewhere below her stomach.

The kitchen smelled wonderful. Rebecca had made a beef and potato stew and freshly baked bread was cooling on the counter.

Phoebe's phone buzzed. Ranger Angie had found a relative of the Anderson family, the family that had previously owned the land where the graveyard was. The great-great-great grandson of a cousin of Elsie and Noah lived in Oregon. Jacoby Hendrick was quite elderly and hard of hearing and Ranger Angie had had to shout a lot to explain her request. Finally, Jacoby handed the phone off to a woman who turned out to be an orderly at his assisted living facility.

Alice Williams from the nursing home had explained that Jacoby, while frail from a fall the past winter, was very lucid at ninety-four. He was very amused that some white folks wanted to bury their child alongside slave babies but he thought that was quite alright. He had asked for a photo of the gravesites because he expected that he would not make it back east, at least not in this lifetime.

Ranger Angie's brother-in-law, who lived in Huddleston, happened to be a minister. He would be pleased to preside over the service. Don't worry, Angie hastened to reassure Phoebe, he was not the bible thumping kind and would go along with whatever gave the family peace. Phoebe thanked her and picked a date the following week.

Damien thought the idea of a service and burial in the woods near the lake was awesome.

"Mom!" he exclaimed, face flush with happiness, "Can we bury Roxie there too?"

Phoebe hesitated and looked at Rebecca. Rebecca was a practicing Catholic, although never strident in her faith. Rebecca nodded.

"I think that would be really great," Phoebe said to Damien. "Eileen would have company."

"Elsie and Noah would help to take care of Roxie too," responded Damien.

Kendall was lost in thought.

"What do you think, Kendall?" asked Phoebe. "Would you like to read what you have been writing at the service?"

Kendall gave herself a little shake.

"What? Oh, yes, Mom. Of course."

Kendall went back to thinking about the text she had sent to Howard right before dinner, the one where she asked him to send her pictures.

•   •   •

Howard did enjoy the photos of Kendall. Then again, he appreciated the art of photography and videography and young boys and girls made such enchanting subjects. Of course, he was not really Howard. This was one of the many names he used for his work. He considered himself lucky, well it was probably more talent than luck that had carried him so far, to such a lucrative career. People were quite vain. Give them the idea that they were special or beautiful and it was amazing what they would do for the camera.

His first subjects had been his brothers and sisters. That was when he was in middle school. Basic cell phone photos at first, then videos. He would hide in the closet while they were in the bathroom. Later, he installed cameras in their bedrooms. He posted his work on a website he hosted. Funny the things that a grown man would find enticing. A toddler with a lollypop, a young boy urinating. He quickly realized there was money to be made. Of course, he never did anything to his siblings, that would have been wrong.

He graduated from high school. By then, he had enticed several young girlfriends to make some soft porn. Once or twice, he got them drunk enough to go at it with each other. Those movies earned him some nice money. He upgraded his equipment, bought a car. He went to college, intending to study photography and film. After a semester or two, he was thoroughly bored with still life and clothed subjects.

He met a barista at a local coffee shop. She worked two jobs to make ends meet for her and her daughter. She was thrilled to have a boyfriend willing to babysit for free.

He took some of his best photos of the little blond girl. She did not seem to mind the camera or the poses, so long as he delivered on the promises of candy and toys. He posted his art on a pay for view website. It was the three minute video of the four year old masturbating that caught him his first big break.

Her name, or at least the one she gave him, was Ann Handsome. She met him at a diner outside of Harrisonburg. There was big money in this business, she told him, but he had to get off the internet. Too many cops posing at predators. She had clients with prurient interests, who were always willing to pay for new material.

He dropped out of college, telling his parents that it was just a semester off to make a bit more money working full time. He started to take photos for schools and daycares as well as for private birthday parties, showers and weddings. Some of the work was legit and he sold plenty of photo and video to regular clients.

He learned to recognize within seconds which children were well attended to and which had parents who were absent or inattentive. The pre-teens were the easiest to access. They were wired and often latch key kids. Time was never a problem. A little money or jewelry or a new electronic something went a long way in making an otherwise reluctant kid willing to make some racy video.

His work was always in demand. He kept it very discreet. The non-official stuff never went on the internet or even into the postal system. He and Ann rarely met in person. They had an elaborate system of post office boxes that they used to communicate.

He made enough money the first year to buy a condo in Lynchburg. A city that liked to think it was the bedrock of religious conservatism. Under the surface, there was more demand for porn than in a more moderate setting.

By then, he had dropped completely out of college. The spare bedroom in the condo was devoted to the business. He had a rare personal meeting with Ann in late spring. It was the first time they had met in a year or more.

She explained that she had several big money clients who were interested in live material. You mean like coming to watch a photo shoot or a video, he had asked. Well yes but more. They might like to participate, have a video taken, a set of custom photos featuring them and their favorite subject.

Howard hesitated at first. This sounded risky. What kind of

security was involved? How were arrangements made? What if something went wrong, if the subject balked? It was one thing when Howard enticed a subject into a relationship with him. Introducing a third party, well that was a different ball of wax.

And that is why there is so much money in this, she had explained. Once a client had expressed a certain interest, several subjects were selected. Photos and videos were provided to the client, usually over a period of months. This served to hook the client, who would be told the process was taking longer than expected and more money was needed. Basic information about the subject was gathered and a scenario developed to bring the parties together. A tailored process was used for each subject to encourage participation. Most of these clients were overseas and wanted the subject brought to their location.

Howard was nobody's fool. He could see where she was going with this. She was marketing her subjects and selling them to the highest bidder. No chance a kid taken overseas to film porn would be brought home to mommy and daddy. Howard did not much care. So long as the money was good and he was making art he was content.

Howard found most of the clients of his product disgusting. They were more animals than people. He felt no emotion towards his subjects. They were just tools to further his art. Most of them would do almost anything if the enticement were right. He never forced them. He had no sexual interest in children or in anyone. He had always been that way. He sometimes entertained himself with the challenge of impersonating someone who cared, who was interested in and attracted to another human being. His role ended when he handed off the subject to Ann's handler for transpiration to the client. He wanted nothing to do with that part, not the names of the client or the destinations of the subjects. Beyond a few personal meetings, he communicated with Ann only via the safe deposit boxes. Plausible deniability.

Kendall was a potential subject. He assumed she was destined for one of Ann's overseas clients. Howard liked the money he earned with these cases. He regularly double dipped, selling the art he made from the subject on the side and pocketing the money from the client as well. He would sometimes drag out the process to squeeze a bit more out of it. He figured Ann was getting the big payoff when she delivered. No harm in a little extra for him.

The only thing different about Kendall was that she had not been a subject Howard found. Ann usually reviewed his art for her clients. She must have more than one Howard working for her and Kendall was probably spillover. He had asked for more money for Kendall, citing the need to do research and spend time away from Lynchburg and his regular business. The money had appeared in the safety deposit box two days later along with Kendall's photo and address.

Finding Kendall on Facebook was easy. A private message introducing himself and referring to Eileen got him friended. Then he started following her on Instagram and Twitter. He got their conversations off the internet as soon as he could. He was relieved when her mother confiscated her phone and computer. He deleted the Facebook account he had used to connect with her. Not only would this reduce his connection to her, her loss of the electronics made her more willing to see him in person and take risks in the process. She had found and hidden her dead sister's phone. He hoped her mother would figure that out soon and take it away. He supposed her mother might monitor her instead but he was ok with that. Being caught talking to him would only make him more enticing to her.

He found talking to his subjects excruciating. Asking them questions the answers to which mattered little. Listening to them prattle on about themselves. Vain little things most of them. And vapid. He entertained himself by trying to figure out what they were going to say before they said it. Kendall was no exception. Moaning and groaning about being misunderstood, treated like a baby. Her mother was out to get her. They had no fun since their dad died and there was less money. He had delivered the first set of photos to the safety deposit box yesterday. It seemed like a normal job.

Chapter Sixteen

Annette

The new arrangement with Daniel was lucrative. He never asked Annette where the kids came from and she never told him about Howard. Or her other Howards. His attorney worked out a deal with the prosecutor in Austin. The kidnapping charge was dismissed, the fines for tax evasion paid.

She bought a little house in Chiang Mai. She did side deals, mostly blackmail of foreigners who got a little over the top with their escapades in Thailand and Indonesia, like the one that netted David. She never met Daniel's clients. She only saw him when he contacted her. But she chafed at working for Daniel, hated not being in complete control.

Daniel asked her to meet him in Singapore. They had dinner in a private room in a hotel. After they had exchanged pleasantries and ordered dinner, he spoke.

"I get the impression that you are no longer happy with our arrangements."

Annette was mildly surprised at his directness.

"I would prefer to be more involved on the client end," she replied

"I imagine so." Daniel took a sip of wine. "I think that unwise. They are an unsavory lot."

Annette shrugged. "Do you really think that I do not know the character of people who buy and sell this product?"

"Precisely. You are all too familiar. My clients would recognize this immediately. They would never respect you."

Annette pretended to consider this at the same time that she struggled to contain the rage consuming her. She closed her eyes briefly and comforted herself with the image of her knife, tucked safely in her straw handbag.

"You have come far. I will concede that," he said. "You do a fine job procuring product that my clients appreciate. You would do well to simply enjoy the proceeds of your efforts."

The waiter placed their salads on the table. Annette tried to eat. Her face felt wooden as she smiled at Daniel.

"I certainly appreciate the business," she said at last. "I was just hoping for more involvement."

"It is best that our arrangements remain the same. I will keep you busy."

The rest of the meal was small talk and a bit of politics. Over cognac, Daniel outlined his latest requirements. He bade her goodnight as she got into a taxi.

She had the driver let her out a few blocks later and she walked back to the hotel. She stood in the shadows outside and saw Daniel talking to the concierge. He got into the elevator and she stepped into the lobby to see the elevator stop on the fifth floor. She went around to the back of the hotel. One of the busboys had propped the door open while he smoked. He ground out his cigarette and went back inside. Annette caught the door before it closed.

She waited a beat and then stepped inside. A housekeepers' cart was outside the laundry room. She peered into the laundry room where a heavyset woman was dozing on a chair next to the dryer. Annette eased the door open. She slid her hand inside the maid's uniform pocket and drew out what she hoped was the master entry card.

She went out the back door and re-entered the lobby. She approached the desk clerk.

"I need to call Mr. Carmichael. May I use your phone?"

"I believe Mr. Carmichael has gone out."

"May I leave him a message?"

"Certainly."

The clerk passed her a pen and paper. She scrawled on the paper and placed the note in the envelope he offered.

"You can give it to him tomorrow," she said.

She watched as the clerk wrote on the envelope and thanked him. She crossed the lobby and had an expresso at the hotel bar. When the clerk left his station, she took the elevator to the fifth floor.

She listened for a moment outside room 508. There was no light under the door.

The key card opened the door on the first swipe. Annette stepped into the suite. Daniel's suitcase was on a stand. The bed was turned down. A pair of pajamas were at the foot of the bed and the bedside lamp was on. A bucket of fresh ice topped the mini-bar. She peered under the bed and slid herself into her hiding place. She rested on her side, knife in hand.

Two hours later, the keypad buzzed. The door clicked shut and the chain slid into place. The bathroom door closed and the shower ran. A pair of feet in hotel slippers moved around the room. Papers rustled. The bedsprings moved and Daniel settled into bed. Ten minutes later, he switched off the bedside lamp. Thirty minutes after he began to snore, she eased from under the bed.

The room was very dark; the shades were closed. She could barely make out the man sleeping on his stomach. He was not a large man but she suspected that he was stronger than he looked. Surprise would be on her side but she still wished she had something to subdue him. She hoped he did not have a weapon. Had he not dismissed her, lumped her into the same category as Glory and the subjects she procured for his clients, she would not be here, rage-fueled.

Daniel moved in his sleep, rolling onto his side. His back was toward her. She stood stock still, holding her breath. Before she could consider her next move, he spoke.

"I know you are in here. I can smell you. I am flattered but you do nothing for me. Don't embarrass yourself."

She grabbed for his hair with her left hand, yanking his head back. He startled violently, flinching from her touch.

"Don't put your whore hands on me," he began.

Those were his last words. She slit his throat and then switched on the bedside lamp. Green eyes focused on her. He worked his lips, but could produce no sound.

"You underestimated me, Daniel. I will not be beholden to anyone. More than anything, I will not be disrespected."

He blinked in acknowledgment as blood seeped into the pillow and sheet. His limbs began to twitch and he reached for her, trying to sit up. It was of little effect.

She stood next to him and watched him die. She wiped the blade on a towel in the bathroom and washed her hands. His briefcase contained pages of handwritten notes, a set of keys and two remote controls. She placed all of these items in her large straw handbag and slipped her feet back into her shoes. A final check in the mirror and she left the suite, hanging the Do Not Disturb sign outside.

Annette left Singapore the next morning, hours before Daniel's body was discovered. By the time the horrified housekeeper found the body, Annette had let herself onto Daniel's compound in Phuket. She dismissed all of his staff, but not without lavish bonuses and glowing reference letters. After hiring her own housekeeper and gardener, and changing all the locks and the security system, she went to her place in Chaing Mai and watched the local papers and CNN international.

Daniel's death was reported but the name released was the one he had used to register at the hotel in Singapore, the one that was on his passport from New Zealand. She searched the internet periodically for any references to Daniel or his property in Phuket. After nine months she was satisfied that the property was hers, along with the contents of the safes she found in his wine cellar.

Chapter Seventeen

Phoebe and Kendall

Pregnant? Kendall was stunned. This on top of all the other crap that was becoming her life. Damien looked part excited and part jealous. He was, after all, the baby. Grandma clearly knew about this before their mother spilled the beans to her and Damien.

Kendall smiled at her mother. At least she could talk to Howard about this, tell him how she really felt. Her father was dead and her mother was pregnant. Great. What a weird family. The kids at school were going to have a field day gossiping about her in the fall.

Kendall excused herself and went to her room. Damien went outside to play with Magnet. Rebecca and Phoebe sat at the kitchen table. Rebecca poured Earl Grey into two teacups. Phoebe wondered where she had found those. She had to admit, tea brewed in a teapot did taste better. She nibbled at a peanut butter cookie.

"You mustn't worry so much," said Rebecca. "It is not good for the baby. Plenty of women raise children alone. So what if you have to move to a smaller house, cut back on expenses. You know that your dad and I will help you."

Phoebe smiled. "I know, Mom. It is just a lot to process. I hope this does not drive a deeper wedge between me and Kendall."

Phoebe felt Kendall pulling away from her a little more each day. She tried to take some of it as teenaged angst and attributed some to displaced grief. She wished she could reach Kendall somehow. The anxiety rose in her chest and her inner voice mocked her, told her that she could not do this, keep up this farce of being a good mother. Look, said that horrid voice, this unborn child's father is a rapist or a murderer or both. She had described the deaths as an accident to Kendall and Damien but sooner or later, they would figure out what had really happened. How would she answer those questions? How would she deal with their anger and confusion?

She took another bite of the cookie, mostly to please Rebecca. She washed it down with the tea and felt the lightest, but unmistakable flutter in her belly. She closed her eyes and touched her stomach. A faint smile played across her lips and faded. Tears sprang to her eyes.

"What is wrong, Phoebe? Are you ok?"

Phoebe opened her eyes.

"Nothing, really. Just hormonal."

She could not bring herself to share her broken heart with her mother, her grief that her beautiful daughter who had proven to be so extraordinarily strong would never meet the child in her womb. Her soul yearned for Eileen. She felt such an overwhelming sense of having failed her oldest daughter and now she was losing Kendall a bit more each day.

The morning of Eileen's service was oppressively hot. The path from the cabins to the graveyard was criss-crosssed with cobwebs. They stuck to Phoebe's face and hair. She carried the urn carefully, picking her way across the rocks and roots in her sandals. Damien held Magnet's leash. Kendall clutched several pieces of paper. Rebecca had a small cooler and a dozen yellow roses.

The little graveyard had been carefully weeded. Ranger Angie and several of her colleagues were in place. Trooper Weyson stood next to them, his hat over his heart. Preacher Elijah talked about family and love and Eileen resting in a peaceful place. Phoebe could only half listen as she fought the urge to throw herself on the ground and sob, to tear at her hair. The headstone was simple granite. "Eileen Marie Beloved Daughter 1998-2014." The hole in the ground looked impossibly deep, yet so small. How could this be all that remained of her child?

Kendall stepped forward. She began in a sturdy voice but her tone became tremulous.

"I loved my sister very much. I did not tell her that enough. I miss hearing her voice and talking to her about music. I can't play video games without her. I don't understand why this had to happen. Our family will never be the same."

Kendall's voice trailed off and she turned to Rebecca and buried her face in her grandmother's shoulder.

Phoebe held the urn to her chest. It was so very light. She closed her eyes and kissed it. Then she placed it into the hole in the ground. The rangers stepped forward to fill it in. Thunder rumbled in the distance. Rebecca placed the roses next to the headstone. The little group dispersed as fat raindrops began to fall and lightening flashed. They were all soaked to the skin by the time they reached the cabin.

It rained all afternoon and into the early evening. Damien was disappointed that the beach was closed. Kendall paced around the cabin. The rain finally stopped a little before nine. Phoebe took Magnet out. She had a flashlight but did not yet need it. Stars were beginning to appear and fireflies were out. She remembered Eileen as a toddler, chasing fireflies in the backyard and shouting with delight when she caught one and it lit up her cupped hands.

Before she realized it, she was on the path to the cemetery. Well, why not say good night to her baby? She switched the flashlight on and the beam danced in the trees. An owl hooted. She paused in the clearing. Maybe this was really just a dream and there was no headstone for Eileen Marie Beloved Daughter. Reluctantly, she trained her flashlight on the graveyard. The roses that Rebecca had placed next to the stone should have been ruined by the rain. They were arranged in a perfect heart shape.

"I know your heart broke."

Phoebe was not even surprised to see Raven.

"I have the same sorrow. It don't ever get better no matter what time go by. But this a good place for her. It peaceful. I expect my young-uns is glad for the company."

"How did you lose your children?" asked Phoebe.

"They took sick when I was forced to be a slave again and live on that old bastard's plantation. Not enough food or blankets that winter. They died on the same day. Noah in the morning and Elsie that afternoon."

"What do you mean you were forced to be a slave again?"

Raven smiled sadly. "My man was a Monacan Indian. He bought me from the old bastard and married me. I thought I was free and our children too. I lived free for seven years. My man took sick later and when he die, the old bastard come back for me. He gave some money to my man's brother and back to the plantation we went. Nobody said a word."

Phoebe heard such anguish in Raven's voice, in a ghost's voice. But it was unmistakable.

"What that old bastard didn't know was that I had another child. Delivered her myself in that slave cabin and sent her to my man's sister the same night. Now she a good woman. Nursed my baby along with her own. But my man's brother hated us black folks. He sold my baby girl right back to the old man. She worked with me at the plantation til she was growed. One morning, she just took off with my grandbaby. Wish I knew what ever became of that baby boy and my Sorel."

Raven continued before Phoebe could reply.

"As long as you have your kids you just go on. You have to. You worry bout them your whole life. Now you, you need to look after the children in your life and the one you got growing in you. I watch over this one here. Don't you fret now."

Phoebe blinked back hot tears. When she opened her eyes, Raven was gone. The yellow roses in the heart shape gleamed in the moonlight.

Phoebe woke unrested. Her back ached from the thin mattress. The plan was to sprinkle Roxie's ashes near the cemetery. This time Phoebe held Magnet's leash and Damien carried the cardboard box. The yellow roses were back in Rebecca's vase, petals intact. Rebecca smiled. There was a slight breeze. The air was much cooler than the day before. The kids took turns sprinkling handfuls of ash. Magnet whined.

The puppy stood suddenly, tail wagging furiously. Phoebe let him off the leash. He ran in circles around the clearing.

"He is chasing Roxie!" said Damien.

Damien's face was lit with joy. Magnet stopped suddenly and cocked his head. His ears pricked up and he trotted back to the cemetery. He licked at the air and then turned his head to the side, groaning in pleasure. He rolled over on his back kicking his legs in the air.

Phoebe looked at Kendall. She hoped her daughter could see whatever Damien had seen but Kendall was looking distractedly at the water through the trees, twirling a curl around her index finger.

• • •

July stretched into August. The days were humid and the cicadas hummed. Phoebe's mom tended to the kids while Phoebe worked. Phoebe felt a sense of desperation at her inability to focus on her caseload. She tried to engage Kendall but the girl was so distracted.

Phoebe made an appointment for Kendall to see a therapist. Kendall had flown into a rage in the car on the way to the appointment and had refused to speak at all during the session.

Phoebe could not find Eileen's phone anywhere but she had the service turned off. Howard had anticipated that and had paid for a new number and plan for the phone. Kendall continued to send him photos. He passed the photos and the information about the new baby via the safe deposit box.

Phoebe was getting a baby belly. Moises remarked that her color was better and her face was no longer too thin. She had managed to refinance the house and thought that they would be able to stay there, at least for a year or two longer. Magnet had grown too. He was Damien's shadow.

Ann told Howard that her customer was ready for Kendall. All he needed was to bring her to an address on the outskirts of Norfolk.

"Hi, Doll," said Howard when he called her late one night in mid-August. "How about we go to Busch Gardens?"

Kendall agreed at once; she had never been there. Her mother hated amusement parks.

The next morning after breakfast she told her grandmother that she would walk Magnet. She met Howard about a mile from the house. Belatedly, she wondered what to do with Magnet. She told Howard that the dog could not stay in the hot car. He looped the dog's leash around a guard rail. One of the neighbors would drive by and see him and call the number on the tag.

The puppy howled and tried to lunge after Howard's Toyota. Kendall felt a bit sorry for him but she was so excited to go to Busch Gardens that she forgot all about the dog. She chattered away and Howard smiled at her, asking a question here and there and occasionally leaning over to kiss her. Howard could not wait to be done with this one; she never shut up.

The ride to Norfolk took about three hours. He parked in the lot of an apartment building. Kendall looked perplexed.

"What are we doing here?" she asked.

"We are picking up a friend of mine. You will really like her."

Kendall was not at all sure she would like Howard's friend. She thought this day was just about her and Howard. She followed him into the building. It was not a particularly nice place and it smelled of fried food. She suddenly wished she was back at home. She was going to be in so much trouble. They climbed the stairs to the second floor and he rapped on the door marked 2-D. The door opened and Howard motioned for her to go first. She hesitated and looked into the apartment.

A slim blond woman with her hair pulled back in a severe bun was standing just inside the apartment.

"Come on in, Kendall. I have been wanting to meet you."

Kendall did not like the sound of that. She turned to look at Howard.

"Go on in, Kendall. I need to use the bathroom. Do you want a Coke?"

She stepped inside.

"Sure."

Kendall was thirsty. She followed the woman into the living room. It was small and dark.

"Sit down," said the woman. "Let me get you that soda."

The woman reappeared in a few minutes with a glass with ice and a can of Coke. She handed it to Kendall. Kendall poured some soda into the glass and took a long sip. Where was Howard? He was sure taking a long time. She felt suddenly lightheaded and laid her head against the back of the couch.

Phoebe was working on a response to a demand letter. The parents of a sixth-grader who had been showing off on the baby swing at an elementary school were seeking damages for the injuries he sustained when he jumped off the baby swing and it hit him in the head. The two students and teacher who had witnessed the incident all claimed he had been told to get off the baby swing and that he had been standing on top of it. Nothing in the medical record reflected any type of injury other than a scraped knee. That and a bruised ego, she thought. The witnesses all said the boy was screaming and crying hysterically and the other kids had laughed.

Her phone rang. It was a man she did not know. He explained that he lived in the neighborhood and had been out for a walk when he found Magnet leashed to a guard rail. He took the puppy back to his house for some water. She got his address and called her mother.

"What do you mean?" demanded Rebecca. "Kendall is walking him."

"How long ago did she leave?" asked Phoebe.

"Let's see, had to be an hour ago. Oh wait, it is already eleven. Maybe two hours."

Two hours? Kendall never ever volunteered to walk Magnet. She was clearly up to something. Phoebe went to fetch Magnet. He must have gotten away from her daughter who was walking him, she told him. But she wondered to herself how he had been leashed to the guardrail. She drove around the neighborhood. There was no sign of Kendall anywhere.

She went home. It was nearly noon. She waited an hour or two and then called Detective Nichols. He came at once. It felt surreal to Phoebe. How could she possibly have another child missing? She reassured herself that Kendall had done this before. Surely she would reappear before dinner.

But she did not come back. Phoebe hated that she had taken Kendall's cell phone away. At least then the police would have something to track.

"We were able to find folks before they invented cell phones. Besides, she has disappeared before and came back."

Nichols was trying to be positive. His officers were canvassing the neighborhood. An older woman had seen Kendall getting into a black car, she thought it was a Toyota or a Honda. That had been around ten this morning. A man was driving.

Phoebe gave Kendall's computer to Nichols for analysis. She told them about Kendall's contact with Howard. A sketch artist worked with Damien to get a description of Howard. An Amber Alert was issued. Night fell with no news.

"There is something I have to tell you," Phoebe said to Nichols.

He sat stock still and silent at her kitchen table. She laid down the passports from the strong box. She told him how she and Eileen had found the passports and the children's underwear in the house in Mitchell's Landing. The words tumbled out in a rush. He did not take any notes or ask any questions.

She waited for Nichols to get angry, tell her she had been withholding evidence. But he did none of that. Tears poured down her face, she felt like she might drown in humiliation. She drew in a shaky breath and Nichols reached over to put his hand on top of hers.

"Phoebe," he began, "you did not cause Kendall's disappearance. Your family is being targeted. Your husband was involved. Someone else is still involved, my guess is Annette Peterson. Maybe you should have told me about these passports a month ago but those items were not found by the officers who searched that place. In the end, this information is something for the families of these kids."

He gestured towards the little stack of blue passports. "I am going to give this information to the FBI. They will work with Interpol. We need to find Annette."

Phoebe could hardly breathe. What if Kendall had been taken out of the country?

One day gone turned into two, and then three. By the time Kendall had been missing for a week Phoebe did not know how she could go on. Damien's sad little face was the only thing that stirred her to get up from the couch where she was spending more and more of her days.

She was afraid to let him out of her sight. There was no way she could go to work. The partners at her firm had been understanding but she knew there would be a limit on their tolerance for lost revenue and the endless drama in Phoebe's life.

Phoebe knew that with every passing hour, her chances of ever seeing Kendall diminished. Phoebe could barely eat and she was not sleeping. She felt wooden. She had started to believe that she must have done something dreadful in a prior life to deserve such anguish. Rebecca's face was pinched with anxiety. Damien hardly spoke and he had started wetting his bed again.

The computer forensics team had recovered deleted messages and photos from Kendall's computer. They updated the Amber Alert to include Howard's photo. They received some calls from Lynchburg. Apparently, Howard was not named Howard but rather Steven Mitchell, a photographer, probably in his mid-twenties. He had not been seen in a week. A search of his condo had revealed an enormous cache of pornographic photos and videos, many of which involved children. Phoebe's heart sank to even greater depths when she heard this. The FBI was now involved and attempting to identify victims. Three of the subjects were missing children. Selena Martinez was mentioned, as was Margaret Lewis. Phoebe felt the last drop of hope drain from her.

Rebecca was guilt stricken. If only she had gone with Kendall to walk Magnet. If only she had noticed sooner that Kendall had been gone too long. If only she had thought how strange it was for Kendall to offer to walk the dog. Phoebe was going to have to send Rebecca home; it was like caring for another child. Phoebe's own grief and anxiety were enough to bear without having to console her own mother.

Chapter Eighteen

Kendall

Kendall opened her eyes. Her head was throbbing. The room was dark. Was it night-time? She drew the curtain back and looked out into a parking lot. It was full dark. Where was Howard? They should have been at Busch Gardens. She reached into her pocket for her cell phone but it was gone. She tried the door. Locked. She banged on the doors and walls and screamed to be let out. There was no response. She tried to open the window but it was painted shut.

She sat down on the bed and began to cry. She missed her mom and Damien. Why had Howard done this to her? She was so stupid. What seventeen year old boy would really be interested in an eighth grader? This was the kind of thing the school safety officers were always going on about, creepy people who stalked kids on the internet. This was exactly what her mom had warned her about.

She had to pee. Bad. Either there was no bathroom or she was locked out of it. She opened the door to the closet and squatted down in the corner. Would serve that mean looking lady right to have to clean that up. It was stuffy in the room. It would start to smell soon, and worse if she had to poop in the closet. She lay back down on the bed and stared at the ceiling.

Dawn was streaking the sky outside the dirty window when she heard a door opening in another room. The door to the bedroom unlocked. It was the mean woman. Kendall did not move. The mean woman had a paper bag. It smelled good. The door closed behind the woman. Kendall's stomach growled. She ate the ham and egg sandwich and drank the orange juice.

Another day had passed before the woman returned. The room stank of sweat and shit.

"Clean up your mess." The woman left rags and a bucket of water with PineSol.

Kendall wept as she scrubbed the closet floor. She was hungry but she was afraid to eat the food the lady left. She did not want to have to clean again. After a time though, she ate the turkey and cheese sandwich and drank the coke.

Kendall lost track of the days. She was rank. There were some old clothes in one of the drawers and she wore some of them. The mean woman brought her food once a day, along with the bucket and rags. The woman rarely spoke, except to order Kendall to clean up. Her face was pinched and her hair was always tied back in a severe ponytail. Sometimes the woman scratched at her left shoulder, like it really itched. Kendall had asked her why she was locked up but the woman did not even look at her.

• • •

Howard was secretly glad that Kendall had been knocked out by whatever Ann put into her soda. He hated to think what kind of a scene she would have made if she saw him leave her in that disgusting apartment. He had been drained enough by all her babbling on the way to Norfolk. He was always glad when a subject was delivered. He was ready for a new project. He was thinking about a movie, maybe doing something on the soft side that would get him some public acclaim.

The safe deposit box for the Kendall job was in Roanoke. He drove straight from Norfolk, barely arriving in time before the Bank of America branch closed for the day. He was supposed to leave all his notes and correspondence about the case in the box and pick up his funds. Ann had warned him repeatedly about the folly of keeping any paperwork on his subjects. He had nodded at her and disregarded what he thought to be a self-serving admonition on Ann's part. Although he left all his original paperwork on Kendall in the safe deposit box, he had already copied it all. He would file it in the self-storage locker he rented in Danville.

You never knew when that stuff would come in handy, he thought to himself as he thumbed the wad of bills. He would deposit the money in a bank account at the Credit Union. He had not eaten since breakfast and stopped at a Waffle House on Route 460. It was getting dark when he got back on the road and headed for Lynchburg. He was ready for a shower and a beer. About five miles east of Roanoke his car began to hesitate. Puzzled, he looked down at the gas gauge. It was nearly half full but the engine and oil lights were on. The car was steadily losing power.

"Fuck."

He did not need this. There was not much between where he was and Bedford. He was going to have to call Triple A. God knew how long they would take to get there. He put his hazards on and got the car onto the shoulder right before the engine quit. He popped the hood and got out. Mechanical, he was not but he could maybe see if something was obviously wrong. He studied the contents of the engine. No clue. He sighed and drew out his phone to call Triple A.

"Need some help, man?"

Howard whirled around. He had not heard another car pull up. Two good ole boys in greasy jeans were approaching.

"I have no idea what is wrong. Oil light and engine light are on."

One of the guys was using the dipstick.

"Got no oil at all in here. Must have a bad leak."

The other guy looked under the car with his cigarette lighter. That seemed like a bad idea to Howard.

"Yep, big old puddle of oil here. Probably the engine seized."

The first guy considered this.

"Yeah. We could give you a lift up to the Sheetz."

"I'd appreciate that."

Howard grabbed his backpack out of his car and climbed into the back seat of the pickup truck. They pulled back onto 460 and he took out his cell phone to call Triple A.

"You don't want to do that."

Howard looked up. The guy in the front passenger seat was pointing a .38 at him.

"I have money. Just let me out of here and I will give it to you."

"How much you got?" asked the driver.

"Three thousand."

Howard was lying.

They seemed to consider that.

"Nah, this ain't about your money," said the man holding the gun. " It ain't personal to us. But you got some folks who want you gone."

Ann. It had to be her. He knew too much. Maybe she assumed he kept records. He nodded. He was not going to beg for his life.

"How much are they paying you?"

"Plenty of money," said the driver. "Plus, you know how these folks are. They got dirt on us they'll use in a heartbeat. We got family too. We got priorities."

"What if I told you that I have more than enough dirt on them, shared it with you? Could get you out of your mess too." Howard tried to keep his voice calm.

"Nope," said the man with the gun. "Sorry, but it is just too complicated. Just like my relationship on Facebook." His companion thought that was hilarious.

The driver had turned off 460 onto a side road. It was full dark now. There was no moon. They pulled onto a dirt road and stopped. It looked like an abandoned construction site. The front seat passenger motioned to Howard to get out of the car.

Howard's life ended with a single shot to the back of his head. Had the good ole boys known how many children Howard had delivered to a near certain life of abuse and torture, they might have been more creative. They heaved his body into an ancient dumpster. They were quite pleased to discover not only the three thousand Howard had tried to ply them with but an additional seven.

The cops noticed his car on the shoulder of 460 later that night and towed it to an impound lot in Roanoke where it sat unclaimed for several months and was eventually sold at auction. Three nights later, a carload of teenagers parked at the abandoned house site to drink a bottle of whiskey. When one of them went into the bushes to take a piss, he noticed a terrible odor. Must be a dead deer out there somewhere he told his friends. It wasn't until late fall that a realtor who had been given the listing for foreclosure of the half-finished house that Howard's body was discovered. The FBI office in Roanoke notified the task force working on the Annette Peterson case that her last known accomplice was deceased.

• • •

Kendall passed the days watching the sunlight through the dirty window. Sometimes she heard children playing outside. Their shouts and laughter made her long for the playground, even in her dumb old babyish elementary school. Once or twice, she heard something like music or a TV through the walls. She had stopped crying. It made her tired and it was not helping at all. She felt rage when she thought of Howard. If she ever saw him again, she would scratch his eyes out. She spent a lot of time picturing herself reporting him to the police.

She slept a lot. It helped but she knew she was just trying to escape the nightmare by dreaming of her real life. One afternoon, maybe the ninth or tenth day she was locked in the fetid room, she dreamed of a little boy and his mother. They were running through a thick forest. She could hear men shouting in the distance. She could feel their fear. The mother, her long brown hair tied back with a strip of black cloth, scooped up the little boy in her arms. He was exhausted, trying not to cry.

In the dream, Kendall was in a cave in the forest. She had to help them. She ran out toward the boy and his mother. She would hide them in her cave. The men were closer, angry.

"They mean to eat him," said the boy's mother.

She was panting with exertion. Her face was gaunt.

"Those men have no soul," said the woman with the long hair.

The cave, she must hide them in the cave. Kendall tried to speak but her voice had no sound. She reached out to take the little boy's hand and drew him toward the cave. He collapsed into her arms. His mother stumbled and fell. Her head struck a rock with a dreadful sound.

"Take Sachel. Hide my boy."

The mother's voice was exhausted and despairing. Blood was running down her face from a deep scalp wound.

Kendall lifted Sachel. He felt light as a feather compared with Damien. She darted into the cave. She covered the little boy's ears as his mother's screams filled the air. The little boy turned his tear-stained face towards her. Sachel's voice was a whisper in her ear.

"There is another way out of here. Think. Look carefully."

He laid his head on her chest and slept.

The boy's mother had stopped screaming. Kendall heard no more shouting. She thought she should check outside to be sure but the little boy was so tired. He had barely stirred. She stroked his cheek.

"I will take care of him now. You must go. Find your way out. You can."

Kendall turned towards that voice, that familiar voice. Eileen smiled at her. She looked older and wore an old fashioned looking dress. Kendall gaped at her. Eileen lifted the sleeping boy off Kendall's lap. Kendall stood up and reached for her sister but she touched only the sunlight.

Kendall woke in a cold sweat. It was nighttime. She had slept through the mean lady's visit. The bucket and clothes were there and a bag of fast food. She must have really been out. She turned the light on and began to look at each corner of the room. The walls were paneled, a cheap fake pine. The dream kept tugging at her mind. Another way out. The doors and the windows were obvious, and blocked.

She went into the closet. She ignored the piss stink and studied the walls. She pushed at them but they seemed pretty solid. The music and TV noises she had heard had come from the left side of the room. She pulled at each of the panels in the back of the closet in the left corner. One was loose and came off in her hand, revealing a rough wall under it, streaked with glue. She looked around her prison for something hard, something to bang against that plank. Not much to choose from but she settled on sliding the top drawer out of the dresser. She began to bash it against the rough plank. It chipped and gave a little bit. She bashed harder.

"What the fuck?"

The voice was faintly irritated.

"Help!" Kendall screamed as loud as she could and kept banging.

"Who dat bangin' at my wall at three inna mornin?"

"Help me, please!"

She heard nothing for a minute or two. Then a sharp rapping and wood splintering. A hole appeared where the panel had been and an eye met hers. It blinked.

"Girl, whatcha doin'?"

More splintering.

"You aight?"

"No," said Kendall. "I have been kidnapped."

"Jesus Christ. Can't I get a decent night's sleep?"

More banging and a portion of the wall gave in. A large black arm reached into the room and yanked her through the hole. She stumbled and found herself in a bedroom similar to the one where she had been held.

"Damn, girl, you stink."

Kendall's eyes filled with tears. The man was a giant in flannel pajama pants and a white tank top.

"How long you been in there?"

"I am not sure. Since Friday the eighth, I think."

The giant shook his head.

"Twelve days. You look like you need a bath and a good meal. I need this shit like a hole in the head. Goddamn."

He did not seem angry.

"Well, I got a hole in my wall and a gal who needs to get out of dodge. Come on, now. Let's take you to my girl's place."

Kendall followed him. Normally, she would never have gone anywhere with a stranger, much less one as large as this one but normal had ceased to be. He had a large battered white van. She climbed in gratefully. He sang under his breath to the Naughty by Nature CD in his stereo. Kendall only recognized the song because she had heard her mother sing along to her iPod. "OPP, you know me." She bobbed her head along with the music.

He turned and looked at her. His smile was broad.

"You know this song?"

"My mom likes this one."

He laughed out loud.

"You ok."

A few minutes later, the old van pulled up to a small white house. The giant opened the door for Kendall. She climbed down and followed him to the front door. A tiny woman stood there. Her hair was in braids and her complexion was olive.

"Jerrod, what is this?" asked the woman.

"This little gal, she need help. Some food and a bath, to start. Then we gots to find her folks."

The tiny woman trained her green eyes on Kendall.

"Child, you look terrible," said the woman.

She drew Kendall into the house. The kitchen was lit by candlelight. There was a bouquet of daisies on a black and red checkered tablecloth. The woman bustled around the kitchen and a plate of scrambled eggs with cheese and ham and toast appeared before Kendall. She tore into the food.

In the corner Jerrod and the tiny woman were huddled.

"Iris, don't be mad. I went out for a drink with the boys and went back to my place. Then I heard this little thing on other side of the wall crying for help."

Iris raised her eyebrows at him.

"I don't want to hear your stories. That can wait. This child needs help."

Her eyes widened. "That is the girl from the Amber Alert."

Kendall half heard all this. She was too busy eating her toast and eggs. They were nearly as good as her mom's. Iris led her to the bathroom and gave her a towel and a t-shirt and sweatpants. The hot water was delicious and the scent of the shampoo intoxicating. When she emerged, she was nearly sleepwalking.

"Lay down for a bit, child," said Iris. "Your name is Kendall, right? Can you give us your mama's phone number?"

Kendall whispered the numbers as she slid under the blanket in Iris's bed. She was asleep before her eyes closed.

Iris and Jerrod were arguing in hushed voices.

"We need to contact the police and get her home." Iris was insistent. "Her mother has to be out of her mind with worry."

Jerrod shook his head. "You know I can't be connected to this."

Iris sighed. "I don't know why I put up with you. Must be your soft spot for kids."

Jerrod leaned in and kissed her on the lips.

"Since you gave away your bed to that poor kid," he said, "I guess we are both on the couch."

Iris sighed. Jerrod was on probation after doing six years for possession with intent to distribute. He was working for Goodwill and trying to land a job with the Post Office. He was supposed to be living with his mother. Although his parole officer knew about Iris, he was not aware that Jerrod kept a separate apartment in a questionable area of Norfolk, where he hung out with his old friends. Iris did not think that Jerrod was using or dealing but she assumed his friends were still part of that life.

Jerrod was torn. If the police were to learn where and how Kendall had been rescued, they would surely find out about his apartment, maybe dig around in his background, talk to his parol officer. On the other hand, whoever had snatched Kendall in the first place deserved to be caught.

In the end, they decided to contact his parole officer first, then Kendall's mother.

Phoebe looked at the caller ID on her phone. A private number at five in the morning. She answered quickly, trying not to think about what the call might mean. It was a woman who identified herself as Iris. Iris was telling her that she had Kendall, that she seemed alright, she was sleeping at the moment. Could Phoebe come and get her, and not call the police just yet? Iris would text her a photo of Kendall and explain everything when Phoebe got there. A moment later, a picture of her daughter flashed across her screen. She was sleeping soundly under a quilt, wearing a borrowed t-shirt. She looked thin but unharmed. Phoebe felt a relief so strong that her knees buckled and she nearly blacked out.

Phoebe loaded a sleeping Damien into his booster seat. For good measure, she put Magnet into the back of the wagon. He had grown a bit. A pit bull was imposing, even if this one had nothing but affection in his demeanor and food and a romp in the woods on his agenda. She texted Moises. She did not call Nichols. She would only do so once she had her daughter back.

Jefferson Thomas had seen it all in his twenty-seven years in Norfolk's criminal justice system. He viewed Jerrod Brown as low risk, one who might be able to turn it around. He had been working and making all his meetings. He wondered what sort of mess Brown was in to be calling him at six in the morning on a Sunday.

Iris opened the door to Thomas. Jerrod was drinking coffee at the kitchen table. Iris offered Thomas a mug. He sipped and listened.

Jerrod explained that he kept an apartment in his old neighborhood, just for a little personal space. Sometimes he liked to play cards there, with his boys. He had gone there last night and was just getting ready to turn in when he heard someone calling for help. Thomas nodded and motioned for Jerrod to go on.

There was a tentative knock at the door. Iris looked through the peephole. She opened the door. Phoebe stood in the doorway, Damien held her right hand and Magnet's leash was in her left. The pit bull began wagging his tail. He sniffed the air and barked happily.

"Pretty ferocious dog you got there," Jerrod said with a smile and held out his hand. Phoebe clasped his hand. Magnet whined and strained at the leash.

"I think he knows someone is here," said Iris. "Go ahead, let him off the leash. We love dogs."

Thomas watched all of this closely. Magnet bounded out of the kitchen and down the narrow hallway. A shriek of delight followed. Phoebe sank to her knees. Damien's eyes widened. A moment later, Kendall stepped into the kitchen. Her curly hair was a mass of tangles and the borrowed sweatpants sagged around her narrow waist. She collapsed into Phoebe's arms. Damien grabbed Kendall around the neck.

"Thank you," Phoebe whispered, looking at Iris.

Jerrod offered his hand and Phoebe stood awkwardly, her belly made her clumsy now. Thomas got up from his place at the kitchen table and offered her his chair.

It was Kendall who told the story. It poured out of her. Her stupid friendship with Howard and how he had tricked her into thinking he liked her and was taking her to Busch Gardens. She was so sorry, mom. The days and days she had been held captive by the mean blond lady. She never thought she would see Damien and Magnet again. When she said this Magnet licked her cheek and wagged his tail. Banging on the wall and having Jerrod answer, pull her out of her prison. Iris made her eggs, so good they almost tasted like her mom's. Phoebe and Iris exchanged a smile at this.

Finally, Kendall ran out of words. She slumped, exhausted, in Phoebe's arms. Iris handed her a mug of hot chocolate and offered one to Damien.

Thomas spoke first. First, he said, he was very grateful to Jerrod for finding Kendall. And to Iris for contacting Phoebe. They had done the right thing, he said firmly. Phoebe nodded in agreement. Thomas would contact the local authorities and Phoebe should contact the Fairfax police.

"Thank God," breathed Detective Nichols when Phoebe reached him. "Can you stay put there for a few hours? We want to delay any public announcement that Kendall has been found."

He went on to say that he did not want Phoebe and the kids to return to Fairfax, not until Annette had been apprehended. Give him an hour or two to work things out.

Phoebe hated to impose on Jerrod and Iris. They had been beyond kind. They brushed off her thanks.

"That gal, she ain't safe yet." Jerrod was firm. "The folks that are behind this, be looking for her. But they won't get to her here. My boys, been out front watching since before we got here last night." He smiled.

"I did not hear that," said Thomas, but his eyes were kind. "You did the right thing. Next week, we will talk about the wisdom of you keeping that apartment but for now, you got no worries with me."

He stood up, and offered his hand to Jerrod and tipped his hat at Phoebe and Iris.

Phoebe was confused. "Who was he?"

Jerrod laughed. "He my parole officer. We cool."

Iris made pancakes and bacon. Kendall and Damien tucked into the food, while Magnet hovered beneath the table. Jerrod fed him a scrap of bacon when Phoebe's back was turned. He winked at the kids.

It was late morning when Nichols arrived to tell them that they were being moved to a safe house west of Norfolk. The house in Fairfax was staked out as was the apartment building where Kendall had been held. The hope was that Annette would show up and they would nab her. Phoebe had her doubts; the woman was pure evil and would not be taken easily. She wondered if they would ever be free of her.

A van showed up an hour later. Iris hugged Kendall tightly and Jerrod kissed the top of her head. Iris pressed a piece of paper into Phoebe's hand.

"Will you let me know that you are safe?" Iris asked.

Phoebe nodded and plugged Iris's number into her cell phone.

"You need me, you just call." Jerrod said firmly.

Kendall smiled at him and then flung herself into his arms.

"Thank you," she whispered.

Chapter Nineteen

Phoebe

The safe house was west of Norfolk, an apartment on the top floor of an older, four story building. They went in through the loading dock and up the service elevator. Nichols told them to keep the blinds closed.

Phoebe felt instantly claustrophobic. Nichols must have sensed that; he told her that an officer would walk outside with her and Magnet whenever she asked. There were three bedrooms, a small living room, and a galley kitchen. A bulky television was in one of the bedrooms. Phoebe hoped that it at least got Cartoon Network.

An officer was placed in the apartment with them. Another pair of officers was outside patrolling on foot and in their vehicle. Phoebe chafed at the restriction against contacting anyone, or using her cell phone at all. Surely Rebecca and Moises would worry. Nichols was adamant. The Amber Alert had not been cancelled; the longer Annette and whoever she was working with thought Kendall was still in their control, the easier it would be to find them.

After Marion had spoken with Kendall, and assessed that she had been drugged, at least initially, Eva arrived and drew blood. Surprisingly, Kendall did not complain. Phoebe watched as Eva examined Kendall, dreading what she might discover. But Eva found no evidence of any physical assault. Phoebe wept in relief when Kendall left the room. Marion patted her shoulder and put her notes into her briefcase.

"You have good kids," Marion said. Phoebe could only smile weakly.

An FBI profiler spent some time talking to Kendall, teasing out details about what Annette had said, how she had looked, what she had done. How long had she left Kendall alone in the apartment? What did Kendall remember about the time in the apartment?

Phoebe puzzled on Annette's motivation. Was it revenge for David's death, or did she have a plan to sell Kendall overseas? David had talked about insurance money; was it possible for Annette to have taken out a policy on Kendall? Was Damien in danger too? Would they have to live the rest of their lives looking over their shoulders, their home, wherever it might be, a fortress?

The profiler, a gaunt black-haired man with still eyes, tried to be reassuring.

"We have her on the defensive. We have names and photos associated with missing kids as well as where those children were taken. Interpol is working the case. We have current information on her whereabouts."

Phoebe willed herself to focus on the good. Damien and Kendall snuggled on the couch. Magnet lay at her feet. The dog raised his eyebrows if Phoebe so much as moved a muscle. The child in her belly rolled regularly but the motion made her edgy. Six hours earlier she was certain that her daughter was gone forever. Now she had this unexpected second chance. Why didn't she feel better?

She could not relax. The apartment felt like a prison. Her skin crawled with anxiety. That night she paced the three rooms until the sky in the east turned pink. It was as if the years of managing all the details of a contained and organized life had worn away her sanity and exposed raw nerve, pure anger. Anger at David, anger at Annette but most of all, anger at herself and her self-inflicted blindness and inadequacy. She fought the urge to scream, to slap herself, to chain smoke, anything to release the boiling inside her soul. She had lost all fear for herself; all that mattered now was the safety and happiness of her children. She would gladly kill herself if it would help them, if it would get Annette to leave them alone.

Her skin erupted. Her hands and feet swelled. She gritted her teeth and willed herself not to show this ugliness, this self-loathing, to the children. She felt the weight of her failure in every cell. She flinched at every sound. Her mind played an endless loop of Eileen's death, of cigarette man and white glove man. She could not let Damien and Kendall out of her sight.

After four days in the safe house, with no signs or sightings of Annette, she thought she might lose her mind. Nichols must have sensed something in her voice, a ragged edge perhaps, an inkling that she was teetering on the very edge of sanity.

Nichols rapped quietly at the door. Phoebe sat bolt upright from the couch where she had been trying in vain to sleep for a few minutes. Magnet wagged his tail. She opened the door to Moises and Nichols. Moises gave her a long look and shook his head. He whirled on Nichols.

"What good is it doing to keep them hidden here? Look at her. She looks like death warmed over. This can't be good for the baby. Those children need to be outside, with their friends, playing. This is no way for anyone to live."

Moises grimaced at the take-out food containers in the garbage and started to wash the dishes.

Nichols looked chagrined. He nodded. Phoebe buried her face in her hands and sobbed quietly.

"This is all my fault," Phoebe sniffed. "If I hadn't ignored the signs that something was really wrong with David, hadn't been all too happy to have him travel, lived my life around him. If I had left him years ago, Eileen would still be alive."

Phoebe wiped at her nose with the sleeve of her sweatshirt. She looked up at Nichols.

"I know you are doing your best to keep us alive. Believe me, I appreciate that."

Phoebe looked down at her hands. She was certain Nichols could see the blood on them. Not just cigarette man's blood as she plunged the knife into his back, but Eileen's lifeblood as she cradled her dying child, even David's blood on the black and white tiles in the bathroom. She closed her eyes on the kaleidescope of memories but they were imprinted on the inside of her eyelids.

"Can we please just go home?" Kendall's voice was soft. "I want to sleep in my bed with my stuffed animals."

"We haven't found Annette yet," began Nichols.

Phoebe waved him off.

"Don't you see? If we stay here, we are still her victims. These kids start school next week. I need to earn a living. We can't stay holed up here forever."

"I can't guarantee your safety." Nichols was resigned.

"We're going home," said Phoebe.

Nichols insisted on sending a team to the house first to sweep for monitoring devices and be certain that the house was secure. He asked them to wait until the next morning to return home.

"That's fine," said Moises. "But I am taking them all to the beach today. Send a detective with us if you want. These children need sunshine and fresh air and some good food. Even that dog can come."

Magnet licked Moises' hand and thumped his tail. Moises fussing made Phoebe smile for the first time in days.

Moises had rented a suite overlooking the southern, dog-friendly end of Virginia Beach. It was a hot day but not humid. They stopped at Target to buy bathing suits and sunscreen. The air on Phoebe's face felt soft. The sea gulls' calling was soothing. She breathed deeply as she walked in the surf.

Later that evening, after Moises had stuffed them with rice and beans and steak and salad, Phoebe kissed her children's sunburned cheeks and tucked them into one of the double beds in her room. Kendall was clutching Damien like one of her stuffed animals. She looked at them for a long time and then closed the door.

Phoebe sat out on the balcony and listened to the surf. Sleep was far away. Magnet whined at her feet, a sure sign that he needed to go out. She peered in at the kids and listened to their deep breathing and then softly closed the door. The shower in Moises' bathroom was running. She would just take the puppy outside quickly and be back before Moises was out of the bathroom.

She kicked her flip flops off and left them on the boardwalk. She let Magnet off his leash and he bounded into the water. Earlier, he had tried to drink from the ocean and turned and looked at her with a wounded expression. He barked once, sharply. She could barely make him out, racing down the beach away from her. She called to him but he ignored her. The night seemed much darker. She glanced over her shoulder. The hotels and boardwalk were gone.

Of course. It would come to this. A figure walked towards her. Magnet barked furiously now. A woman with a knife in her hand. Phoebe felt a strange relief. At last a chance to confront the woman who had tortured her children, brought out the monster in her husband, robbed Phoebe of her peace of mind and changed their lives forever.

"You." The thin blond woman stopped in front of Phoebe. She had a strange scar on her left shoulder that gleamed in the moonlight.

"You are the one who ruined all my plans. When will you learn that no one stops me? Those children are mine; David was mine. You took him from me."

She stepped forward menacingly. Her eyes glittered feverishly.

"No," said Phoebe. "You may have manipulated and used my husband but these children are most certainly not your children. None of the children you have stolen and abused are yours. You have no right to hurt or use or take another human being."

"Bitch! You don't know how you are talking to! I cannot be stopped and I will not be disrespected."

"She may not know who you be, but I sure 'nuff do."

The man's voice was familiar but Phoebe could not see him in the darkness. She strained to see his face.

Annette whirled around.

"Look at your arm," said the man.

He stepped forward and Phoebe saw his face. Amos grabbed Annette by the shoulder and held her arm up in the moonlight. He twisted her arm savagely and Annette dropped the knife.

"Marked for the devil you is. Just like that no-account man you was running with. Pity Phoebe and her poor child got to him. He died a whole lot kinder than he deserved to."

Phoebe heard shouts in the distance. Amos turned in the direction of the voices.

"Ah yea, here they come." His teeth gleamed in his dark face.

Out of the darkness ran a young woman clutching a little boy in her arms.

"Here we are, Amos. I hope we are in time."

The woman was barefoot and wearing a long dress. She was panting and her chest was heaving.

"Give me that child and catch your breath." Amos held out one arm; with the opposite hand he gripped Annette by the hair.

"Come here, Sachel," said Amos.

The little boy's eyes were wide and fearful.

"Don't let them get us, please," said Sachel.

"Ah, don't worry. Ain't you they are going to get."

The young woman stepped closer to Phoebe.

"Mom," she whispered in Phoebe's ear. "It is going to be alright."

Phoebe's heart fluttered in her chest. "I must be dreaming," she murmured as she reached for Eileen.

"It's not a dream mom. It's the other place, the world before and the world after and the world between."

"I don't really understand," began Phoebe.

Amos's voice boomed out. "Here is the one you want."

A group of four or five men appeared. They were painfully thin and wore tattered clothes. They had sticks and rocks in their hands. Annette struggled in Amos' grip. She scratched at her scarred shoulder.

"Let me go!" Annette's scream was shrill.

"Ain't no mercy for the likes of you."

Amos thrust Annette towards the men. They fell upon her but Amos stopped them for a moment.

"This one is more evil than you are. Take her away from here. Just know the reckoning, it always come."

The men dragged Annette away. Her screams of terror and rage reached them for a while and then faded.

Sachel was the first to speak. He tugged at Phoebe's arm.

"Are you Eileen's mama?"

"Yes, sweetie I am. It is so good to see her." Phoebe smiled at him.

Sachel regarded her gravely.

"I am sorry she had to leave you. You see, the hungry men, they took my mama. But Eileen, she kept me safe."

Sachel buried his face in Eileen's skirt.

Phoebe's eyes filled with tears. "She will take good care of you."

Phoebe turned to Amos. "Thank you for letting me see my daughter, for watching out for her."

Amos nodded solemnly. "The good, it always shine through. You won't likely see this one again. But you still have work to do in the world in between, folks that need your help in quieting the pain in their hearts and answering the questions in their souls."

Phoebe reached towards Eileen. She could almost feel Eileen, like the embrace of a moonbeam. Her daughter smiled and shone in the starlight. Eileen reached down for Sachel. The little boy waved at Phoebe and then Amos, Eileen and Sachel turned and walked away. Phoebe closed her eyes against tears and when she opened them, they were gone. Magnet was next to her. He looked down the beach and wagged his tail.

She turned back towards the hotel. Of course it was there, lights shining. Magnet trotted happily at her side.

Two weeks later, the Norfolk police reported the discovery of the skeletal remains of a white female washed up on the beach after a storm off the coast. Forensic evidence indicated that she might have been the victim of cannibals; there were human teeth marks on some of the bones. Phoebe feigned surprise when Nichols told her a week after that that DNA indicated that the remains were of Annette Peterson. Nichols told her that he had never worked such a strange case. Phoebe knew he still suspected that she knew more than she had told him but he never pressed her.

Summer was giving way to fall. Kendall clung to Phoebe and avoided places she had previously begged to be driven to, like the mall or the movies. Phoebe got Kendall a new phone and computer but Kendall barely touched them. Instead, Kendall started keeping a journal and insisted that Magnet and sometimes Damien sleep in her room. Phoebe did not think her daughter was depressed. She was not withdrawn or sad; it was more that Kendall was surrounding herself with the things that comforted her.

The kids went back to school. Kendall cried when Phoebe kissed her goodbye in the kiss and ride line but she came home calm and Phoebe could hear her up in her room, doing her homework while she chatted with a friend on Skype.

Phoebe went to Damien's second grade parent-teacher conference. She smiled quietly when the teacher showed her Damien's drawings of Magnet and Roxie chasing butterflies. Phoebe shrugged when the teacher asked if the dogs were in a graveyard.

"That one, he has a vivid imagination," was all that Phoebe said to the teacher.

Phoebe's belly grew larger and her runs with Magnet got slower. The leaves turned. The house seemed more settled. Magnet grew into his paws but was still a puppy at heart.

Nichols stopped by from time to time with updates on Interpol's search for the missing children. Two had been located and were being reintroduced to their families. The mother of one of the girls located had sent a note thanking Phoebe for stepping forward with information. Phoebe began to feel slightly better, almost an easing of her conscience and a loosening of her taut heartstrings.

Eileen's sixteenth birthday would have been the first weekend of November. Phoebe planted yellow and purple mums next to her gravestone. They spent a weekend at the lake. Phoebe visited the graveyard hoping for a glimpse of Raven or a sign of the children. There were none.

The morning they left, Kendall woke agitated.

"Mom, I had the weirdest dream. There was this old lady, over where Eileen is buried. She was looking for you, said she had seen some lost young people in the woods." Kendall's voice trailed off.

Phoebe waited. Kendall looked out the window towards the woods. Kendall pointed.

"See, right over there?" said Kendall.

Phoebe could not see anything. Damien stood up.

"You mean those kids? Those big kids over there?" Damien's voice rose in excitement.

"Yes," said Kendall.

"They're teenagers," said Damien. "and they're playing with Elsie and Noah."

He walked out to the porch and down the steps into the clearing. Magnet trailed him. He stopped, talking. After a bit, he nodded and returned to the porch.

"They were kids who got taken from their parents and died somewhere else," he reported. "Selene and Jason and I forget the other ones' names. Elsie and Noah's mom said you might know them, could tell her if they were good souls."

Phoebe smiled. "Go tell their mom that I know of these children and they deserve to be here."

Damien skipped happily off the porch. Kendall trailed behind. Phoebe sank into a rocker and watched. Sunlight dappled the clearing and boat engines roared in the distance. She closed her eyes in gratitude for having been a part of all of Eileen's life and even more for knowing her child's final resting place.

But Raven, Phoebe though, Raven needed to know what became of Sorel and her baby boy. Maybe this was what Amos meant when he talked of the work in the world in between.

Thanksgiving was chilly but clear. Phoebe put the turkey in the oven and went for a hike with Magnet. Rebecca was making apple pie. She fussed at Phoebe to take her cell phone and not to go too far.

Phoebe and Magnet picked their way down the dirt road near the site of the old field hospital. The collie in the yard of the ranch house barked frantically. She wondered if she had lost her ability to see the past. After all, she had not seen any of the children or Raven at the lake. Magnet drank noisily from the creek. He paused, lifted his head. Water dripped from his chin as he stared intently at the bushes on the opposite bank. A figure stood in the shade, a woman in a grey dress.

Phoebe stepped into the stream. The woman held up her hand.

"Ma'am, don't be wetting your feet in your condition. Best be mindful of that child."

Sorel's voice was gentle, more serene. She looked older than Phoebe remembered.

"Are you alright?" Phoebe asked.

"Oh yes, I am. Thanks be to you. Only regret I have in this world is not knowing what became of my boy, that little child I sent north so long ago."

There was a hint of wistfulness in her voice. "And I know I will never again see my mama." She smiled. "I do dream of my Petrel."

Phoebe reached for Sorel's arm. "I have seen your son. He did me a great kindness. He was a man of courage."

"I did pray he was raised right. I hoped he would be a good man, stand up for himself and what is right. I worried so." Sorel nodded firmly.

"And your mama, would that be Raven?" asked Phoebe.

"Yes, ma'am. Last I saw of her she was setting by the grave of my brother and sister."

"And she is still there. But now she keeps watch over more children. My oldest is with her. Your mama is such a source of strength for me. She made me see the good in the world when everything was so terrifying and I was lost."

Sorel sighed. "It do give me some comfort to know this."

Magnet barked sharply at two deer bounding in the underbrush. When Phoebe turned her eyes back from watching the flash of white tails, Sorel was gone.

Christmas approached. Dr. Sayers thought the baby would be born in late January. Moises and his mother came for Christmas Eve. It was unseasonably warm, actually balmy, and they had coffee and cake on the porch. Carmen cleared away the last of the dishes, insisting that Phoebe stay off her feet.

"Flaca, is that a light in the woods?" Moises pointed.

"That is the neighbors' house. You can only see the lights when the leaves are down. They must be having a party."

The sound of music and glasses clinking echoed through the backyard.

Later, when the kids had hung their stockings and Carmen and Moises said their goodbyes, Phoebe went back out onto the porch. The light still shone but the night was quiet. She thought she might walk out into the yard when a shadow fell across the porch.

"Don't mean to startle you," said Petrel. "Just don't think you should be wandering the woods in your condition."

Phoebe unlatched the screen door. Petrel settled into the chair next to her. He moved more stiffly than Phoebe had remembered. He scratched Magnet's ears and the dog moaned with pleasure.

"Petrel, do you have any children?"

"I have two. And five grands and one great. They keep me busy. My Veronica died young."

"Did you always live here, Petrel?"

Petrel shook his head. "I was raised in Pennsylvania. I never did know my mama. The Quaker family that raised me said she put me on the underground railroad from somewhere down near Danville. I don't know if that's true but some folks used to call me high yellow."

"This is going to sound funny," Phoebe said. "But I can tell you for sure that your mama was a kind, strong woman. She was a Civil War nurse, right around here. She spied for the Union. And your grandma was something special. She watches over lost children, including my eldest, who died last summer. I am forever grateful to her."

"That don't surprise me one bit. You have a bit of the sight. Just like I think my great grand baby Collette will."

They sat for a few more minutes. Petrel stood and doffed his hat.

"That baby will be along soon now."

He eased off the porch into the darkness.

It was right after New Year's when Phoebe's water broke. Her labor was too swift to allow for another c-section. The little boy with dark hair slipped into the world squalling lustily. Moises brought Kendall and Damien to Phoebe's bedside. They peered at their baby brother. The infant looked intently at their faces.

"What is his name, Flaca?"

Phoebe looked at Damien and Kendall.

"Noah," said Damien.

Sachel was Kendall's choice.

When the spring flowers bloomed, Noah Sachel made his first trip to his oldest sister's resting place. Phoebe placed him on a blanket while she and Kendall weeded the small cemetery. Damien raced around, Magnet chasing him. Noah Sachel chortled and Damien laughed out loud.

"Roxie is licking him!" shouted Damien.

The baby's eyes followed all his siblings, even the one Phoebe did not see, as they darted in and out of the trees with Magnet.

"That a fine baby boy you got there." Raven was kneeling next to the stone with the lamb on top. "What do you call him?"

"Noah Sachel," Phoebe answered. Raven smiled.

"Raven," Phoebe began, "I know what became of your daughter and your grandson. They were both courageous and kind. She was a nurse and your grandson, well, he saved my life. I am proud to have met them."

Raven's smile was as brilliant as the sun on the lake. "Oh, child, I have wondered so long. I am mighty grateful to learn this."

Raven stood and Phoebe reached to embrace her. It was not a solid hug but Raven was there, Phoebe could feel her. And then, Phoebe was alone by the gravestone and the kids were back, asking for pizza.

Noah Sachel was not a fussy baby but he was not a sleeper. He was content to watch Phoebe from his swing as she worked at her computer. One evening, not long after visiting Eileen's grave, she paid for one of those people searches for "Collette Johnson". She scrolled through the results and smiled.

"Dear Ms. Johnson," her email began. "I am researching local Fairfax history for a book. I believe you may be related to Petrel Johnson, who owned a speakeasy near where my home now stands. I would welcome the opportunity to talk to you about my research."

Phoebe hit send. Noah Sachel giggled and kicked his feet. He grabbed his toes and gave her a wide, toothless grin.